MW00681493

# MERRYWWEATHER
# LODGE
# ANCIENT REVENGE

by

## Pauline Holyoak

**WHISKEY CREEK PRESS**

www.whiskeycreekpress.com

Published by
WHISKEY CREEK PRESS

Whiskey Creek Press
PO Box 51052
Casper, WY 82605-1052
www.whiskeycreekpress.com

Copyright © 2010 by *Pauline Holyoak*

*Warning: The unauthorized reproduction or distribution of this copyrighted work is illegal. Criminal copyright infringement, including infringement without monetary gain, is investigated by the FBI and is punishable by up to 5 (five) years in federal prison and a fine of $250,000.*

Names, characters and incidents depicted in this book are products of the author's imagination or are used fictitiously. Any resemblance to actual events, locales, organizations, or persons, living or dead, is entirely coincidental and beyond the intent of the author or the publisher.

No part of this book may be reproduced or transmitted in any form or by any means, electronic or mechanical, including photocopying, recording, or by any information storage and retrieval system, without permission in writing from the publisher.

ISBN 978-1-61160-006-3

**Credits**
Cover Artist: Nancy Donahue
Editor: Sylvia Anglin
Printed in the United States of America

# Dedication

I dedicate this book to my parents, Reg and Elsie Wellings. The diamonds in my collection of treasured memories.

My heartfelt thank you to: My parents, for a wonderful start in life, for teaching me how to love unconditionally, how to be honest, humble yet proud. To my husband Ted, for having so much faith in me and my writing, for telling me time and time again, "This is a terrific read and it would make a great movie." (I'm still trying to manifest that one.) To my most precious gifts, my children Matt and Katie. You fill me with pride. To my loving sister Tina and her family, for never doubting me. To my aunt and uncle Ron and Helga Wellings, for my magical childhood holidays at Scotland Lodge, the place that inspired me to write this book. And last but not least to all the staff at Whiskey Creek Press, for liking my book enough to want to publish it.

# Prologue

Slowly I climbed the old wooden stairs that lead to the attic. My heart pounded harder with each step. It took me a moment to get up the courage to grip the knob. The heavy door creaked as I pushed it open. I reached around the corner and fumbled for the light switch. The room was exactly the way I remembered it, although it smelled a little stale and dusty.

Five years had passed and Auntie Em hadn't moved a thing. The Eliss family portrait still hung on the wall beside the door. The white linen draped over the little brass bed, and the fine lace curtains had yellowed slightly from the sun. Annabella's china face and painted blue eyes glared up at me from her throne in the corner of the room. The framed photograph of Jonathan, Belinda and me echoed fond memories. I wondered if Jonathan was still around and if he was as gorgeous now as he had been back then.

I gazed at the torn wallpaper that exposed the cubbyhole where the gruesome discovery was made. I was a mere child

1

of fourteen back then, but the memories of what happened here are as vivid as if it were only yesterday. A cold ripple of intense fear tricked down my spine as I recalled the events of my last bittersweet holiday at Merryweather Lodge.

# Chapter 1

*Five years earlier*

It was a long and uncomfortable ride from the airport, especially after being cramped in the window seat of a jumbo jet for nine hours. The old car smelled like pipe smoke and the hot humid air made the black leather seats stick to my skin. Uncle Reg never stopped talking; his bald head bounced back and forth like a bowling ball in front of me. The conversation was mundane and had become a boring hum. Until:

"Took an axe to her, I heard."

My ears perked up.

"Oh my God, any suspects?" Dad asked.

"Not yet, but they're looking for her stepson. Never was right in the head, that lad."

Uncle Reg was looking at my dad, who sat next to him. He didn't seem to be paying any attention to the road, which was nerve wracking, considering it curved, looped and dropped like a roller coaster.

"How's Emy taking it?"

"It's stirred up some old memories, if you know what I mean."

"I bet."

A gruesome murder was interesting, but I wasn't about to ask any questions, just in case Uncle Reg turned around and looked back at me. We would have ended up in the ditch for sure then. I glanced at Mom; she had fallen asleep with her head pressed against the window, cushioned by her glossy red purse. I was glad she hadn't heard the conversation because Mom smokes when she's anxious, and the last thing we needed was smelly cigarette smoke stinging our eyes. I gazed out of my partially opened window, as the fresh earthy smell of newly plowed soil drifted in. My body was uncomfortable and weary but my mind was in a world of fantasy, captivated by the enchanting view. There were cottages with thatched roofs hemmed in by manicured hedges, clusters of cone shaped trees topped with ice-creamy pink and white blossoms, snake-like rivers flowing through rich vegetation, gentle rolling hills dotted with sheep and crowned by dense woodlots, all against a backdrop of warm pale blue. So this was England.

I had waited for this day for as far back as I could remember. My dad's parents immigrated to Canada when he was sixteen years old. His older brother, my Uncle Reg, stayed in England with his wife, my Auntie Em. When Auntie's dad died, she inherited the farm and Merryweather Lodge. It is situated on Salisbury Plain, not far from historical Stonehenge. My parents had come here a couple of times before I was born and once when I was a baby. Uncle Reg and Auntie Em have visited us twice, at our country home just outside of Edmonton. My mom adores her sister-in-law; she calls her a "hardy English rose" although I have never quite understood why, as Auntie can be harsh and unkind to Mom at times. Perhaps it's because, like the rest of us, she knows that her sister-in-law is tough on the outside but all soft and mushy on the inside. I was named after her, Emily Anne Fletcher.

"Almost there," Uncle Reg announced.

We drove up a narrow dirt road shadowed by tall trees. An old wooden sign pointed the way: *1/4 mile Merryweather Lodge.* I rolled the window all the way down to get a better look. It was just as I had imagined, enchanting and blissfully romantic, like a scene from a fairy tale. Ivy and climbing wild roses draped the gray stone cottage; its tiny windows were complemented by diamond divisions and black wooden shutters. Massive clumps of shrubs, flowers and lilac bushes showed splendid color and gave off a delicious perfume. A white picket fence surrounded the cottage, adding to its charm. Just beyond the cottage, on one side, sat lush green hills patched with bushes and sprinkled with sheep. On the other side, in contrast, was a sea of flowing meadow with an island of thick, dense wood in the center.

"Come on, m' luvs, let's have a look at ya," Auntie Em demanded loudly, as soon Uncle Reg turned off the ignition. She was standing at the cottage door, waving with one hand and wiping the other down her gingham apron. We squeezed our stiff bodies out of the car. The air was fresh and fragrant. Mom ran her fingers through her long, blonde hair and inhaled deeply with an air of satisfaction. Dad lifted his arms, stretched, yawned, and then proceeded to unload our luggage.

"Never mind them there cases, Ron, Reg will fetch 'um," Auntie shouted. "Come on in; take a load off yer feet."

I swung open the little wooden gate and walked up the cobblestone path. As I gazed up at the straw roof, I noticed an odd little window just under the thatch. It was different from the others. Newer, I thought. It gave me a strange, uneasy feeling. Just then, Auntie Em reached up and threw her short chubby arm over my shoulder. She smelled like apple pie.

"My, haven't ya grown and ya don't look a day over sixteen."

Was she joking, I wondered, or had she forgotten that I was only fourteen? It's really hard to tell with English people. My mom said that they have a weird sense of humor. Everyone giggled so I guessed she was joking.

Inside, the cottage was cluttered but cozy. The walls were covered with old paintings, black and white photographs and heavy floral wallpaper. An elegant antique sideboard displayed an array of delicate figurines and cat ornaments on top of a dainty white doily. An oversized stone fireplace sat in the corner, accompanied by a chunky rolled-arm sofa, a chair dressed in chintz and an elegant wing-back holding a worn patchwork blanket. Colorful woven rugs warmed the rustic oak floors. The smell of lemon polish, mingled with old wood and pipe smoke, hung in the air.

Dad put his hand on Auntie's shoulder, and said, "We were sorry to hear about Lizzy Lunn."

Auntie swallowed and glanced at me. "We'll talk about it later."

*This must be the murdered woman they were talking about*, I thought. Obviously it was too shocking for 'sensitive' ears.

"These are our kids," Auntie said, pointing to the cats.

"Can I pet them?" I asked.

"Of course. I'll introduce you." Her jolly round face beamed, like a proud mother. "This is Wooky. Gotta watch him, he's cantankerous." The large black male was stretched out on the back of the sofa, glaring at us. I walked over and stroked him carefully.

"That's Winky over there. She's the shy one." She pointed to a black and white ball of fur buried in the fireside rug. "And this is our baby." Auntie crooked her finger. "Come 'ere, Winny, come and meet our Emily." She puckered her lips and made a kissing sound.

Like a well-trained dog, the cat jumped off the window ledge and came over to me. She arched her back and started weaving through my legs, purring and demanding attention. I picked her up gently and stroked her soft, snow-white fur.

Uncle Reg piled our luggage on the floor, next to the shiny polished sideboard.

"Time for a cuppa, Mother," he said, wiping his bushy brow with a large white handkerchief. I wondered why he called his wife "Mother." They didn't have any children but my mom did tell me that Auntie had given birth to a stillborn baby a couple of years after she and Uncle Reg were married, and there were the cats, I suppose.

In the kitchen, a crisp white cloth covered a rough wooden table; on top, a blue earthenware jar displayed a bunch of golden daffodils. Their delicate fragrance mingled with the mouth-watering aroma of freshly baked pastry. We gathered around the table, drank lemon tea from tiny china cups and ate warm powdered biscuits, covered in strawberry jam and thick Devonshire cream, off of pretty floral plates. After tea and what seemed like hours of babbling, Auntie showed us to our rooms.

"You two can sleep in 'ere," she said to Mom and Dad.

The parlor, like the sitting room, was snug and old-fashioned. She pointed to a plain couch in the corner; it had dark knobby fabric, wooden arms, and looked out of place amongst the antique furniture.

"This is one of them there new-fangled pullout beds. There's sheets in the airing cupboard, and I've made room in the bathroom for Penny's paraphernalia." She was referring to Mom's endless supply of cosmetics. My mom is a beautician and gets everything at discount prices. I couldn't wait until I was old enough to try it out, but I wasn't sure if I would ever wear it in public. It just seems too fussy for me.

"Thank you, Emy," Mom said sweetly.

"The hot water tank's full, if anyone wants to take a bath," Uncle Reg shouted from the other room.

"They'll be too tired for that," Auntie shouted back

abruptly. Then, in a lower voice, "Keep the door shut or you'll have a bed full of cats."

Mom cringed; she hated cat hair, or anything else that might flaw her perfect appearance.

"I've done the attic up for you, m' luv," Auntie said as she pulled the handle of my suitcase out of my hand. The stairs were narrow and steep.

"Let me carry that, Auntie Em," I said, feeling guilty.

"I've carried many a load up these 'ere stairs, Emily Ann, I ain't afraid of a bit of hard lifting." She grunted and struggled with every step. The heavy wooden door creaked open as she pushed it, sending a strange wave of apprehension washing over me.

"Here we are, luv, hope ya like it. We've been using it as a storeroom. Took me and your Uncle Reg a fortnight to clean up the rubbish."

"It's… It's beautiful, Auntie Em!" I assured her, but there was something odd about this room…something ominous.

"The furniture was left here by the folks that owned the farm before Dad bought it. It's very old and worth a bob or two." Auntie nodded her head and strolled toward the door. "Let me know if you need anything. And don't lock the door." She turned and gave me an odd grin. "It's old and can be tricky to open."

I felt a vague uneasiness.

The walls were covered in pink and blue candy-striped wallpaper. A small crescent-shaped window was curtained with white ruffled lace. Low wooden beams crossed the sloping ceiling. A kidney-shaped dressing table with a huge oval mirror and a tiny cushioned stool sat against one wall, a single brass bed draped in lace and embroidered linen against the other. In the corner, a toy rocking chair cradled a porcelain doll, dressed in faded red velvet. She seemed to be scowling at me with her painted blue eyes.

A large gold framed portrait hung on the wall beside the door. It looked like something you'd see in an art gallery. I walked over to take a closer look. In it, a tall dark-haired man with a curly moustache stood stiff and starched. A beautiful woman with blonde hair and piercing green eyes sat in a high-backed chair in front of him. Beside them stood a young red-headed girl, wearing a long green dress and holding two snow-white kittens. At the bottom in bold handwriting were the words "The Eliss Family".

Suddenly I felt a presence behind me. Slowly, cautiously, I turned; no one was there. Then I felt a cool breeze coming from the window. *That's strange,* I thought, *the window was closed when I came in.* As I pushed back the delicate curtains, I took a deep breath to clear my anxious, overtired mind.

A whiff of wild roses and lilac drifted in with the cool, damp air. I grabbed the latch to close the window. It wouldn't budge. I checked the hinge; it looked okay. I pulled again, but still it wouldn't move. It felt like someone was pulling it back from the other side. I pulled; it pulled back. I swallowed hard, let go and stood back, perplexed, shaking my hand as if to rid myself of whatever it was. Too nervous to change into my nightclothes, I crawled into bed fully clothed and pulled the covers snugly around my neck. For comfort, I decided to leave the light on.

* * * *

I awoke to the sound of a cock's crow and the smell of bacon. Slanted rays of early sun filled the room with light. I assumed that someone had come in to check on me during the night as the light was off and the window was closed. I gazed around the room suspiciously. All seemed well.

Brushing off the events of the night before, I proceeded to unpack my suitcase. There was no closet or wardrobe, so I placed my clothes neatly in the dressing table drawers. The huge mirror in front of me reflected a tired, pale face, with fading freckles and puffy green eyes, surrounded by a messy mop of ginger hair.

On top of the dresser, a tarnished silver tray displayed a beautiful brush and comb set with the initials M. E. engraved on the back. I picked up the brush and started to untangle the knots. I hated my red hair. As soon as I was old enough, I was going to dye it golden blonde, like my mom's or jet black like my best friend's, Skye Jenkins. As I stared at my reflection in the ornate mirror, it started to become blurry, distorted. I dropped the brush and narrowed my eyes, trying to focus. For a moment it looked like there were two of me, but the other one was older and much prettier. I blinked rapidly. My image became clear again. *Must be prolonged jet lag.* Then, out of the corner of my eye, I noticed that the doll that had been sitting on the rocking chair was gone. That did it! I grabbed a t-shirt and a pair of jeans, threw them on and rushed out of the door.

"Well, good morning, young lady," Dad said cheerfully while mopping up his egg yolk with a thick piece of home-made bread. I pulled out a chair and sat beside him. Auntie Em slapped two pieces of crisp-fried bacon on the plate in front of me. I screwed up my nose, looked at Mom and then at Dad.

"Our Emily has become a tree-hugging vegetarian," Dad said, in a sarcastic tone. I gave him an evil eye.

"Well, I never. What brought this on?" Auntie asked.

I paused, then sat up straight. "I watched a program on TV that showed how animals were slaughtered. It was bar-baric. I swore I would never consume the flesh of another species again."

Auntie rolled her eyes. "Sorry I asked."

She slid my bacon onto Dad's plate, then dumped a cou-ple of eggs, sunny side up, on a clean plate and shoved it in front of me.

"Ya do eat eggs, don't ya?"

"Yes, thank you."

"Watch for the little chicky inside," Dad said, then he chuckled. My dad can be a real jerk. He ridicules anything that goes against his conservative views.

I gave him another evil look.

"What's up, honey? You look pale, like you've seen a ghost," Mom asked, changing the subject while she poured me a cup of tea from a large brown pot.

"I'm fine, just a little tired, that's all. Where's Uncle Reg?"

"He left for the fields, of course, ages ago," Auntie said as if I should have known. Winny jumped up on my lap under the table. I stroked her fur; she purred contentedly. Auntie Em came over and lifted the corner of the tablecloth. Winny's innocent blue eyes glared at her.

"Don't you think for a minute that I can't see you under there. Ya know yer not allowed near the table." She shook her finger at the disobedient cat. Now I knew why they're called "the kids".

With a Visitors' Guide and map in hand, Mom and Dad started to plan our agenda.

"Tomorrow, we'll get the bus up to Portsmouth. Friday, we'll visit Stonehenge. On the weekend, we'll…" Dad paused and looked over at me pitifully. "But today, we'll stay here and recuperate," he said, giving me a nod and a smile.

After breakfast Auntie suggested that we all go for a walk.

"Grab your macs and wellies," she said. "My legs have been playing me up all morning. Must be a storm brewing."

My coat was in the attic room. I felt nervous about going back up there. "I don't need a coat," I announced, heading for the door.

"You'll do as you're told, young lady," Dad ordered.

I sighed loudly, stomped into the sitting room, lifted Wooky off the back of the sofa and draped him over my shoulder like a fur stole. He gave me a lengthy, indignant meow. I did not want to go back up there alone and a cat was better than nothing. The stairs groaned. I ran my fingers down Wooky's silky coat and hummed, to comfort myself. The foreboding wooden door stood before me, like the portal to a dark kingdom. Without warning, Wooky let out a piercing hiss and scurried down my back, digging his claws into my flesh for support! I winced and screamed.

Mom came running to the bottom of the steps. "Emily, what's wrong?"

"I'm okay. The cat scratched me, that's all." His claw marks tingled painfully on my back.

"Hurry up, honey. We are all waiting for you," Mom said, as she walked away.

To ease my anxiety, I visualized Mom still standing there as I ran up the remaining stairs.

I flung open the door, rushed over to the bed, grabbed my coat from the brass bed post and headed for the door. As I did, I noticed the Eliss Family portrait was hanging upside down. *This is creepy,* I thought, but for some unimaginable reason I felt impelled to stop and move it. Lifting it carefully off the hook, I turned it the right way up. The young girl's painted face seemed to draw me in. It looked angelic, almost radiant. Mesmerized, I gazed into her bright green eyes; as I did, an intense feeling of utter sadness gripped me. Tears filled my eyes. A cold draft and the scent of lavender drifted by me. Something brushed against my back. Too frightened to turn around, I flew out the door and scurried down the stairs as fast as I could.

# Chapter 2

Outside, the dense humid air shadowed the farm in an eerie haze. We were engulfed in a cloudy mist as we wandered through the back yard, down the beaten path, past a big red barn and over to the chicken coop. Mom cleared her throat and held her nose as a disgusting smell greeted us. Auntie pulled a large white hanky out of her apron pocket and held it over her mouth as she snickered and rolled her eyes.

We helped feed the chickens and collected eggs in a large wicker basket. I sucked my stomach in, held my breath for as long as I could and tried hard not to touch anything. Inside, the coop was littered with sticky gray pooh and the stench was overpowering. It was too much for Mom; she stood back and lit a cigarette. Auntie Em, with her bizarre sense of humor, had named some of the hens after people she knew. There was Maud, Martha, Elsie, little Lindy, Lizzie and the one with her "head in the clouds," Emily Anne. I hoped that Emily would not be the one selected for Sunday dinner.

Later, we met Uncle Reg in the pasture where he was

tending the sheep. The lambs were almost full grown now, but still cute and frisky. I loved their pink ears and sweet little faces, and their jubilant antics made me think I might like to name some of them. They had a lot more personality than the chickens and they didn't smell. We watched Sam, Uncle Reg's Border collie, put on an impressive demonstration of herding. Sam was not allowed in the house because he chased the cats, and although he was cared for and appreciated, they treated him more like a farm hand than a member of the family. I thought this was unfair.

The haze had lifted now, giving way to bright sunshine. Just as we were about to leave, a couple of silhouettes waving their hands emerged from over the hill. Uncle Reg and Auntie Em waved back and beckoned them over.

"Glutton for punishment you are, John McArthur," Uncle Reg shouted while shading his eyes from the sun. "Thought I'd given you the day off?"

As the two men got closer, I could see that the shorter one was middle-aged. He was wearing gray baggy pants, a red tartan sweater and a tweed cap. The other one was young, about seventeen, I guessed. He was tall, muscular, with silky-black hair and was dressed in blue jeans and a black, long-sleeved T-shirt. The closer they got, the cuter he looked.

"I ain't come to work; I've just come to meet the family. We missed them the last time they were over, as we'd gone on holiday."

Mom straightened her wide-brimmed hat and brushed the dust off her jacket. Dad went over and boldly stuck out his hand. "That was thirteen years ago, Ron Fletcher."

The man removed his cap, revealing a dappled bald head. "John McArthur. And this is my son Jonathan, or little Jonny as we used to call him." He looked up at his son and laughed heartily. "But he ain't so little anymore."

We all shook hands. Jonathan's hand felt warm; its touch gave me goose bumps and an odd feeling of recognition, as if we had touched before.

"John's my right-hand man. Don't know what I'd do without him," Uncle Reg said. "Him and his wife look after the farm when we go over to visit you lot."

Mom stamped out her cigarette and cleared her throat. "Oh, are you the people that moved into the pretty cottage over the hill, where the Havshaws used to live?"

"Yep, been here eighteen years now."

"They left when their young daughter got pregnant, didn't they?" Mom asked, in her subtly prying, quiet voice.

I stood twirling strands of hair between my fingers, trying to appear interested in the conversation but really just wanting to stare at Jonathan. He was so incredibly handsome.

Mr. McArthur nodded his head and gave her a forced smile. There was a pause of uncomfortable silence. Then Auntie coughed into her hanky and walked over to Jonathan. Pointing at him with her stick, she asked in an authoritative voice, "Why ain't ya at school, young man?"

"Teachers' convention," he answered softly.

"Cool! You get them, too?" I blurted out excitedly.

Jonathan gave me a lazy grin and lowered his eyes to the

ground. *Why did you have to go and say that?* It sounded so im-mature.

As the men walked away, Auntie shouted, "Tell Maud I'll have ya over for dinner before they go back, I will."

"Right you are," John shouted back.

"And bring your son," I whispered under my breath. I couldn't wait to tell my best friend Skye Jenkins about this guy.

Uncle Reg and Sam went back to tending the sheep. We strolled over the rich green hills toward the meadow. A heavenly canopy of baby blue hung over us. Mom kept her eyes on the ground, watching for and being careful to avoid the blobs of sheep droppings that littered the landscape. Every once in a while she would stop to light up a cigarette or tuck a stray blonde lock under her hat. She was lagging behind the rest of us. It didn't help that she was wearing a pair of Auntie's old wellies, which looked ridiculous with her tailored spring jacket.

"Getting tired, are ya, Penny?" Auntie asked in a sarcastic tone.

"I'm afraid I am…my feet are starting to ache." She glared at Dad. "Think I'll turn back. Coming, Ron?"

That wasn't a question, it was an order. Even though most people walked all over Mom, she had Dad wrapped around her finger.

"Time we all went back for a nice cuppa," Auntie said.

I hooked my arm around hers. "Can we go through the meadow and over to the woods?" I asked.

She wiped her weathered brow with the back of her hand and sighed deeply. "Oh, that's a long walk, luv."

"Well, maybe we can have a rest first." I looked at her with pleading eyes. "Please, Auntie Em."

"All right, all right. You'll be the death of me, ya will."

I never really understood all the lingo that my aunt and uncle used. But I knew that if they were referring to me, it was a form of endearment.

"We'll see you guys later," Dad hollered as he walked away with Mom on one arm and our raincoats on the other.

"We'll put the kettle on," Mom mumbled between coughs.

Auntie shook her head. "That's what smoking fags does for ya. Filthy habit, it is." Then she lowered her plump little form slowly into the soft cool grass, laid her walking stick down beside her, dug deep into her apron pocket and pulled out a small white paper bag. "Sweet, luv? They're butter-scotch—your favorite."

English butterscotch is so rich and creamy…I salivated as I anticipated its smooth milky texture melting in my mouth.

Auntie gazed lovingly at the rich landscape in front of her as she dug the sticky toffee from between her dentures with her rough finger nails. This would be the perfect time to ask her some questions, I thought. I wanted to know more about Jonathan. And the events in the attic room kept creeping into my mind, even though I was trying hard not to think about them.

"Auntie, do the McArthur's have any other kids besides

Jonathan?" I asked, not wanting to be too direct.

"They have a girl, Belinda, or Lindy, as we used to call her when she were small; twelve she'd be now, born on September the third she was." She lowered her eyes, as if that date had some painful significance. Then she looked up and grinned. "Lovely little thing, she is."

"How old is Jonathan?" That was a bit too direct, but it just came out.

"Too old for you, our Emily." She gave me a wide grin. "He's eighteen, I think." I wondered why she knew the exact day that Belinda was born but wasn't even sure that Jonathan was eighteen. "Funny lad, is Jonny."

"In what way?" I asked as I picked the heads off of a clump of daisies.

"Got more in 'ere," she patted her heart, "than he has up 'ere." She patted her head. "When he were little, he would catch insects in the house, put 'em in jars, then take 'em outside and let 'em go." She put her hand over her mouth and giggled. "Now he's going to art school. Paints flowers and trees, he does."

What's wrong with that? I wondered.

She patted me on the knee. "But he's a good lad, really."

"Who are those people in the portrait hanging in the attic room?"

"Those are the folks that owned the farm before my dad bought it," she said in a hesitant but matter-of-fact way.

"What do you know about them? Was the attic room the little girl's bedroom? And what happened to your friend

Lizzy?" I asked, all in one breath.

Auntie heaved her chubby body up from the ground, brushed herself off, and then announced firmly, "That's too many questions. We're off now!"

The meadow was a sea of multicolored grass, mixed with all manner of wildflowers. The gentle breeze created waves beneath our feet, lifted my hair and caressed my face. It was laced with a fresh earthy scent. Winny had found us and was following close behind, stopping every once in a while to paw an insect or chase a butterfly. When we got to the edge of the woodlot she stopped, then turned to leave; to my surprise, Auntie did too.

"Aren't we going in?" I asked, my lips tight and my arms folded.

Auntie turned around, squinted, pointed her stick at the woodlot and said in a harsh tone, "There is nothing in them there woods but trees."

I stood my ground. "But I love trees. Please, Auntie Em." I wasn't going to give up. There was something about that place; it felt like a secret portal to a magic realm, enticing me.

She softened and lowered her stick. "All right, all right. But only a little way, mind you."

The tall evergreen, chestnut and beech trees towered over us like formidable giants while beams of sunlight streamed through their branches. The smell of pine and damp moss permeated the air. A woodpecker's tat-tat-tat echoed in the distance. Clusters of wildflowers, foliage debris and damp leaves decorated the ground and clung to the soles of my shoes. *It was,* I thought, *like an enchanted forest.*

Caught up by the magic, I frolicked and fluttered my arms like the ethereal wings of a wood fairy. I saw myself dancing with tiny brown elves, surrounded by hundreds of mystical woodland creatures who giggled and tinkled their bells. I have a private spot in a cluster of trees at our acreage home, where I've acted out this fantasy often. It didn't bother me to act childish in front of Auntie. She seemed to enjoy my immature antics. And I knew that she was worried about me "growing up too fast".

"It's magical in here, Auntie Em."

She screwed up her nose and glared at me. "Magical it is not," she said in a harsh tone.

"What's wrong?" I asked.

"I get a bit claustrophobic in 'ere. That's all, luv." She forced a smile and wiped her clammy brow with her hanky.

"Wow, look at that," I said, pointing to a clearing with a massive tree in the middle. Its roots protruded and spread like the tentacles of a giant octopus. I felt drawn to it.

"Let's go take a look," I said eagerly.

"No!" She grabbed my arm. "We've gone far enough. They'll be thinking we've got lost."

I was confused by her angry tone. "Wait." I spotted a cluster of primroses. "Mom will love these." I ran over, knelt on the ground and started picking their velvety stems. Their delicate scent drifted up to greet me.

"I said let's go, Emily Ann!" She was getting mean and anxious.

Then I heard what sounded like someone tramping through the bushes, the rustling of branches and breaking of twigs. "They've come looking for us," I said.

Before I had time to stand up, Auntie grabbed my arm, whisked me up off the ground and pulled me forcefully in the direction from which we came.

"Come on, girl. Let's hurry."

"Auntie, what's wrong? You're hurting me."

"Run, Emily!" Her tone frightened me. I picked up the pace. The sound was getting louder. I glanced over my shoulder. I couldn't see anything. Auntie huffed and puffed in front of me. With one hand she had a tight grip on my wrist, with the other she paved our way through the twisted vegetation with her stick.

A strange feeling that I had been here and done this before swept over me, like a murky wave. It felt terrifyingly familiar, a sort of sinister déjà vu. My throat was dry. My nostrils filled with the smell of fear as my heart raced faster and faster. A sense of urgency consumed me. All I could hear was the pounding of my own heart and the quick raspy breathing of the stampeding woman in front of me. Blurs of browns and greens flash before us. The twisted, overhanging canopy of the giant trees cast fragmented glimpses of bright blue overhead. Through the tangled bushes and brambles we flew, my eyes fixed on the slowly growing cavities of light guiding us to safety, our invisible enemy in close pursuit.

"Go, Auntie, go!" I shouted impulsively. My wrist was sore. My feet ached. Finally, full sunlight surrounded us. We had reached the clearing. Auntie bent over, dropped her stick and put her hands on her knees. Panting, she tried to catch her breath. I walked over and placed my hand on her shoulder. "Are you okay?"

She nodded and lifted her head. Her weathered face was damp with sweat; wiry gray curls were sticking to her forehead.

"What was chasing us? Why were you so afraid?"

She looked down and mumbled, "Wild animals, m' luv."

"Wild animals? Here?" I questioned.

Then she tightened her thin lips, gave me a serious look and said firmly, "I don't want you going back in them there woods again. Is that clear?" Drawing me tight to her chest, she hugged me and ran her short stubby fingers down my red hair. "Promise me, luv."

I nodded my head.

"You're worth your weight in gold to me. I won't 'ave anything happening to ya, I won't."

I gave her a quick peck on the cheek.

Her tired eyes seemed to light up. "Let's go home, luv, away from these 'ere woods."

\* \* \* \*

I had mixed feelings of both wonderment and apprehension as I sat on the back door step, gazing around the yard. It was the last week in May; the late afternoon sun was hot for that time of year. My journal and pen sat patiently beside me, waiting for me to spill my secrets and fears in its pages. Winny was curled up like a large cotton ball on my lap, sleeping contentedly.

On one side of the yard, a sturdy cherry tree stood, laden with heavy pink blossoms and skirted by a ring of violets. On the other side, an improvised washing line was held up by a large forked branch. It was accompanied by two white wicker chairs and a wooden table with a basket of pegs and a straw hat on top. In the middle, a vegetable patch sprouted tiny green soldiers, all in a row. Clumps of bright yellow butter-cups and creamy white daisies dotted the lawn. I could see Winky's black and white coat, nested amongst a bunch of bearded iris. It reminded me of Green Gables. *Anne of Green Gables* was my favorite book when I was a child. I could relate to Anne Shirley. She was a lot like me, strong willed and full of imagination. And she had red hair, too.

I inhaled the floral fragrance that floated in the air. It was all so pretty and peaceful, like the enchanted kingdom I had dreamt about. But there was a subtle, mysterious essence about the place, too obscure to describe and I couldn't shake off the strange feeling that I was being watched or the thoughts of the incidents in the attic room and the woods. It was like a fairytale with a sinister twist.

"You'll get sun stroked if ya sit there too long, ya will."

Auntie's voice jogged me. She was carrying a large tin tub filled with steaming soapy water, which she hauled across the lawn and plunked beside the clothes line.

"What's in there?" I asked.

"Hankys, socks and knickers."

I was sorry I asked. She went back inside, drying her wet hands with the bottom of her apron. A strong scent of lavender drifted past my nose, followed by a warm sensation that spilled over my body, like a heat wave. A creepy sick feeling overwhelmed me. It felt like something was consuming my flesh. Winny hissed and flew off my lap. I felt light-headed and shaky. Then, darkness.

When I came to, I was sitting on the grass next to the tub of water. My hands were wet and covered in tiny soap bubbles. Winny was under the tree; she was licking her soggy wet fur vigorously. Dazed, I wobbled over to her. She looked like a rodent with huge, blue eyes. Carefully, I lifted her up, cradled her on my lap and dabbed her drenched white coat with my skirt. Perplexed, I refused to believe the obvious and decided that we both got "sun stroked". I stayed outside, waving my skirt in the sun until it was dry and I was safe to go inside.

The delicious smell of home-baked biscuits greeted me as I stepped inside the door.

"Ah, Emily, there you are. I have a question for you," Dad said, peeking over the *Daily Times* with his reading glasses perched precariously on the end of his nose. "Would you like to go to a pub in Chillsbury this evening?"

"Are you kidding? I'm only fourteen, remember?"

"Children are allowed in pubs here," he said.

"As long as they don't get drunk," Auntie shouted from the kitchen. Dad lowered his paper and chuckled. A tuneless rendition of "I've Got a Lovely Bunch of Coconuts," came gushing through the kitchen door. Auntie Em always sang while preparing tea. Her voice was awful but her heart was pure gold.

"Sure, I'll go," I said. The thought of staying in the cottage alone was unsettling. "And I promise not to get drunk!" I shouted so Auntie could hear me.

The song was replaced with girlish giggles, then, "Tea's up!"

I sighed a blissful *aaahhh* as we drove through the picturesque village of Chillsbury. A narrow winding road carried us past pretty thatched-roofed cottages with well kept gardens and a row of black and white Tudor houses with miniature doors and spider-web windows. An array of colorful blooms oozed out of window boxes, pots and hanging baskets. Hedgerows of brilliant green lined the streets. A cobblestone lane with old fashioned lamp posts twisted its way upward among curio shops, confectionaries and tea houses. A group of young boys were playing cricket beside a colorful bandstand on the village green. A quaint old church built of red bricks displayed beautiful stained glass windows and a short clock-faced steeple. It was surrounded by a low stone wall. Inside the wall, time-worn headstones dotted the grass. The smell of hot oil and vinegar drifted through the open window as we drove past a corner fish and chip shop. The place was alive with old-world charm and reminded me of a miniature Christmas village without the snow.

We pulled up to a pub with white-washed walls and a tin sign that read: *The Grayhound.* It had a picture of a skinny dog underneath. A little old man towing a brown and white hound tipped his hat as we stepped out of the car.

The inside of the pub was small, dark and dingy. The air

was thick with cigarette and pipe smoke, making my vision blurry and my eyes itchy. All kinds of memorabilia, antiques and old farm tools covered the walls and hung from the low-beamed ceiling. We sat at a round wooden table, with an ash tray full of cigarette butts and monogrammed beer coasters on top. Hearty laughter and spirited conversation buzzed all around. Uncle Reg went up to the bar and ordered drinks and Cornish pasties for everyone.

"Tell them to bring us a clean ashtray," I said. "This one's gross. It makes me want to puke!"

"Yes, your ladyship," he answered sarcastically.

Mom stuck her long red fingernails into her purse and fumbled for her cigarettes. Auntie grimaced at her critically. A couple of bedraggled old men wearing worn tweed jackets and jolly red faces sat at the table next to us. They were drinking thick black liquid with a frothy head from tall glasses. Uncle Reg introduced them as neighboring farmers and old mates, Bob Thomas and Ted White. Ted wiped the foam from his bushy black moustache, leaned toward Dad and started asking him questions about Canada.

Bob looked over at me, smiled widely and asked in a croaky whisper, "Have you seen Mary Eliss wandering about?" Then he broke out in vigorous laughter, exposing his crooked yellow teeth. The smell of stale beer drifted toward me from his breath. I turned my head and wrinkled my nose. Auntie straightened her back, stretched her short stubby neck and glared at him across the table.

"Don't you go filling the girl's head with all that nonsense, Bob Thomas," she said.

The name rang a bell. "Who's Mary Eliss?" I asked.

Gazes darted back and forth. Then I remembered. I looked over at Auntie and asked, "Is she related to the people in the portrait?"

She scratched her wiry gray head and sighed. "We may as well tell 'er, because if we don't, someone else will."

Everyone nodded. Mom looked concerned and bit down on her lip. I was all ears. Auntie shoved her half-eaten Cornish pasty to the side, gulped back her shandy and wiped her mouth with her hanky. Then she gave me a serious look.

"I'll tell ya, but I don't want ya having nightmares. It's only a tale." She squeezed her brown eyes into tiny slits. "Well, legend has," she said, her voice resonating with intrigue, "that the Eliss' daughter Mary was mad. Possessed by an evil spirit, they claimed. She was said to have killed the family pets. Then she went on to kill her folks and bury them in the woods." Her voice took on an eerie sarcastic tone. "People say that they've 'eard her cries and seen her wanderin' in the woods at night."

I gasped, clutching at my throat. Mom reached over and put her hand on mine.

"Emily, it's just a story. The girl might have had some kind of mental illness. People didn't understand things like that back then."

"Just one of the old yarns, luv," Bob Thomas said, chuckling.

Uncle Reg turned his head toward the door. "Well, look

who just walked in." It was Mr. McArthur and his gorgeous son Jonathan. He motioned them over to the table. It felt like a million butterflies were fluttering inside my stomach as they walked through the grimy haze toward us.

"Grab a couple of chairs. Take a load off," Auntie ordered.

Dad stood up. "What can I get you? Stout? Bitters?"

"A pint of Guinness for me."

"I'll have a Lager, thank you," Jonathan said. What a hottie, I thought, as my pulse started to race. I took some discreet, deep breaths but they didn't stop it. There was something about this guy, something different, something mysterious. The black high-neck sweater he wore complemented his tanned complexion and made him look like an Arabian prince. Oh, how neat it would be to touch that skin, just one little touch. I shook away the thought as his dark eyes met mine. Then he smiled. His open mouth stretched his sexy cleft chin and revealed perfect white teeth. My lips quivered as I pressed them together hard and smiled back. I didn't want him to see the ugly hardware in my mouth. I tried not to stare but I couldn't help it.

Mr. McArthur put his tweed cap on the table and scratched his dappled bald head as he asked nervously, "Did you hear the news?"

Everyone shook their heads.

"They've found Lizzy's stepson. Got him in custody."

"Do you think he did it?" Dad asked.

Ted White butted in. "Not bloody likely. She was killed

on March twenty-first." His gaze moved around the table. "Ring any bells, does it?" Then he mumbled something about the devil's kids.

Suspicious looks were exchanged. Bob Thomas looked at me with his beady little eyes and said teasingly, "Maybe it was Mary Eliss."

The two men laughed. There was a moment of silence. Then, wham! Auntie slammed her hand on the table. Drinks bounced. Everyone jumped. Tapping her beer coaster on the hard surface, she lowered her eyebrows and said, "I've lived on that there farm most of my life. If there were any ghosts around, I'd 'ave seen 'um by now."

Jonathan's mouth twitched with humor. I looked at him and shrugged my shoulders. His eyes met mine and his mouth eased into a warm smile. I felt a touch of heat on my cheeks and was glad the pub was dimly lit, because blushing was so immature.

Uncle Reg lifted his doddery body from the chair. "Bloody load of rubbish, if you ask me," he said, stubbing his shiny brown pipe with his fingers. "I'm ready for a cuppa, Mother," he announced, grabbing his gray overcoat from the back of his chair.

I didn't want to leave. I just wanted to sit there staring at Jonathan, listening to his soft voice. He was so gorgeous. But who was I kidding; eighteen-year-old guys, especially really cute ones, do not date fourteen-year-old girls. Especially ones with red hair, freckles, braces and no boobs.

Before we left, Auntie invited them over for Sunday dinner. "One o'clock, sharp," she said.

"Right you are. I'll tell Maud," Mr. McArthur replied.

The dusky crimson sun was setting in a mass of dark gray clouds, and the hills were pricked with the lights of scattered farm houses. I gazed out of the car window, my mind abuzz. Jonathan was coming to dinner. I would get to meet his mom and little sister whom, I had decided, I would cleverly befriend. This was a tactic a lot of my friends used to get to know a guy better. Then I switched gears, remembering that Lizzy's stepson had been arrested but Ted said he didn't do it because she was killed on the twenty-first of March. March twenty-first…it sounded familiar…ah yes, Spring Equinox. But why would that have anything to do with a murder? Or did this date have some other significance?

# Chapter 3

By the time we got back to the cottage, jagged streaks of lightning were splitting the dusky sky and thunder rumbled in the distance.

"Told ya there'd be a storm," Auntie boasted as she pried her stubby form out of the car. Sam ran to greet us, wagging his bushy black and white tail enthusiastically. He shoved his damp cold nose into my hand.

"You wouldn't leave him outside in a storm, would you?" I asked.

Uncle Reg plunked his brown cap on his balding head and drew his collar around his neck.

"No, lass. Come on, old fella," he said as he whistled and tapped his side. "You'll be bedding in the hay tonight." Sam heeled and the two of them trotted off side-by-side toward the barn.

I shivered as the wind-driven rain stung my face. Large rain drops splattered hard on the gravel driveway. The fresh smell of wet pavement filled the blustery air. We gathered our belongings from inside the car and scurried to the house. Dad opened the door and flicked the light switch but nothing happened. We were cloaked in darkness.

"Don't worry, I have matches," Mom said as she fumbled inside her purse. Her face took on a wraithlike sheen when she lit a match. Auntie stumbled as she reached for a candle. They were placed strategically around the cottage as the newly-installed electricity failed frequently. When the candles were lit, their luminance filled the room with a soothing glow. I felt the soft touch of Winny's warm fur rubbing against my leg and bent to pick her up. She brushed her cheek on mine and purred; her very presence comforted me.

"Who's for a cuppa?" Auntie asked, carrying a thick beeswax candle into the kitchen. She lit the small gas stove and placed her faithful kettle over the bright blue flame. My mom calls Merryweather Lodge "The place that time forgot". I can see why now, since it's like we've stepped back in time fifty years.

I was starting to get a little nervous about going back to the attic room. The shadowy darkness and thrashing and banging coming from outside made it all the more threatening. The prickly sensation of tiny goose bumps ran up and down my arms every time I thought of it. Suddenly the back door burst open. I jumped as a blast of fear gripped me. A large dark frame stood at the door.

"It's raining cats and dogs out there."

What a relief. It was only Uncle Reg, windswept and dripping wet. Taking a large white hanky out of his coat pocket, he blew his red nose noisily like a trumpet.

After tea Mom handed me a brass candlestick, two candles and a box of matches.

"How long will the power be out?" I asked.

"It could be off all night, honey. You're not scared, are you, Emily?"

"No! I'm fine." My lips quivered and my hands trembled as I lit the wick. I thought about asking Mom to stand at the bottom of the stairs but I knew that she'd fuss. "Does my little girl need tucking in?" she'd ask in her mushy voice. I hated the way she babied me.

A feeling of apprehension consumed me as I climbed the stairs. "It's all in your head, it's all in your head," I mumbled as I visualized Mom standing at the bottom. A voice from within me whispered, *Don't go in, don't go in.* Slowly I opened the door, took a deep breath and entered the room. Closing my eyes, I said a silent prayer before flicking the light switch.

In hopeful anticipation, I opened my eyes. It was still dark, cool, damp and scary. The window was ajar and the delicate lace curtains rustled in the chilly breeze. Tentatively I walked over and closed the latch. Looking around the room, I noticed that the doll was still missing and the picture was upside down again. I wondered if someone was playing tricks on me, but who and why?

My candle cast eerie flickering shadows around the room. Shivering, I walked over and placed it on the night stand and sat on the edge of the bed. Wrapping my arms around myself, I tried to calm my beating heart. The legend of Mary Eliss came to mind, but I quickly brushed it aside. I couldn't allow such thoughts to enter my head tonight. I remembered what my friend Skye would say: "When I get really scared, I close my eyes and breathe deeply. Then I imagine myself on a tranquil river bank, with a soft blanket, a picnic basket full of goodies and Matt Hasselman by my side." Matt is the hottest guy in our school and Skye is obsessed with him. Skye gets these ideas from her New Age mom, who practices neat stuff like meditation, reiki, chakra work and the art of creative visualization. I find it so intriguing, but my parents think it's bizarre.

I visualized a forbidden seductive scene with Jonathan McArthur by my side, slipped into my fleecy night gown and crept into bed.

I gasped and flew off the mattress, startled by the touch of something cold and hard lying next to me. I landed with a bang on the floor. Grabbing the covers with my trembling hands, I drew myself up and slowly peeled back the quilt. It was the doll, but how did she get there? Now I was really spooked. Perhaps Auntie put her there to keep me company.

Scooping her pale porcelain body up into my arms, I cradled her. She smelt like the garden and there was something about her that felt warm and comforting.

As I ran my hands over her rich velvet dress, I felt a lump in the back. Eagerly I untied the tiny fasteners. It was a piece of yellowed paper, neatly folded. I held it under the candle. The handwriting was meticulous but the ink was faded and there were splatters of it like little black spiders on the paper.

It read…

>She came to me in the night and stole my diary. Now I have nothing to confide in but you, Annabella, and this mere piece of paper. She has killed my dear Tommy and Mossy. I loved them so. Mother thinks I have gone mad. She locks me in my room and refuses to let me go to school. When she looks at me, there is hate in her eyes. Father, though compassionate, goes along with whatever she says. I think he is afraid of her. I can't stand it any longer. I will find a way to escape from this hideous creature and my mother. Help me, God.
>
>Desperately, Mary

My hands shook as I refolded the paper, put it back under the dress and considered the words. As my nimble fingers fastened the tiny clasps, I caught a whiff of lavender. Then I felt an invisible hand on mine. Its silky-soft fingers caressed me gently. For a moment I felt comforted by the sensation, but then my senses kicked in and I panicked, tearing my hand away from whatever it was and dropping the doll on the floor.

Then I heard a faint scratching sound. Mice, I thought. Auntie said that if it wasn't for the cats, they'd be overrun by mice. "Oh God, please let it be mice."

The sound got louder and louder. Now it sounded like someone running their nails down a blackboard. Part of me wanted to make a dash for the door but the stubborn, irrational part of me was curious. There was a mystery here and my gut told me that this mystery had something to do with me.

Terrified and trembling, I pricked my ears and followed the sound's direction. It was coming from inside the wall next to the dressing table. I crept over to the nightstand, grabbed the candle and knelt by the wall to get a closer look. There was a small bulge in the wallpaper.

As I ran my fingers over the notch, the sound stopped. The silence was all the more ominous.

Impulsively, with trembling hands, I ripped the wallpaper off the wall. Underneath lay a cubby hole door with a tiny brass latch. Cautiously, I lifted the latch and opened the door.

I shot back, overwhelmed by a strong stench of cat urine. Holding my nose, I shone the candle into the disgusting dark hole. There were bones inside, lots of little white bones. Feeling light headed and sick to my stomach, I shuffled back.

Then, the comforting hand that I had felt before touched my shoulder. I tipped my head and rubbed the warm illusion against my cheek. It was soothing and fragrant. Suddenly and sharply, it pulled away. The overhead light flickered on just then, illuminating the room. An uncanny feeling of something standing behind me overwhelmed me. Slowly, fearfully I turned.

Gasping, wide-eyed, I froze to the floor.

A terrifying specter hovered in front of me. It was a woman dressed in a long white dress, covered in blood-red splatters. A rope-like sash hung around her waist. On her head she wore a wreath of dried berries. Her long fair hair was matted and hung limp over her ashen face. Her green eyes glared at me from their deep sockets, surrounded by dark gray rings. The smell of cat pee filled the air.

My voice trembled. "Who are you? What do you want?" She grinned, exposing rows of uneven yellow teeth.

"Colceathrar, Colceathrar," she hissed.

I tore myself from the floor and dashed to the door, shaking from head to foot and screaming at the top of my lungs. Mom came running as I flew down the stairs.

"What's wrong, Emily?"

Breathlessly I threw myself into her arms. My heart pounded against her chest.

"There's a ghost in my room!"

Dad bolted past us. "There's no one here, Emily," he shouted from the doorway.

I grabbed Mom's hand and held it tight as I guided her into the room. It was gone, and furthermore, the wallpaper was back on the wall, the doll was in the rocking chair and there was no unpleasant smell. Mom hugged me and stroked my sweaty hair.

"You had a nightmare, honey. It was all the talk about that silly legend."

I pushed her away. "No, it was here!" I ran over to the doll and ripped open the back of her dress. Nothing.

Was I hallucinating or losing my mind? Was I going to get sick like Grandma Fletcher did? How old was she? I think it started just before they moved to Canada and she went downhill from there. I don't want to die like she did, in a mental institution somewhere.

My mind was spinning. It had all felt so real, the ghost, the doll, the note, the wallpaper…so real. There was one thing I knew for sure: I'd never come back into this room.

Auntie was standing at the bottom of the stairs, weighed down by her heavy tartan housecoat. She was clasping her handkerchief over her mouth. That was what she did when she worried about something or when she was discreetly taking out her false teeth. She thought she was hiding it, but we all knew what she had done when she shoved her hanky into her pocket and her lips collapsed.

"What was all that about?"

"It's okay, Emy. Emily had a nightmare, that's all," Mom said, patting me on the head like a dog.

I jerked my head away from her hand. "It wasn't a dream!" I insisted.

"All right, m' luv. You go and sit down and I'll go make everyone a nice cuppa," Auntie said. That was her remedy for everything.

"I told them in detail what I had seen and read. But they just patronized me. Auntie was the only one who showed any emotion. She held her hanky over her mouth, eyes wide and brows raised. I had to admit it was hard to believe, especially when there wasn't a shred of evidence to back it up.

Dad and Mom reluctantly moved my stuff in with them. I used the cushions from the pullout couch to sleep on.

"Leaving that nice bedroom isn't going to make your bad

dreams go away," Mom protested. But it did, even the weird recurring dream with giant boulders and naked dancing ladies that I've had since I was very young seemed to have been silenced.

* * * *

The next morning we took the train to London and spent the day sightseeing. I put the events of the night before out of my mind and tried to act as a normal tourist, snapping pictures and reading brochures and plaques. I was surprised to see how plain Buckingham Palace was. I thought the Queen's residence would be more majestic than that. It looked more like a government building than a castle.

The following day we went to Stonehenge. It was only a short drive away from the farm. My parents spent hours admiring the huge monoliths but I found them dull and boring. Dad made it worse by quizzing me.

"Emily, which ones are bluestone and which ones are sarsen?"

"Who cares? Let's just go."

"It would benefit your education to care, young lady."

It wasn't just that they were uninteresting. The massive gray rocks made me uncomfortable, too. They seemed to be surrounded by a strange, dark aura similar to what I had felt in the attic room, and they looked like the boulders in my recurring dream. Auntie said that she remembers when there were no tourists, fences or fees here. You could touch the giant stones and sit amongst them. I wonder how that must have felt.

After that, we went to the New Forest. That was good fuel for my nature fantasies, as it's inhabited by hundreds of beautiful wild ponies.

Over the next few days, we covered most of the tourist attractions in and around Salisbury. But what I enjoyed most was spending time alone on the farm. I loved playing with the cats, watching Sam herd the sheep and feeding the chickens, which I renamed after friends of mine. The countryside was a wonderland, a haven; it made me feel safe, uninhibited, free to dream and let my fantasies run wild. And this enchanting land had all the things I needed for my make-believe world to come alive.

I tried hard to push the thoughts of what had happened out of my mind, but Mary's note and horrid pictures of the hideous creature kept creeping in, and every time I walked past the attic stairs my pulse raced. Often I would have the feeling that someone or something was watching me. A couple of times I'd ask whatever it was to show itself, then I'd feel foolish and brush it off, blaming what my mom calls my "silly imagination". A small part of me wanted to go back to the attic room, investigate and try to solve this mystery, but even the thought of it made my gut clench and sent cold shivers down my back.

Finally it was Sunday morning and the McArthur's were coming for dinner. My mind was spinning and my heart danced at the thought of seeing Jonathan again. What should I wear? How should I act? Meek and shy, mature and responsible, or be my usual self, outgoing and bold? What kind of girls did Jonathan like? I knew so very little about him. But I did know a lot about twelve-year-old girls. His little sister would be my target to impress. If I could win her affection, perhaps through her I could win his.

"You'll cut your fingers off if you don't watch what yer doing."

Auntie's voice jogged me. We were in the kitchen making apple pies. I was peeling and slicing while Auntie rolled the dough with an old wooden rolling pin. I had to smile when I looked at her, her head crowned with prickly hair pins and metal rollers, and her face flushed and dusted with flour that mingled with drops of sweat to shimmer on her brow.

"Would you like me to go open a window?" I asked. "You look really hot."

"No, it's just the change, luv." She lifted the bottom of her dependable apron with her doughy fingers and wiped her brow. "A woman's plight, it is. M' mum suffered with it for years, bless her soul."

*Why doesn't she just call it menopause?* I'd heard her complaining about it to Mom: hot flashes, night sweats, mood swings and facial hair. Wow, and I thought puberty and menstruating were awful. I couldn't imagine how Mom was going to handle such an unattractive condition. She had been primping herself all morning for company that Auntie described as "down-to-earth, simple folk." Dad was helping Uncle Reg in the fields. They had strict instructions to be back in the house before noon.

"What happened to your mom and dad, Auntie Em," I asked.

"M' mum went off the deep end, had a heart attack and passed on! M' dad just up and died," she said, in a harsh tone. I didn't want to pry in case I upset her. Auntie, like the cottage, was full of secrets.

The old oak table was draped in a white linen tablecloth embroidered with grapevines and set with Auntie's best Royal Albert china. Nine chairs were squeezed together and pushed underneath. Dog-eared cookbooks and sentimental treasures decorated the counter tops and window sill. A Welsh cabinet packed with blue and white dishes occupied the space next to the window. An antique radio blurted out big band sounds from the top corner shelf. Auntie hummed and boogied to the music, swinging her hips and tossing her head as she mixed mint sauce and sipped sherry wine. The kitchen was alive with the succulent aroma of apple, cinnamon, roast beef, mint and Yorkshire pudding. Thick rich gravy simmered on the stove.

Mom walked in wearing a yellow sun dress complemented by a shiny white belt and beige high heeled sandals. Her lips shimmered bubble gum pink, and her long blonde hair shone like spun gold. She looked like a glamour girl from the fifties. Mom was so into appearances. My friends at home would always say, "It must be cool to have a mom that's so attractive." Personally I'd rather have a mom like Mrs. Jenkins. She's into all kinds of fascinating things and isn't the least bit superficial.

"Need any help, ladies?" she asked, smiling sweetly. Auntie glanced at me, rolled her eyes, then gaped at Mom.

"Well, finally decided to show up, did ya? And dressed up like a dog's dinner no less. You're a bit late; it's all done." Mom walked away sheepishly.

I had to say something. "That wasn't very nice, Auntie Em."

"Oh, cod's wallop, I was just takin' the micky. She knows I didn't mean anything by it."

I guessed that meant she was joking.

The squeak of the garden gate and the sound of voices gave me butterflies. There was a knock on the door. Uncle Reg in his clean plaid shirt rose from his seat, perched his pipe on the ash tray and went to answer it.

"Come in, come in; take a load off."

The woman at the door handed him a small bundle wrapped in a striped tea towel. Uncle Reg put his nose to the cloth.

"Mmmm, smashing," he said with a wide smile. The smell of warm, homemade bread drifted in from the doorway.

"Right out of the oven," the woman said in a deep stern voice that seemed right for her tall stout frame and tough weathered face. Her graying hair was bundled in a tight knot at the back of her head. She wore a simple blue cotton dress, dotted with little white flowers that ballooned at the chest. She had prominent hazel eyes that looked like Uncle Reg's, and she reminded me of a photograph of my grandma Fletcher before she got sick, which was odd as they were not related, or so I assumed.

I was surprised by the appearance of the young girl behind her. Wisps of uneven blonde hair with red streaks framed her face. Long, thick lashes fringed her large, greenish-brown eyes. The short skirt, tank top, accessories and lip gloss she was wearing made her look much older than her age and she looked nothing like her brother, who was tall, dark and especially today, extremely handsome. She glared over at Wooky who was sprawled out in his usual spot on the back of the sofa. He glared back at her with a look that seemed to say, "Back off, bitch," then he let out an indignant meow and scurried off. There was something familiar and unsettling about this girl. I could have sworn that we had met before.

"Well, don't you all look spiffy," Auntie said as she untied her best frilly apron and laid it on the back of the chair.

"It's not every day that the boss invites you to dinner," Mr. McArthur said, his cheerful face lighting up.

Uncle Reg put his hand on Mr. McArthur's shoulder. "Boss, no less. And all this time I thought we were partners." They chuckled and shook hands.

We were introduced to Maud McArthur and Belinda, who grunted and gave me a dirty look. Then we squeezed ourselves around the table. With her manicured fingers, Mom delicately brushed cat hair off the seat of her chair before sitting down. Jonathan sat directly across from me. I tried hard not to stare, but it wasn't easy. Uncle Reg said a short grace. "For what we are about to receive, let us all be thankful. Amen."

Drinks were poured, bowls were passed, cutlery clicked and chitter-chatter was exchanged. When I declined the roast beef, Mrs. McArthur glared at me critically and mumbled with a mouth full of food, "That's a lovely piece of English beef. Your aunt is a marvelous cook."

"I don't eat meat." I hoped that Jonathan would not find this odd.

"It's a stage. She'll get over it," Dad piped up in a jocular tone.

"Don't know what's good for 'er, she don't," Auntie said. I decided not to defend myself in case I sounded stupid or blushed.

I felt Belinda's bulgy eyes staring at me from across the table. I looked up and glanced at her. With lips wrinkled and eyes narrowed, she shot me an icy glare. A cold shiver ran down my back. It was as if I had just been touched by something diabolical. *What's her problem,* I thought. It was evident that it wasn't going to be easy to befriend this kid.

"Did you ever phone that bloke about replacing your window, John?" Uncle Reg asked.

"Not yet, but I'm gonna."

"He did a good job in our attic and he's not dear."

Mr. McArthur dug a piece of roast beef out of his teeth with his broken fingernails and asked, "Did ya ever find out who broke that window in your attic?"

"Nope. Bloody mystery, that."

Mrs. McArthur shook her head. "It was likely some of them hooligans from Salisbury. Them that ride those new-fangled motorbikes, destructive beggars, they are."

Auntie cleared her throat. "Now, now, Maud. We don't

know it were them."

Dad put his hands at the back of his head and leaned back in his chair. "A good stint in the Army is what they need."

I looked at Jonathan and rolled my eyes. He shook his head, then turned to Uncle Reg and asked in a mellow voice, "Didn't you say it looked like it had been broken from the inside, Mr. Fletcher?"

"I'd have to be balmy to say something like that, wouldn't I, lad?"

Auntie dropped her knife and fork. "A few bricks short of a full load, maybe, but not balmy," she said, chuckling. The English, I had noticed, have an unusual way of poking fun at other people without being disrespectful. And they all seemed to know by some mysterious cultural link when the fine line between insult and humor had been crossed.

Laughter echoed around the table. Jonathan and I just carried on eating and ignored the sarcasm. I looked up from my plate. There was a tender strength in Jonathan's face that was vaguely familiar and I felt a subtle, silent connection with him, a sort of strange spiritual link. I wondered if he felt it, too. After dessert, Auntie stood up and started clearing the table. I proceeded to help her.

"That's all right, luv. Your mum can help me with the dishes." Mom gave her a sour grin. She wasn't used to doing dishes by hand and complained privately that the dish soap was ruining her nails.

"Why don't you kids go outside and play football or something?" Auntie asked. "There's an old football in the cupboard by the back door."

Belinda's cold eyes widened and her top lip turned up, as if she had been asked to take out the garbage. I decided to break the ice. "Don't you like playing soccer," I asked? She screwed up her nose in distaste.

"No! And it's not soccer, it's football."

"Whatever," I mumbled.

Jonathan raised his firm muscular body from the table. "You used to. Come on, Sis, let's show Emily how it's played."

"All right, since there's nothing better to do."

I shaded my eyes with my hand as we stepped outside into full dazzling sunlight. The sky was cloudless; the air was filled with the sweet smells of spring. Looking around, I asked, "Where's your vehicle?"

"We walked. It's just over a mile, or about two kilometers to you," Jonathan said. His face lit with a wide, friendly smile. I could feel my heart flutter inside my chest and blots of scarlet touching my cheeks. I turned my head quickly so he wouldn't notice. Oh God, when will this childish blushing stop?

"All right, you lot!" Auntie hollered as she stormed out of the front door waving a camera. "Stand over here," she demanded, pointing at the garden gate. Belinda tossed her blonde hair, placed both hands on her hips and let out a long mournful sigh. Auntie squinted and pointed her stubby little finger. "Now don't you go getting your knickers in a twist, young lady. It won't take a minute."

Jonathan walked toward her, waving his hands behind his back, motioning us to follow. He leaned against the white picket fence. Belinda and I stood on either side of him, shadowed by his powerful wide shoulders. His arms opened like the wings of a majestic bird, then dropped gently over our shoulders. They were tanned and powdered with fine black hair. His touch, the warmth from his body and the tantalizing scent of his deodorant sent shiver ripples through every cell of my body. I was in heaven.

"Say cheese!" My moment of bliss was over in a flash. Auntie dropped the camera into her apron pocket and went back inside.

Jonathan started dribbling the ball, then he bounced it off his knee and onto his head. I stood there in awe, watching his muscles ripple under his thin white tee-shirt. Oh, how much I wanted to touch him, just one little touch.

"All right, showoff, you've got the slapper drooling. You can kick it now!" Belinda shouted as she pushed her sunglasses to the top of her head.

"Hey! That's not nice," Jonathan hollered in an angry tone.

I had no idea what a slapper was, but I couldn't think of anything quick or witty to say, so I decided to keep my mouth shut and brush it off. Squinting her eyes and biting her lip, Belinda kicked the ball forcefully back to her brother. Smiling and trying to look like he was enthused, Jonathan kicked the ball to me. I tried not to show my inexperience by keeping it on the ground. Back and forth it went. Everyone seemed to get a little more relaxed with each play.

Then, as I drew my leg back ready to kick, a strange tingling sensation ran through my body and into my foot.

Wham! I booted the ball. It flew through the air at a tremendous speed, hitting Belinda in the chest, knocking her off her feet and flat on her back. She screamed. I ran over to her, stunned.

"I'm so sorry. Are you okay? I have no idea how that happened."

Jonathan didn't move. He just stood there with his mouth wide open. I put my hand on Belinda's shoulder. She brushed it off angrily and scowled at me.

"Fuck you! You freckle-faced bitch, I'll get you for this."

Ow, that hurt. My fingers curled into a tight fist. I wanted to slap her and give her a piece of my mind but I moved back, took a deep breath and restrained myself, not wanting to run the risk of offending Jonathan. "She's a lovely little thing," Auntie had said. Was she kidding? This mini diva was nasty! She lifted her small frame from the ground and hobbled off, slamming the garden gate forcefully behind her. I walked over to Jonathan. He was sitting on a grassy knoll, combing his thick dark hair. He seemed unconcerned.

"What's with your sister?" I asked.

He shrugged his shoulders. "Puberty, I guess. Hey, how did you do that?"

"Do what?"

"Kick the ball like that."

I blew a long sigh. "I have absolutely no clue." Without thinking I sat down beside him, drew up my knees and sank my face into my hands. Oh, how much I needed a friend to talk to. Someone to share my freaky experiences with, someone who wouldn't think I was mad. Could I confide in Jonathan? Would this hot guy listen to an ugly freckle-faced fourteen-year-old? I said a silent prayer before I opened my mouth.

# Chapter 4

"Hey, are you all right?" Jonathan asked sympathetically.

I pulled my hands away from my face and looked into his soft dark eyes.

"I guess, well, not really." There was a moment of awkward silence while he waited for my response. Then he glanced at his watch.

*Say something, Emily, quickly.* "Have you heard about the legend of Mary Eliss?" I blurted out.

He smiled. "Yep, and all the others."

"Others?"

"The old folks around here are superstitious. They make up all kinds of stories."

I lowered my head and ran my fingers through the silky cool grass. "But there is something really weird about this place and I've seen some things, horrible things."

His forehead wrinkled. "What things?"

I took a deep breath and told him what I had seen in the attic room and all the other creepy things that had happened to me. He didn't look at all surprised or shocked by what I was saying. He just sat motionless, listening intently, wearing a serious expression.

"Well, I suppose you think I'm crazy, too!" I said in a bitter tone.

He just shook his head, grinned, combed his thick ebony hair with his fingers and lifted himself from the ground. "Why doesn't he say something?" I mumbled, as my pleading gaze wandered all over the large sensual form towering above me. Then he bent down and patted me on the head, like you would a dog or a little child.

"Gotta go, kid. Talk to you later." He turned and walked with haste toward the cottage. My heart felt heavy. Tears of embarrassment welled up inside me. It was evident that to him I was just a mixed up little kid.

"Jonathan!" I shouted, impulsively. My hand hit my mouth as I realized how immature it was to call out to him.

He turned his head and hollered, "You're not crazy, Emily. I do believe you!" My eyes widened, filling with tears of relief and joy. Warm and wet, they trickled down my freckled cheeks as I clasped my arms around myself and rocked back and forth on the grassy knoll. He believed me! He believed me! The words rang in my head.

I sat for a while, wrapped in thought, watching the orange glow of the sun slip slowly behind the clouds. The air was cool and the grass was touched with early evening dew. I needed time to think.

When I returned to the cottage, the McArthur's had left.

Everyone's head turned when I walked in the door. Auntie was sitting in her favorite chair, darning socks. Wooky was curled up on the tapestry foot stool beside her feet.

"Where 'ave ya been, luv? We were gonna send out a search party."

"I was just sitting outside. How's Belinda?" I thought it was only polite to ask, although I really wasn't interested.

Auntie bit off a length of wool with her teeth and threaded her needle. "A bit sore, she is."

Dad peered at me over his reading glasses. "She said that you deliberately tried to hurt her."

"No, I did not!"

Mom stood up. "Now, now, honey. I'm sure it was an accident. You can apologize to her tomorrow."

"Fat chance," I mumbled as I wandered into the parlor to seek seclusion.

The room was a true hideaway, full of cozy, comfortable things. There were framed family photos, delicate ornaments, soft armchairs with needlepoint cushions, colorful hooked rugs scattered over the rich hardwood floor, and the odd, newfangled, pull-out couch. A large glass vase stuffed with voluptuous powder-pink peonies sat on the polished sideboard, filling the room with their rich perfume. Small bundles of lavender tied with faded ribbon hung from the tiny window. They looked stale and out of place.

The cottage was more a reflection of Auntie's heritage than her no frills, no nonsense, farm-wife personality. She had been taught at a young age how to crochet, arrange flowers, sew, bake English delicacies, keep a tidy house and set a proper table. Her mother, I assumed, must have been a gentler, more refined soul—a modest domestic goddess, or something like that. Auntie did say: "Like chalk and cheese, me mum and me, we were."

I grabbed my backpack from beside the arm chair and pulled out my journal and pen. A familiar black and white fur ball was nested in a hand-knitted blanket on the couch. "Hi, Winky, can I join you? Mom would have a fit if she saw you in here." She lifted her white chin and glared up at me as if to say 'Who cares what she thinks?' I snuggled down beside her and scratched behind her velvety ears. She purred contentedly. I opened my journal.

*May 26*

*Dear friend,*

*Merryweather Lodge has lost its fairytale magic. Somewhere beneath its enchanting exterior lies an ugly, dark soul. I feel both good and evil in this place and it scares me. Furthermore, I'm changing, torn between two worlds. Part of me wants to stay in the safe and comfortable place, where I am free to be me—this place where I can paint cows purple and color outside the lines, where I can eat mounds of ice cream and chocolate without feeling fat or guilty, where the fairies at the bottom of my garden are not silly products of my imagination, but real colorful little creatures with magical lives. The other part of me fights to move into the confusing, insecure adult world, where the boundaries are like barbed wire fences and the pressures, huge. But now I feel I must give in and step outside the gate and into the great beyond, as I have fallen in love. And this kind of world is no place for a child. Jonathan McArthur is leading me away. I can smell his manly scent and hear his soft, sexy voice as I visualize his warm naked body lying next to mine. Pleasurable sensations wash over parts of me I never knew I had. No, this is no place for a child.*

The floorboards creaked. Someone was coming. Quickly I grabbed my backpack and shoved my confidant into its zippered pocket.

"Just came in for a pack of cards, luv. We thought ya were asleep."

I put my hand over my mouth to stop myself from giggling. Auntie's words were slurred, her lips had caved in and the bulge in her apron pocket revealed her secret. I was tempted to ask her where her teeth were.

"I was just getting ready for bed."

She shivered. "You'll catch your death of cold with that there window open."

"The window's not open." I turned. The window was open and furthermore, the lavender had disappeared. "Where's the lavender that was hanging there?"

"Lavender? I wouldn't have that stuff in the house if ya paid me. It's bad luck. Been dreaming again 'ave ya, luv?"

Auntie left the room shaking her head. I pulled the heavy

cushions off the couch, tucked a flannel sheet under them and plunked a fluffy pillow on top. After slipping into my night-gown, I grabbed the soft downy quilt and crawled under-neath. It smelt like fresh air and sunshine. My eyes searched the window. How could bundles of lavender just disappear? Was I hallucinating, dreaming or going crazy like my grand-mother? Or were these visions keys to the dark mystery that shrouded Merryweather Lodge? Why was I the only one ex-periencing this freaky stuff? But Jonathan believed me and he did say we'd talk about it later. Perhaps he knew something that no one else did or perhaps he'd had some strange experi-ences himself. I needed to see him again and ask him. But what if he was lying to me to make me feel better and laugh-ing at me under his breath? I'd die of embarrassment for sure. This vacation was like something out of the twilight zone. My mind was spinning; my eyelids were getting heavier and heav-ier.

When I woke up, I was alone. Mom and Dad's bed linen was folded neatly on top of the pull-out couch. I blinked the sleep out of my eyes and squinted at the brass clock on the sideboard. It was ten thirty. I'd slept in. There were muffled voices coming from the kitchen. Dragging a cushion from my makeshift bed across the floor, I sank onto my knees and opened the door just enough to hear what was being said.

"Had to let him go, they did."

"Why's that then?" I hadn't heard this woman's voice before.

"He 'ad an alibi and the blood they found under 'er fin-gernails were that of a relative, they say."

"He was a relative, weren't he?"

"A blood relative, you dingbat!" There was laughter, a moment of silence, and then Auntie spoke. "The only blood relative that I know of is 'er brother that lives in America."

"And all her cousins and second cousins from around here, your Reg being one."

"Oh yeah." There was a pause. "And Maud. She was the last one to see 'er alive, ya know."

*Is she saying that Maud and Uncle Reg are related? It can't be.*

"They'll be wanting to question her, then."

"Maud would have your guts for garters if you crossed 'er, but she ain't capable of something like that. Besides, she was in Portsmouth visiting John's sister when it 'appened. Mark my words, this were done by the same ravin' lunatic that did the others in. I told Lizzy to keep 'er bloody mouth shut, poor thing."

"Others?" I muttered. My knees were cramping up. I shuffled awkwardly, knocking the door handle with my elbow and hitting my funny bone. A sharp pain shot up my arm. "Ouch!"

"What was that?"

"Is that you, our Emily? It's about time you got up."

Oh great, just when it was getting interesting. "I'll be out in a minute!" I slipped into my clothes, grabbed my toiletries and headed for the bathroom, straining my ears for any curious morsel. But all I could hear was whispering and the clink of cups and saucers.

"Blimey. It's alive," Auntie said in her sarcastic tone.

"Where's Mom and Dad?"

"Gone to town, they 'ave. They won't be long. Come 'ere, there's someone I want ya to meet."

A little old lady was sitting at the table. A paisley shawl with long tassels covered her shoulders. Snow-white hair was pulled up in a bun and sat on top of her head like a doughnut. Long dangly earrings hung from her ear lobes; strings of multicolored beads circled her short neck. Round glasses perched on her little pug nose.

"This is Mrs. Tilly, from two farms down." She held out her wrinkled little hand and smiled sweetly. "This is our Emily. Named after me, she was."

Mrs. Tilly's glasses slid to the end of her nose. Two milky greenish-blue eyes peered over them and studied me eagerly. "Well, if she ain't a Ross, I don't know who is."

Ross was my Grandma Fletcher's maiden name. She patted the seat of the ladder-back chair beside her. I dragged it from under the table and sat down next to her.

"I never knew my Grandma Fletcher. She died before I was born."

"Maybe it were for the best," Auntie said as she plunked a large glass of milk in front of me. "Eggs, luv?"

"No, just toast, please."

Auntie gave me one of her reprimanding half smiles. "Eats like a bird, 'er does."

"Didn't you like my grandmother, Auntie?"

"Truth was, Sarah didn't like me. Wanted us to immigrate to Canada with them, she did; 'er blamed me for talking

Reg into staying 'ere. Nutty as a fruit cake, she was."

Mrs. Tilly drew close to me, put her white boney fingers on my hand and looked at me compassionately. Her eyes were a little creepy and looked like tiny turquoise marbles in a puddle of water. "Elizabeth Eliss was a little mental too. Ran in the family, it did."

I gasped. "Eliss? The ones that used to live here?"

Aunties' eyes ballooned. She pulled out her hanky and put it to her mouth.

"Yes, that's right. Your great grandma was Elizabeth Eliss' sister."

I could see Auntie shaking her head vigorously out of the corner of my eye. "I'm related to Mary Eliss?"

Mrs. Tilly glanced over at Auntie, then she stared into her cup and chewed on her bottom lip. I waited for an answer. Auntie cleared her throat. "What ya got planned for today, Emily?"

I bolted to my feet. The chair fell with a thump behind me. "Why is everybody so secretive?" I glared at Auntie and raised my voice. "Why didn't you tell me I was related to the Elisses?"

Mrs. Tilly put her hand on her chest and sank back against her chair. Auntie smacked the hard surface of the table with her stubby hands, narrowed her eyes and said in a stern voice, "Sit down, ya cheeky madam!"

Timidly I picked up the chair and lowered myself into the seat. I've got to stop being so volatile, I told myself.

"I didn't tell ya 'cause ya didn't need to know." She bent

over the table tight-lipped, grabbed the brown earthenware teapot and poured herself another cup of tea. There was an uncomfortable silence.

I gulped the rest of my milk. "Can I go now, please?"

"And where would ya be going?"

"For a walk." I unfolded my long legs from under the table and stood up. "It was nice meeting you, Mrs. Tilly."

"So long, dear. We'll meet again, I'm sure." There was a sweet but sly smile on her lips and a strange gleam in her eyes.

"Don't ya go near them there woods, do ya 'ear!"

"Yeah, I hear."

"Teenagers. They live the life of Riley these days and got no respect for their elders, they don't," Auntie whispered, loud enough for me to hear.

Then I heard Mrs. Tilly's soft voice. "She has the gift. I can see it in her eyes."

"Rubbish! The only gift she 'as is the gift of the gab."

What was she talking about? What gift? "Whoops!" I flinched as I stepped outside the door. Winny was curled up in a heap on the step. "You're lucky I didn't stand on you, kitty." Her pale-blue eyes stared up at me, as if to acknowledge what I had said. She got up, humped her snow-white back, gave a long lazy yawn and stretched. I rubbed my fingers together and made a kissing sound. "Coming for a walk, Winny?" Like a faithful dog, she trotted after me. I had never met such an agreeable cat.

The path from the farm to the meadow zigzagged up a

slight incline. Masses of colorful wild flowers were spread all around like a patchwork blanket. The fresh air was heavy with floral perfume and abuzz with the soft hum of honey bees on the wing. A warm breeze caressed my face. Caught up in the moment, I hummed and skipped, turning my imaginary rope over my head and under my feet, like a playful little child. Sometimes I wished that I never had to grow up, that I could always be like this, fancy-free in my world of make believe. Winny's white coat was spotted with the downy tufts of dandelion seeds. I picked a stalk and blew softly. "He loves me, he loves me not."

On a whim I threw myself on the ground, cushioned by the thick floral quilt. Winny climbed on my chest. I reached for the willow stick that was lying beside me and cleaned her fur gently with its nodules. Kneading her paws into my stomach, she purred contentedly. I gazed up. Puffs of marshmallow clouds sailed across the vast blue sky, like ships on a calm ocean voyage. A yellow and blue butterfly flew past Winny's nose; she gave it a quick swipe, just missing its fragile wings. Thank goodness.

It felt so calm and peaceful here but a voice inside was vibrating with a message that I didn't understand. Then I heard what sounded like a whisper. I listened intently. It was a soft surreal sound. Gradually it became louder and clearer.

Suddenly, Winny arched her back. Her fur stood erect. She flew off my chest. I sprang to my feet. A gush of cold air swirled around me. Shivering, I mumbled, "Who's there?"

"Run! Run!" it commanded. My feet wouldn't move. A

sickening heat crept over me. I felt light headed, dizzy, then darkness.

When I came to, I was holding a blood-stained stick tightly in my hand. Dazed, I looked around for Winny. She was lying still, in a bed of clover. Blood-red dots stained her pure white coat. I threw the stick into the long grass and crouched down beside her. At first she hissed, and then she cowered down and gazed at me pitifully. I gathered her up gently into my arms and cradled her like a newborn baby. Her sad eyes met mine. "Oh, Winny, it wasn't me. I wouldn't hurt you. Don't you know I love you?"

I started to run, being as careful as I could not to jolt her. My heart ached; there was an empty feeling in the pit of my stomach. Tears of utter sadness trickled down my cheeks. The colorful sea of gentle waves was now a turbulent ocean, thrashing against my feet. Seagulls screeched, circling overhead. "She'll be okay. She'll be okay," I repeated. Using positive affirmations was a way of getting what you want, according to Skye's mom.

I dashed out of the meadow with my arms stiff and unwavering, down the zigzag path that led to the cottage. I couldn't look at Winny now, in fear that she might have stopped breathing. The cottage was becoming clearer. I could see Auntie pegging washing on the clothes line. "Auntie Em!" I screamed. She didn't hear me. I screamed louder, then she turned, dropped her peg basket and ran toward me. My legs felt like rubber, my arms were numb. I fell to the ground, exhausted.

"Good God, child. What's 'appened?" Her sturdy little hands cupped my elbows and lifted me up. Cautiously she took Winny out of my arms.

"Is she going to be okay? Please let her be okay." I sobbed. Mom spotted us from the kitchen window and came dashing out of the cottage in a panic.

"Emily, Emily! What's happened to you?"

"Now, don't ya go getting your knickers in a twist, Penny. There's been a bit of an accident. Take 'er into the house and I'll get Ron to take us to the vet. Hurry now," Auntie said with authority.

Mom's hand caressed my back. "Are you okay, honey?"

"I'm fine. Just go and get Dad." I hobbled into the sitting room and collapsed into the wide arms of the wing-backed chair. My body felt limp, drained of its life force. My mind was spinning. I closed my eyes and tried to visualize Winny chasing butterflies in the garden, happy and healthy. But the picture was blurred. Mom stormed into the room, wearing a concerned expression. She stood in front of me with her arms folded across her chest. "I want you to explain to me what happened, please, honey."

What could I say? I couldn't tell her the truth. She'd think I was mad, and I couldn't believe it myself. How could I have hurt Winny, even unconsciously? It was unthinkable. Someone must have knocked me out and planted the stick in my hand, or worse still, something had possessed me. I remembered the voice telling me to run.

"Emily Ann, I'm talking to you."

"Hmm, I found her like that in the meadow; a wild animal must have attacked her."

"Well then, you must have saved her life. She'd have probably died if you hadn't found her. You stay here and I'll go make you a nice cup of tea."

I felt sick. My head sank into the soft cushions. My eyelids drooped.

The screeching sound of worn brakes woke me up. I flew off the chair and over to the window. It was Dad and Auntie Em. She was carrying a bundle wrapped in a red tartan blanket. I dashed out the door. "Is she okay?" I pleaded.

Auntie smiled widely and nodded her head. "She'll be all right, m' luv. There's no broken bones. Whatever it was just cut the skin on her back. The vet told us to keep her in the house for a couple of days and gave us some ointment so she don't go septic."

I breathed a sigh of relief, pulled back the red blanket and stroked the top of her soft white head with my finger.

Mom was waiting at the door. "Emily said that a wild animal must have attacked her."

Auntie Em looked at me suspiciously. "Oh, is that right?" I could tell that she knew I was lying. I lowered my head, as feelings of guilt and shame ran through me.

It didn't take Winny long to recover, but the incident left me in a state of confusion and fear. Something was haunting me and making me do horrible things. But something else was trying to protect me; that I was sure of. What was going on here?

I missed Skye and all my other friends. I missed my dog. I even missed school, which was unthinkable under normal circumstances. We came here in May because the flights were cheaper and it was convenient for my dad to get time off work. I brought lots of homework but it's boring when you don't have a friend to do it with. This place was getting annoying. There was no computer, an old TV that only got three channels and only one phone that I'm not allowed to use except for emergencies. It was like being in a time warp. I was counting the days until I could leave this ominous place and return to my normal, predictable environment.

There was one thing that held me back though, something I didn't want to leave: Jonathan McArthur. Merryweather Lodge had lost its charm but Jonathan had captured my heart. I had to see him again. I just had to.

One day we were in Salisbury shopping for souvenirs. Uncle Reg had slipped me a ten pound note before we left. I bought each one of my friends a pen with a Union Jack motif engraved on it, and I found a piece of rock from Stonehenge for Skye. It was supposed to have mystical powers, or at least that's what the package said.

After we came home, Auntie made us one of her special cream teas. It was a high fat, high carb delectable delight consisting of buttered crumpets, tomato and cucumber sandwiches, custard tarts, chocolate éclairs and scones covered in strawberry jam and thick Devonshire cream. Now I was stuffed and felt uncomfortably fat. I stood at the kitchen sink and submerged a delicate rose-patterned plate into warm soapy water. I had offered to clear away and wash the dishes, because I had nothing better to do and so that Auntie and Mom could watch their favorite show, *Coronation Street*. I could hear Auntie giving Mom a running commentary. Mom had become addicted to English soap operas, but I couldn't understand half of what they were saying and they were all so superficial.

I pushed open the little window with my soapy hands. The smell of fresh air and sunshine greeted me. A row of spotless white sheets hung from the clothes line and fluttered in the gentle breeze. Pretty pink blossoms littered the ground below the large cherry tree, while glimpses of early fruit hung from its sturdy branches. I looked into my mind's eye and imagined I could see myself standing under the canopy of branches. A long white flowing gown, decorated with silk and lace, was draped over my womanly form. A halo of little white daisies crowned my head and I was holding a bouquet of white gardenias. Jonathan, a man now, was standing beside me, wearing a black tuxedo with white accessories which made him look stunningly handsome.

We turned and faced each other. Slowly he leaned forward, revealing his warm masculine scent. His lips, moist and tender, touched mine, sending a quiver through my entire body. My vision shifted. We were in a pink and white room, standing beside a large bed covered in lace and spotted with rose petals. Jonathan was removing his clothes seductively, in front of me. I watched in awe, examining every part of his beautifully proportioned body.

I knew what to expect, as I had seen pictures of naked men before. Under an old sewing basket in my mom's closet was a stack of dirty magazines. When I first found them I was shocked and repulsed by my discovery. But now, when I'm home alone, I sneak into the bedroom and browse through the erotic photos. I wonder why something so taboo feels so good.

Jonathan was now standing stark naked in front of me. I shivered with excitement and moved toward him. His lips parted. "Colrea. Colrea," he whispered. Colrea? Who was she? The name touched a familiar chord that resonated within me.

Crack! I blinked and looked down. My hands still submerged in soapy water were holding two pieces of a broken plate. A sudden cold draft swept around me. The water in the sink turned icy cold. I sensed the essence of something in the room with me. An unpleasant smell filled my nostrils, stale and medicinal, like my grandfather's bedroom just before he died. My legs started to tremble.

# Chapter 5

I pulled my wrinkled hands out of frigid water and crept slowly, cautiously, toward the door. My body was stiff, my eyes glued to the exit. I was afraid to let them wander in fear of what I might see. I breathed a sigh of relief as I closed the door behind me. Leaning against its safe hard surface, I put my wet hands over my chest to calm my rapidly beating heart and drew in long deep breaths to regain my composure.

Mom and Auntie were still in the sitting room staring at the television screen. They were holding tiny crystal glasses filled with glowing sherry wine. Auntie's cheeks were rosy, her nose bright red and the curls of her wiry gray hair had unraveled in all directions. She looked like a clown. Mom was sitting cross-legged, her back perfectly poised against the sofa. Wooky was sprawled across the back, just above her head. She must be either drunk or oblivious to get that close to the cat, I thought. English slang and odd accents bellowed from the television. A warm orange glow and the scent of wood smoke emanated from the fireplace, giving the room a warm cozy atmosphere.

"Hi, honey, have you come to join us?" Mom asked, then swallowed a lady-like burp.

"No, I need Auntie Em to come and look at something in the kitchen."

Auntie leaned forward, lifted a cheek from the chair and let out a loud *puff*! "Better out than in," she said. Mom put her hand to her mouth and rolled her eyes in disgust.

"What's that about the kitchen, luv?"

"Could you just come and see, please?"

"All right, all right. There's no rest for the wicked." She eased her dwarf-like body out of the chair and wobbled toward me. A loose white thread hung from her petticoat. I grabbed the handle of the kitchen door nervously, flung it open and stood back, allowing Auntie to go in first. I followed close behind her, my gaze darting around the room. There was no cold draft or foul smell, only the broken plate lying in the dirty dish water. I should have known that this would happen.

"What do ya want to show me?"

"Ummm, I broke one of your good plates. I'm really sorry."

She stood in front of me with her arms folded, scowling. "Ya dragged me away from the telly to tell me that?" My hand shot to my face as I tried to fight back tears of utter frustration. Auntie reached up and patted my shoulder. "There, there, luv. It were only a plate. No good crying over spilt milk."

I stepped back, pulled my hands away from my face and looked her right in the eyes. "There was something here!" I sighed. "Something gross."

She wiped her sleeve across her clammy brow, shrugged her shoulders and said in a firm tone, "Codswallop. What ya've got, m' luv, is a funny imagination. Plays tricks on ya, it does. It's the brainy ones like you that suffer with it." She pushed her hand under her cardigan sleeve, pulled out a blue striped hanky and put it over her mouth as she dragged her fuzzy-slippered feet out the door.

Tears of frustration gathered in my eyes. I didn't want to stay in this house a moment longer, but what choice did I have? What was I going to do? I clenched my fists and stamped my feet on the hardwood floor. "Who are you and what do you want from me?" I cried. Then I paused for a moment, just in case. Nothing. I dashed into the parlor and threw myself onto the couch, grabbing the soft downy quilt for comfort. I remembered my daydream and Jonathan's voice. It was only a vision but his voice sounded so clear. Colrea...why was that name so familiar?

I had to contact Jonathan; I had tons of questions to ask him, but how? I wouldn't dare go to his house and Uncle Reg didn't want me using the telephone unless it was "a must". They had to pay for all their local calls, so they'd know if I used it. Oh, what the heck. We would be gone before they get their next bill. Besides, how much could it cost to phone someone so close? The telephone sat on an antique curio table which also served as a resting place for keys, pens, matches, a little book of phone numbers and other miscellaneous items. It was by the front door and far enough away from the sitting room that if I was real quiet, Mom and Auntie wouldn't hear me. It would be so much easier if they had a cordless phone. *Things are so primitive here.*

I crouched down, rested my back against the wall and quietly lifted the receiver.

"Hello." It was Mrs. McArthur. My stomach fluttered.

"Hi. Is Jonathan there, please?"

"Speak up, I can't hear ya."

I raised my voice, slightly. "Could I speak to Jonathan?"

"Jonny!" she screamed, right into my ear.

"Hello."

More stomach flutters. I cleared my throat to stop my voice from quivering. "Hi. It's Emily."

"Who?"

"Emily Fletcher. Reg and Emy's niece."

"Oh. Hi ya."

"I'm phoning to ask if you have time to meet with me. I need to talk to you about something." A moment of deafening silence. "It won't take long." I crossed my fingers.

"Okay," he said in a grudging voice.

"How about..." I glanced at my watch, "seven thirty by my uncle's barn?" More silence. "Don't worry; I'm not going to seduce you." *Oh boy, did I just say that?*

A meek, throaty laugh echoed through the receiver. "What's it about?"

"I can't tell you on the phone."

"All right, I'll be there."

"Thanks," I said humbly as I yelled a silent *"Yes! Yes!"* I lowered the receiver quietly and tiptoed into my make-shift bedroom. I had one hour to prepare—to decide what I was going to say, but more importantly, what I was going to wear.

I decided to wear my bright yellow cashmere sweater. I've been told it enhances the color of my eyes and makes me look older. It was a birthday gift from my friend Katherine Westbury. Katherine is the only girl in our grade who has her own credit card. Her parents are loaded. She's quite over-weight, has a poor self-image and thinks everyone hates her. So she buys expensive gifts for people in exchange for their friendship. Skye and I have been trying to help build up her self-image, which isn't easy when secretly we struggle with our own.

I stuffed my bra with a couple of tissues to give my classy sweater more shape. In contrast, my low cut jeans with a studded belt added vogue and sex appeal. I stared at my re-flection in the cabinet mirror. Secretly, I hated my face—the freckles, the cabbage eyes, the boney cheeks and the ugly sil-ver braces that stopped me from smiling and chewing gum. And to top it all off, yesterday I found a zit on my chin. I squeezed it and made it worse. It's a telltale sign that I have my period. I prayed that Jonathan wouldn't sense it. Skye told me that boys can sense when a girl has her period; something to do with our animal nature. I loathe getting my period. It is, as Auntie said, "A woman's plight."

I plastered my face with mom's best concealing foundation, darkened my lashes and brows, smoothed lip gloss over my mouth and took one last look in the mirror. *Oh no, I'm becoming a girly girl.* But I liked what I saw even though it made me feel like a fraud. As long as I didn't smile open-mouthed, I'd be okay.

I stuffed a text book under my arm and headed for the door. "I'm going outside to do some homework," I shouted.

"Okay, honey," Mom shouted back, which was followed by a gulping hiccup. Mom loved her wine almost as much as she loved her cigarettes. I was relieved that they hadn't seen me; they would have questioned my appearance, for sure. I glanced at the clock hanging by the kitchen door. It was seven thirty-five. I was running late, and furthermore, I'd spent so much time preparing my body, I'd forgotten to prepare my speech. What was I going to say?

I flung open the door and hurried out into the refreshing evening air, sucking mouthfuls of it into my lungs. My heart was racing with anticipation, my mind abuzz, but I stuck out my chest and walked with confidence through the back yard, down the trodden path toward the barn. The air was filled with the earthy scent of damp grass, and patchy shadows darkened my way.

I glanced up at the vast dark-blue sky. A tiny twinkling light appeared—the first evening star. I stopped and closed my eyes. "Star light, star bright. First star I've seen tonight. I wish I may, I wish I might, have this wish I wish tonight. I wish that this evening will be perfect and that somehow I will be able to plant a seed of passion deep within Jonathan's heart." A sharp cramp in my gut prompted me to add, "And that he won't be able to sense that I have my period."

As I got closer to the building, doubt and apprehension crept into my mind. I wondered if he'd even show up or if I'd say something stupid and scare him off. The huge red barn with its hipped roof loomed in front of me like a formidable monster. I bent down and leaned my text book against the rough wooden doors. The pungent smell of damp hay filtered through the cracks.

Standing by the door, I hugged my shoulders to keep out the cold. I was knee deep in a tangle of overgrown grasses and my thoughts were tying themselves into knots. What would I do if he didn't show up? What questions should I ask him and how should I ask them? Should I give him a compliment or hint at how much I liked him?

"Boo!"

I screamed, jumped, and grabbed my chest in case my heart popped out. "You scared me to death. It's spooky enough around here as it is."

"I'm sorry. Couldn't resist."

Heat crept into my checks. *Don't blush, don't you dare blush.* Jonathan's wide shoulders filled a dark blue hoodie; black jeans clung to his firm thighs. His warm smile sent my pulse racing. He was pushing a rickety old bike with a slender seat, curved handle bars and rusty wheels.

"That's yours?" I asked with a hint of sarcasm.

He rolled his eyes. "It's my dad's." There was a cool, disapproving tone to his voice.

"Sorry. I didn't mean to offend you."

"You didn't."

I needed to break the ice, without saying something stupid. "My aunt told me that you were going to art school."

"Yeah, I'm studying fine arts."

"Cool! I'm going to be a writer or a vet. I haven't quite made up my mind yet. Do you have any pets?"

He lowered his head. "I've had three cats but they've all died."

"Oh that's so sad. I have a six-year-old German Shepherd named Merlin."

"Brilliant. What did you want to talk to me about?"

*He was getting impatient; I have to make this interesting,* I thought, while twirling strands of red hair between my fingers nervously. "I just want to ask you some questions, if that's okay. All kinds of weird things are happening to me but no one believes me, no one except you, that is. And everyone is so secretive around here."

He lowered his bike into the long grass, leaned his back against the slabs of red wood, and pushed his hands into the deep slits of his hoodie pockets. "How can I help?" He was trying to act poised but I could tell he was uncomfortable.

"What do you know about Lizzie Lunn's murder?"

"Not much, but I do know she was chopped up with an axe in her parlor. My sister found her."

I shivered. "You're kidding. Oh, that must have been horrible."

"Yeah, it had quite an effect on her."

*Maybe that's why she's so deranged.*

"Who do you think did it?"

"Dunno, but they're trying to pin it on her stepson."

"You don't think it was him?"

"No, they're only blaming him because he's simple. People with mental disorders are scapegoats. It's not right." *He's compassionate,* I thought, *and not afraid to show it. A quality I admire in a guy.*

"What about the others?"

"What others?"

"The other murders."

He lowered his head and shuffled his feet. "Oh yeah, there's been a lot lately. One for every season. Some say it's the B.D.O."

"The who?"

"The British Druid Order. They're big around these parts."

I thought for a moment. "Weren't the Druids Celtic priests who were thought to have built Stonehenge?"

He grinned. "Yep, these guys are their successors."

"Wait a minute. Lizzy was killed on the twenty-first of March which is the Spring Equinox. That would be a Druid holiday, right?"

"Right. Like I said, one for every season, Spring Equinox, Summer Solstice, Autumn Equinox and Winter Solstice. That's why some people are suspicious."

"You seem to know a lot about them. Do you think they

had anything to do with it?"

He clicked his gum. "Nope, I shouldn't think so. They're all about animal rights, saving the earth, astrology, herbs and sun worshipping; pagan stuff. Folks around here call them the Devil's children. The locals will ridicule anything they don't understand. Ignorance is all it is."

I nodded my head in agreement. "Do you believe in that kind of stuff, protecting the environment, animal rights and things like that?"

His eyes sparkled and met mine. "Yeah, I do," he replied in a serious tone.

I held his glance and gave him a wide, closed-mouthed smile. "Me too." I knew it, he was a kindred spirit. I had found a connection, a common bond.

He pushed a strand of stray hair away from his face, squared his shoulders and folded his arms. "What else did you want to ask me?"

I had to think fast. "Do you know who all's related around here?"

"That's tough. I think they all are to some degree. I know that my mum and Lizzy Lunn were cousins and my great grandmother was the legendary Mary Eliss' mother's sister."

I gasped. "You're kidding! Apparently she was my great grandmother's sister too. Oh great, does that mean we're related?" *It can't be.* Then I remembered Mrs. Tilly's conversation with Auntie about cousins and second cousins.

He laughed. "And what's wrong with that?"

"Nothing. We'd be like, just distant relatives, right?"

"Very distant," he said, as if he knew what I was thinking. But how distant was distant enough?

I'd almost forgotten the most important question. "How come you believed me when I told you about the spooky stuff that was happening to me?"

"There's lots of spooky stuff going on around here."

"Like what?" I asked eagerly.

"You're not going to get scared if I tell you, are you?"

"Are you kidding, after all I've seen?"

There was a moment of anxious silence. Then he cleared his throat and spoke with staid calmness. "The ghost of a young girl haunts this place. When I was a lad, she used to play with me. We'd climb trees together, play tag and football. She told me never to tell anyone about our friendship or she'd never play with me again. I wasn't scared of her; it felt normal for her to be here." His voice took on a deeper serious tone. "One day she lured me into the woodlot, and I was in there for two days."

My eyes grew. "What happened?"

"Dunno. They found me curled up under a huge oak tree, unconscious. The only thing I could remember was following her into the woods."

"Wow! What did she look like? Do you still see her?"

"She's about twelve, wears a long old-fashioned dress and her hair's red." His gaze swept over me. "Like yours."

"Was it Mary Eliss?"

"I don't know, she never told me her name. Funny though, I hadn't seen her in ages, but just lately she's been showing up a lot."

"Where?"

"Well, yesterday I saw her standing by my parents' bed-room door. I had a feeling that she was trying to protect me from something. Don't know why."

I stared at him intently, captivated by his presence, taking in every morsel of information.

"And now she's here."

"Where?"

"Standing right behind you."

I froze. "You're joking, right?" He lifted his hand and pointed his finger. Ever so carefully, I turned around. Nothing!

Jonathan threw back his head and roared with laughter. I lunged at him, banging my fists on his chest playfully. "That wasn't funny." His powerful hands gripped my arms and squeezed. I flinched. "Ow!"

"Sorry," he said, easing his grip and grinning widely.

"Have you told anyone about the girl?"

"No, they would have just said I was imagining it. Some-times I think the old locals have some sort of secret code of si-lence among themselves. The minute you talk about any weird occurrences, they clam up or change the subject."

"Yeah, I've noticed."

"It's odd, really, as most of them are very superstitious."

His voice was wonderfully soft and clear. I stared into his face longingly. It was so close to mine that I could smell the spearmint gum on his warm breath as it brushed against my face. I could almost taste the mint and feel his full mouth on mine. His dark eyes blazed. His lips were moist and ready. I closed my eyes, drew my face closer to his and waited. A curious sense of recognition overwhelmed me as my body trembled with passion. Then, I felt the weight of two strong hands on my shoulders, pushing me away with gentle authority. I shuffled back, shocked and embarrassed. He looked at me pityingly.

"How old are you, Emily?"

I straightened my back and put my hands on my hips. "I'll be fifteen in August!"

"Yeah? Well, I'll be nineteen."

"So what?" I felt the pain of rejection stabbing at my heart. Humiliation and anger welled up inside me and tears gathered in my eyes. *I won't cry. No way will I cry!*

"I think you'd better go back. Your folks will be wondering where you are." His voice was kind and sympathetic.

"I'm not a little kid, you know."

He gave me a courteous smile, pulled his rusty old bike out of the tall grass and dragged it forcefully onto the beaten path. "Leave it alone, Emily. You'll only get yourself into trouble. And be thankful you don't live here," he shouted as he mounted his bike and pumped the pedals.

"I haven't finished my questions yet! Do you know someone called Colrea?" I hollered. His head turned quickly, then back again. Was that a yes? Had he heard that name before? His dark silhouette rode off into the dusk like a lone cowboy on his trusty old steed.

I grabbed my text book and tucked it under my arm. What was I thinking? As if a catch like that would want to kiss an unattractive girl of my age, with mole hill boobs and a mouth full of braces. *I'm so stupid.* But there was something, my inside voice told me, a sort of yearning in his eyes and the way he stared at me without blinking, as if he were trying to figure out where he'd seen me before. There was an attraction; I could feel it in my gut.

The air was cool now, and under the loose sleeves of my cashmere sweater tiny goose bumps covered my arms. Above my head, an array of twinkling diamonds dotted the infinite navy-blue canvas. Sheep bleated in the distance. Sam's friendly silhouette came running up to greet me. Uncle Reg must be home; that meant it was getting late. "Sorry, Sam, I can't play with you tonight." I patted his black and white head as I hurried by. His sad brown eyes stared up at me, pleading for attention. "I'll play with you tomorrow, I promise." I felt sad for him, having to be outside all night, alone. If only he'd stop chasing the cats.

I couldn't sleep that night. The chatter box inside my head wouldn't shut up; it kept going over and over everything that had happened. I tried desperately to put some of the pieces of the puzzle together. Half dreams, bodiless voices, scraps of conversation were exchanged. Fragments of my recurring dream, scary elusive visions, faded in and out. I tossed and turned, dozed, then awoke and dozed again. The heavy breathing followed by disgusting snorting sounds coming from my dad didn't help. It was so annoying. I wanted to throw my pillow at him.

Finally, glimmers of daybreak filtered through the tiny diamond panels of the window and a rooster's rise-and-shine *cock-a-doodle-do* echoed from a distance. I pushed the little light on my watch as I struggled to my feet, bug-eyed and yawning. It was five o'clock in the morning. My mouth felt fuzzy and dry and tasted like rotten eggs. I slipped my heavy terry housecoat over my shoulders, gathered my toiletries and clothes, and headed for the bathroom. The house was cool and hushed except for the hypnotic, repetitive tick-tock, tick-tock of the antique grandfather clock.

I was startled to see Uncle Reg sitting at the kitchen table. His jolly round face, with its web of purple-red veins, droopy moustache and bushy brows, lit up when he saw me. His large work-worn hands were wrapped around a mug of steaming hot tea. A pile of thick-crusted white toast, smothered in creamy melting butter, sat on a chipped plate next to a soft boiled egg wearing a tiny knitted hat to keep it warm. I gazed at the delightful arrangement of tulips that had replaced the jar of daffodils. Their long proud stems with slender green leaves were topped with crowns of red and orange and inside their crowns tiny black trumpets played a silent tune of contentment.

"Good morning, our Emily. How come you're up so early?"

"Couldn't sleep." I poured myself a glass of orange juice and sat down beside him. His watery old eyes studied me.

"You should have stayed in the attic. Your aunt went to

great lengths to make it all prim and proper for you and I'm sure it would have been more comfortable."

I grinned and swirled the orange pulp around in my glass. "I'm sorry."

"What's up, lass? You look a little down-in-the-dumps."

I knew better than to talk to Uncle Reg about my experiences. He was a kind and gentle man, but like my dad, down to earth, black and white, and conventional with old-fashioned values that were etched in stone. He'd tell me I was crazy for sure. "I'm just bored and tired."

His shiny bald head nodded while his old face split into a wide grin. "Not much for a young lass to do around here, I'll admit." His forehead wrinkled. "Why don't you ask John's young'un to come over or go to the pictures with you? One of us will drive you."

I frowned and laughed to myself at the thought of what Belinda would say if I asked her to go to the movies with me. "I don't think she likes me and we don't have anything in common."

"Rubbish! What's there about you not to like?" His one eye closed in a teasing wink. "Bet you'd go with her brother." He leaned forward and whispered, "I've seen the way you look at him."

Uncle Reg was obviously more perceptive than I had given him credit for. "Well, he is kinda cute, for an older guy," I said with a grin.

He leaned back in his chair and laughed heartedly. It doesn't take much to amuse Uncle Reg. *This might be a good time to do some probing*, I thought. *There were still so many unanswered questions, so many things I wanted to know.* "Uncle Reg, can you tell me about the history of Merryweather Lodge?"

"Your dad hasn't told you?"

"No, he doesn't talk about his childhood. Grandpa used to talk about "the good old days" but I can't remember much of what he said, since he died when I was seven."

He put his little finger in his ear and wiggled it about, then reached for the heavy brown tea pot and poured himself another cup of tea. "Well, I can only tell you what my dad told me and what I've heard from local folk."

He leaned back in his chair. "Merryweather Lodge was built by my great grandfather, Thomas Reginald Wellard. He'd planned to live in this cottage until he could have a more stately home built. But as the story goes, he fell in love with this little cottage and gave up the idea of building a bigger house. And he was a bit of a skin-flint, or so they say. So he lived here, married a local girl and had three daughters: Elizabeth, Eliza and Sara. The youngest, Sara, was my grandma, your great grandma. Because he had no sons, he left the farm to his oldest girl, Elizabeth, who was already married to a young farm hand named Preston Eliss. They had one daughter named Mary who was a bit simple, or so they say. One day they just up and disappeared, the little lass and all." He scratched his head. "No one knows what happened; they just vanished. Folks seen fit to make up all kinds of far-fetched tales to explain their disappearance. You've heard one of them."

"The legend of Mary Eliss?" I asked.

He nodded his head. "Thomas had stated in his will that if anything happened to Elizabeth, the farm was to go to his next oldest, Eliza. But she didn't want anything to do with it, so she sold it to your Aunt Emy's dad. Never gave a penny of her profits to her younger sister. Kept it all to herself, she did."

"That must have really upset your grandma," I said.

"You'd think so, especially after she married a farm hand who worked for Emy's dad." He picked up his spoon and stirred his tea, slowly. "Funny how fate has a way of putting things right. Must have been meant to stay in the family, I suppose."

"I guess so." I'd had enough of the history. Now it was time to ask some serious questions. "Uncle Reg, have you seen anything unusual around here?" I asked in a low voice.

He screwed up his face. "Unusual?"

"You know, sinister stuff."

His gold-green eyes gave me a hostile glare. "There is nothing sinister going on around here, young lady."

*Not much,* I thought, and I could tell by the defensive tone in his voice that he was lying. My eyes met his with unwavering challenge. "Something sinister is going on around here. What about all those murders?"

He eased himself out of his chair, wiped the butter from his mouth with the back of his hand, cleared his throat and said firmly, "Time for me to get to work. There are lots of chores, if you want something to do."

"That's okay," I mumbled.

He walked over to the back door, took his faded old cap and heavy woolen cardigan off the brass hook attached to the door, turned around and gave me a serious look. "Don't go asking a lot of questions; just mind your own business." He forced a smile as he pointed at me with his walking stick. "That's a good lass." Now I knew that Uncle Reg was concealing something.

As I walked through the dark narrow hallway past the attic stairs, I felt compelled to stop. Usually I hurried past, shuddering, my eyes not daring to look up. But this time my feet wouldn't move and the stairs in front of me drew my eyes up like magnets. The door was ajar. Auntie must have forgotten to close it. I'd seen her going up there a couple of times, once with a brown paper bag in her hand. I remember wondering what she was up to.

The foreboding portal beckoned me but my feet didn't want to budge. I told myself I'd just run up, flick on the light, find Mary Eliss' note, reveal the cubby hole, glance around for any other clues and get out of there as quickly as I could. I closed my eyes, said a silent prayer, took a deep breath, straightened my back and repeated: "There is nothing to be afraid of. There's nothing to be afraid of." My heavy foot trembled as I pried it off the floor and placed it on the bottom stair.

# Chapter 6

"Going up there to chase the ghosts away, are ya?"

I was startled and drew back. "I was just going to shut the door." Auntie looked up the stairs, gave me a toothless grin and shook her head. The attic door was closed.

"There's someone on the phone for ya."

"For me?" I dashed through the narrow passageway into the front hall and grabbed the receiver. Who could be phoning me this early?

"Hey, Fletch, how's it going?"

"Skye!" I hollered enthusiastically. "Hey, it's only six o'clock in the morning. What's up?"

"Yeah, well, its eleven o'clock here and I've been waiting all evening to phone you. You guys are seven hours ahead of us."

"How's it going? What's happening at school? Do you miss me?" I asked eagerly.

"Of course I do. There was no school today. It's a teachers' convention."

"Cool."

"Have you found your fairytale kingdom?" she asked.

"Yeah, with ogres and dragons and all."

"Wow!"

"Oh my God, Jenks, I've got so much to tell you. You won't believe what's going on here. And there's this really hot guy," I blurted out all in one breath.

"Can't wait to hear all about it, but I got something to tell you and I can't talk for long—five minutes max, Mom said."

"Don't tell me. You've got a date with Matt Hasselman?"

"I wish." Her voice took on a low serious tone. "Mom and I went to see a psychic this afternoon."

"Wow, too cool!"

"It wasn't. We tried to contact my grandma, but we got yours instead."

"You're kidding!"

Skye's voice quivered. "She said, 'This is Sarah Fletcher. I have a message for Emily'."

I gasped. "A message for me?"

"'Tell her to stay out of the woods. Martha's looking for revenge.' At least, I think that's what she said. Her voice was sort of vague and distant."

"No doubt. Who's Martha?"

"I'm not sure that she said Martha, but that's what it sounded like. I thought you would know who she was talking about."

"I don't know anyone called Martha, but I think I know what woods she was talking about."

"You do? Oh my God, Fletch, it was so creepy. I almost puked."

"I bet. Hey, what else did she say?"

"Nothing, that was all. My mom thinks you're in some kind of danger, and we're worried about you. Is there anyone who could give you some sort of protection?"

"No one will believe me."

"That sucks. Oh shoot, my mom's calling. Gotta go now."

"No! Don't go," I pleaded. "I've got so much to tell you."

"Sorry, Fletch. See you in a few days. Hang tight and don't go in any woods."

My heart sank as I lowered the receiver.

Later that day I escaped to my favorite spot in the garden. On the west side of the cottage, through a white ivy-covered arbor, along a narrow cobblestone path, sat an old iron bench. It was surrounded by clusters of flowering shrubs and lilac bushes. A honeysuckle tree cascaded over its back like a water fountain.

This was my private spot, my own deliciously fragrant, secluded corner. I came here often to get away from the hum-drum adult conversation, nagging silent whispers of the cottage and the strange unseen shadow that followed me around. It was the perfect place to read, catch up on my homework, rant on the pages of my journal and daydream. I sat in silent meditation, savoring the simple pleasures of the moment, my mind void of anything in particular as I sipped a glass of English ginger ale. Its bubbles tickled my nose as I put it to my lips and tasted its gingery tang on my tongue.

I have always had a secret spot like this. A private place in the lap of Mother Nature, where I feel safe and protected from the outside world and all its hostility, competition, materialism, kids that laugh at my freckles, orange hair and spindly flamingo legs. And a mother who tries to improve my looks with subtle suggestions and tells me how other girls have camouflaged their imperfections. Like animals, Mother Nature is non-judgmental and loves me unconditionally.

I gazed around at the tapestry of unbridled color. Multiple shades of green, delicate wild flowers, mingled with daffodils, pansies, hyacinths, violets and a large patch of deep blue lavender stocks. Baby birds chirped hungrily from their nests. Pesky insects buzzed and scurried to and fro, performing their inherent tasks. They were a nuisance but not vicious like the blood-sucking mosquitoes and black flies back home. The sky was a brilliant celestial blue and the air was alive with the sweet scents of the garden. From here, everything looked so surreal, so enchanting. This is how I'd always pictured it. On my bedroom wall I have a collage of various post cards of England and photographs of Merryweather Lodge. I used to lie on my bed and imagine myself living here, falling in love with a handsome Englishman, writing fantasy novels, befriending the animals, conversing with the fairies and living happily ever after. On top of the collage in fancy handwriting, I wrote, "England, the land of magic, dreams, Kings and Queens." I never imagined that my fairytale kingdom would have a dark side. How can something so beautiful be so sinister?

As I sat on my contemplative throne, surrounded by Mother Nature's profusion, I caught a glimpse of something peeking from behind an overgrown privet-hedge. "Who's there?" I shouted. Then I heard giggling, like that of a little child. Slowly, from behind the hedge, a girl appeared.

She was about twelve years old. Red ringlets hung over her shoulders, some of which were pulled up to one side by a big red ribbon. She was wearing a green old-fashioned dress with a pretty lace collar. I recognized her immediately as the girl in the Eliss family portrait. Strangely enough, I felt no fear.

"Where did you come from?" I asked.

She said nothing. Her face had a vacant expression. Her glassy green eyes didn't blink; they seemed to stare right through me. "Mary Eliss?" I asked.

She turned and started to run, waving her hand behind her, beckoning me to follow.

"Wait!" I shouted as I ran to catch up with her. She flew over the garden gate and headed for the meadow.

A strange feeling of urgency pulled me in her direction. I had to keep up with her; I couldn't let her get away from me. Faster and faster she went, skimming over tall grasses like an enormous green bird, her corkscrew curls flowing behind her like wings.

My legs were starting to ache, and inside my chest I could feel my heart racing at a tremendous speed. I stopped, bent over, put my hands on my knees and tried to catch my breath. When I looked up I couldn't see her, but I knew in which direction she was heading.

I drew in a long deep breath and took off after her, fighting my way through tangled grasses, nettles and clumps of wild flowers that thrashed at my legs like tiny whips. Dry air shot into my lungs. The air around me seemed to cry out, *Catch her. Don't let her get away.* I felt like a little child in urgent pursuit of its mother.

Finally, I spotted her standing in front of the woodlot. My feet froze to the ground. I could feel the muscles in my head tighten as I gazed at the dark, eerie shadows of the giant trees.

She moved closer to the woods, then turned around and whispered sweetly, with the voice of an angel, "Come, Emily, come."

I remembered my grandmother's warning but I couldn't help myself; a force much greater than mine seemed to pull me forward.

My feet thawed. I started to run—into the dark shadows, through a maze of twisted thicket, stumbling over fallen logs. Prickly shrubs tore at my skin. Pine cones and twigs crunched under my feet. There was no magic or fairies in the woods today, only dread, gloom, and the fearful threat of unseen ghouls grabbing at me from their hiding places in the shade.

Mary Eliss moved fluently through the woods, looking over her shoulder frequently to make sure I was still following. Her feet did not appear to touch the ground.

"Wait, wait," I kept shouting as I trudged hastily, fearfully, after her. For a moment I lost sight of her. Then I heard what sounded like weeping.

I stopped, looked around and listened carefully. The

sound seemed to be coming from an opening in the bushes. I said a silent prayer and advanced tentatively.

She was sitting on a log under a massive oak tree. It was the one I had seen when I came here with Auntie. Tears trickled down her pale pink cheeks.

"No, please, no," she cried pitifully.

"What's wrong?" I asked, walking toward her. She held out her hand, palm facing me, cautioning me not to come any closer. In a trancelike state she got off the log, stood in front of it, raised her fragile little finger and pointed to the ground. Then in the same trancelike state she sat back on the log. "What is it? Is something buried there?" I asked.

She didn't reply. She just screwed up her face, bit down on her lip and bowed her head as if in agony.

"Oh my God. No, please, no," I mumbled as a sharp jab of fear stabbed me. The hideous apparition that had appeared in my room was now standing behind her. She was holding an axe; slimy yellow mucus oozed from between her teeth and trickled down her chin. Her cold, evil eyes widened as she lifted the axe.

I gasped and shouted, "Run, Mary Eliss, run!"

She just sat there, still and expectant. Then she put her hands over her face and let out a bloodcurdling scream as the sharp silver edge of the blade fell, burying itself deep into her skull. I could hear the bone crack; warm blood spurted from the cavity and splattered on the ground. She collapsed onto the mulch in a heap. The creature lifted her head and glared at me, her green eyes ablaze within their deep dark holes. She raised her axe and moved toward me.

"Colceathrar, Colceathar," she cried.

I swallowed hard as my stomach lurched with a sick dread. Then I turned and ran, heading in the direction of the tiny rays of sun filtering through the trees.

She kept coming.

Tangled shreds of terror and desperation knotted inside my gut as I ploughed my way though fallen debris and low hanging branches. I could smell her foul odor and hear her hissing chant getting closer and closer. A strange flood of adrenaline gushed through my veins like fuel, propelling me forward.

Abruptly, I stopped. My legs were still pumping but I was unable to move. A prickly bush had caught the inside of my coat. I was stuck. Panic consumed me as my trembling hands yanked at the material franticly.

I could sense her presence now. I was going to die, chopped up into pieces by a ghost in the dreaded woodlot.

"Help! Help!" I screamed.

The axe was above my head. I felt woozy, like I was going to pass out. I squeezed my eyes tight and shuddered.

The axe fell, brushing past my arm. *How could she have missed me?* It was as though the blade had been purposely moved to avoid me.

Suddenly a powerful invisible force yanked at my coat, ripping it from the bushes' thorny grasp. I bolted away.

"Don't let her catch me, please God, don't let her catch me," I pleaded breathlessly.

Dashing through the tangled bushes, leaping over fallen trees, I somehow mustered up enough strength to stay ahead of her. Finally, I reached the opening, and into the meadow I flew.

My legs gave way and I collapsed into the soft moist grass, feeling dizzy and sick to my stomach. There was no sound now except for the rustling of the long grass in the breeze. Nervously I turned around and faced the dreaded forest, expecting any moment to see the disgusting ghoul dash out at me, but she never came. She was gone, at least for now.

I breathed a sigh of relief and heaved myself up; my feet ached, my legs stung, my whole body felt sluggish and drained of its life force, but I was alive and free of 'her'.

"Thank you, God," I whispered as I headed for the cottage.

When I reached the end of the meadow, I saw Dad running toward me from the barn.

"Where have you been? We've been looking all over for you," he said in an angry voice. His scowling eyes examined my bedraggled appearance. "What happened to you?"

I flung my tired body into his arms and laid my head on his soft cotton shirt. He smelt of perspiration and hay. "Oh Dad, you won't believe what just happened to me." I thought for a moment, then stood back and met his eyes. "No, you won't believe me; so what's the point of telling you?" He put his strong hairy arm around my shoulder and drew me in.

"How can I believe you if you won't tell me what happened?" We started walking back toward the cottage. Mom and Auntie Em spotted us and hurried to meet us. Mom was in a state of panic. She flicked the long strand of ash that teetered from her cigarette, drew a raspy breath and spoke.

"You found her. Oh, Emily, where have you been?" Her manicured fingers shot to her mouth as she looked me up and down. "What happened? Are you hurt?" she asked as she brushed the hair off my sweaty face and picked debris off my sweater.

I pulled back. "I'm okay."

"Oh, would ya stop fussing, Penny?" Auntie said, fumbling inside her apron pocket for her hanky. "Blimey, ya do look like ya've been pulled through a bush backwards. Ain't been in them there woods, 'ave ya?"

I clenched my teeth, squared my shoulders and raised my chin defiantly. "As a matter of fact, I have. Mary Eliss took me there to show me what happened to her. The hideous creature that I saw in the attic room killed her. She chopped her with an axe." Mom gasped. I scowled at her. "And then she came after me." Their mouths were agape, their faces vacant. I shook my head. "It's like talking to a brick wall." I glared at Auntie. "As you would say."

She raised her eyebrows. "Cheeky madam!"

Dad smoothed down the strands of graying black hair that covered his bald patch with his long sturdy fingers. "The two of you can go back. Emily and I are going to have a little chat," he said with feeble authority.

"I think she should have a nice bath," Mom said as she lit

another cigarette and inhaled the nicotine deeply into her lungs. Dad gave her one of those 'Please, honey' looks.

Auntie grabbed her arm. "Come on, chimney pot, we'll put the kettle on." Mom sighed as she walked away reluctantly.

Dad put his arm around my shoulders. "Now, Princess..." *Oh boy, this has to be a lecture.* It'd been a long time since Dad had called me Princess. It was his pet name for me when I was little. "You've been spending too much time alone, and your imagination is working overtime. It's this place." He stopped, rubbed his fingers over the tiny bristles on his chin, and gazed around at the lush landscape. His face glowed with a warm nostalgic expression. "It does have a certain mystique." Exhaling a long deep sigh of contentment, he looked me in the eyes. "Enchanting, I suppose you'd call it." This was a part of my Dad that I didn't see very often. He always tried to keep his softer side under cover.

"Do you miss it, Dad?"

"Sometimes I do."

"What was it like growing up here?"

His eyes lit up. "I can remember your Uncle Reg and me playing cowboys and Indians in the pasture. We used the sheep for horses. We'd have competitions to see who could stay on the ewe's back the longest, and we gave them all names. There was..." He stopped himself from getting too mushy. Then he cleared his throat and said, "We had lots of chores to do back then. It was hard work."

"Where's the cottage that you grew up in?" I asked

abruptly before he had time to think or say anything else.

"Old Mrs. Tilly lives there now. I don't think she'd ap-preciate us snooping around, though."

"I met her. She's really sweet. I bet she wouldn't mind."

"Bittersweet, maybe, and she would mind."

"What do you mean?"

"Oh, nothing."

"Dad, you always do that. Tell me what you meant."

He chuckled. "Well, if you really must know, she's the local fortune teller, witch doctor, midwife, psychic and all that other nonsense."

"Wow!" I was intrigued.

"It's all a load of garbage, Emily."

"Oh, Dad, you're so shallow. How do you know about her?"

"She's lived around these parts for years. Her husband used to own a farm on the west side. He died just before we moved to Canada. It was too much for the old girl to keep up, so she sold the farm and bought our little cottage. Old witch Tilly, we used to call her. Funny, she looks the same now as she did back then and she must be well into her eighties by now."

We had reached the back yard. Dad sat down on one of the white wicker chairs by the clothes line; I lowered my weary body into the other. A pair of Auntie's large white bloomers danced and waved at us as they blew like sails in the breeze. Wooky was parading around, his head held high with an air of arrogance that seemed to say, "I'm the boss cat, and don't you forget it." The green soldiers in the garden were growing tall and proud: carrots, lettuce, beans, onions, all lined up in regimented order. The cherry tree was heavy with early fruit. A delicious aroma of apple pie and cinnamon drifted toward us from the sill of the open window.

We sat there in a moment of uncomfortable silence, then Dad stretched out his long legs and cleared his throat. But before he could utter a word, I asked, "Did you use to play in the woodlot?'

He looked a little shocked and perturbed at my question. "No, I did not, and neither should you."

"Why? What's in there?" I asked with a hint of sarcasm.

He grinned at me, tight-mouthed, and shook his head lazily from side to side. "There's nothing in there, Emily. It's just big and unfamiliar. You could easily get lost in there."

*Nah, I'm not buying it. He's hiding something.*

The heat of the sun was beating down on the back of my head. I grabbed the old straw hat from the round wooden table and plunked it on top of my head. Then I gave Dad a hard striking glare. "There is something in there buried beside a log. Mary Eliss pointed to it."

He sighed, put his arms on his knees, leaned forward and scanned my face sympathetically. "If these hallucinations continue, when we get home we'll get some help for you."

That did it; I was mad. I jumped up and put my hands on my hips. "You think I'm hallucinating? I was just chased and almost killed by a gruesome ghost. What do I have to do to convince you that it was real?" I sniffed and stomped my feet. "I'm not crazy!"

He frowned. "Have you finished?"

"Yes!" I said in a nasty tone.

"Then sit down!" His voice softened. "It's hereditary, I'm afraid. We were hoping that the schizoid gene would skip you but it seems to be manifesting already. I'm sure your grandmother and great grandmother didn't start having delusions until they were much older. But it's nothing to be afraid of, Princess. It can be stopped if we get you on medication right away." He bit down on his lip thoughtfully. "They don't know why it only affects the women in the family."

"Dad, listen to me," I pleaded. "I know I don't have schizophrenia. The things I'm seeing and feeling are real. And maybe they were for my grandmothers, too. Have you ever thought of that?" I stood up. "Skye's mom said I have unique abilities, like those of a mystic."

"Skye's mom's a crack pot."

"There is a mystery to be solved here, Dad, and I'm going to solve it."

"There will be no mystery solving, young lady. Just forget about what you think you saw and don't go near those woods again. Do I make myself clear?"

I stood my ground. "But if there is nothing to hide, why is everybody so secretive?"

"No buts, Emily. You've had enough excitement for one day. It's time to go back to the cottage. And don't go telling your mom any more stories. She'll have a heart attack." I hesitated, but when his lip quivered and his eyes narrowed into an I-gave-you-an-order expression, I knew it was no use.

I turned and walked away, mumbling through clenched teeth, "Jonathan believes me. Jonathan believes me."

"What was that, young lady?"

"Nothing. I'm just talking to myself. That's what crazy people do, isn't it?" Tears gathered in my eyes. "What would it take for them to believe me?" I mumbled. "My death?" I couldn't believe how much it hurt that no one believed me. It felt lonely and desolate. I couldn't hold back the tears. They trickled down my flushed cheeks, cool, moist and unrelenting.

Everyone sat in solemn silence at the dinner table. It was as if someone had been diagnosed with a terminal illness or died. I pushed the mound of fluffy mashed potatoes lazily around my plate.

"Not hungry, luv?" Auntie asked.

I shook my head. Uncle Reg pulled out a tooth pick and started digging the lamb out from between his teeth. It made me want to throw up.

"Would you like to come to work with me and Sam tomorrow, lass? The lambs are not so little anymore. High-spirited teenagers they are now, just like you." Everyone snickered.

I forced a phony smile. "No, thanks."

Mom dabbed her crimson lips with a paper napkin. "Dad and I are going into town for some last-minute gift shopping. I'm sure you'd like to come with us, wouldn't you, honey?" I shrugged my shoulders. "I know. I'll run you a nice bubble bath after supper. That will make you feel better," she said in her baby voice.

I'd had enough. I plunked my fork down, sniffed, and then sprang to my feet. "Would everyone stop patronizing me? I'm not crazy and I know that some of you," I twisted my mouth and peered around the table, "have seen what I've seen or at least know there is something weird going on around here."

No one said a word. They just sat there speechless, with dumbfounded expressions on their faces. Auntie put her hand under the table, fumbled in her apron pocket and pulled out her distress hanky. Dad's face was red and his glare drilled into me. He lifted his scolding finger and pointed it at me, but before he could say anything Mom put her delicate hand on top of his and lowered it down on the table.

"Hormones, dear, that's all it is," she whispered.

"It will all come out in the wash," Auntie mumbled under her hanky.

I marched out of the kitchen, stamping my feet on the hard wooden floor, rushed into the parlor and slammed the door behind me. I couldn't stand their pitiful looks and how they treated me like a little child. I grabbed my journal and pen from my backpack and threw myself on the fat roll-armed chair. Snuggling into its cloudy soft cushions, I stuck the pen in my mouth, popped the nib and opened my journal.

*June 1ˢᵗ*
*Dear friend,*
*Only three more days to go and I will return to the wonderful routine of my ordinary life. Part of me is reluc-*

tant to leave. The other part wants to run away as fast as I can, never to return. My family thinks I am hallucinating. They are all so shallow and unenlightened. I keep smelling lavender and feeling a comforting presence. Maybe it's my guardian angel. If it is, I wish she'd stop whatever it is from haunting me. I know now that *The Legend of Mary Eliss* is wrong. She did not kill her family and she wasn't crazy. She was killed by the hideous creature. Today she lured me into the woodlot to show me something, but the creature came after me before I could find out what it was. Perhaps it was a clue to the mystery. Grandma Fletcher's spirit tried to warn me not to go into the woods and to be aware of someone named Martha. But I don't know anyone named Martha. It's all so spooky. My recurring dream is getting more frequent now. It's still vague, but I'm remembering bits and pieces of it now and when I wake up I can feel its essence, as though I had just been there, inside my dream, living it. Fragmented pictures— of young girls with long blonde hair dancing and chanting, of men in dirty white robes, of dead cats and of running barefoot through huge blocks of stone—flashed through my mind like snippets of a horror movie. If only I knew its meaning.

Amongst all this dark ominous stuff is a ray of light. The drop-dead gorgeous Jonathan McArthur, my prince charming, my first love. Although he probably thinks I'm too young for him and not pretty enough, his aura feels strangely familiar and my inside voice keeps telling me that we are somehow connected—not by genetics but by

*spirit. Unlike Victoria Weber and some of the other wild
girls in my school, I do not intend to have sex until I'm
much older and have been dating for a long time, but I
can't stop thinking about it. Keeping my emotions under
control has been like trying to harness a wild animal.*

I heard the clicking of high heeled shoes coming in my direction. Mom tapped on the door, opened it slightly and poked her head through. "I've run you a nice hot bath, honey."

I winced at her goo-goo voice. "You didn't have to, but thanks anyway."

The walls of the bathroom were painted a dark moss green. Fluffy white towels and a bar of carbolic soap sat on an old ladder-back chair in the corner. Beside the door sat the toilet, with a long chain hanging from the tank high above it. It made a tremendous whoosh when it was flushed. On the other side of the door, a white enamel sink with copper taps wore a gathered skirt of green gingham. Fragrant steam rose from the claw-foot bathtub in the middle of the floor.

I hung my clothes over the back of the chair and lowered myself slowly into the warm soapy water. The scent of wild roses drifted up to meet me. It felt so good. Bathing like this was a new experience for me, as I usually showered. The luxurious bath oil ran through my fingers and toes like fine silk. Tiny bubbles tickled my chin as I submerged my tired form into the soothing elixir.

My body relaxed, but my mind babbled on. Who was

this hideous creature and why was she after me? What was beside that log that Mary Eliss was sitting on? If I didn't get some answers before I left, my mind wouldn't rest.

I had to go back into the woodlot. But I couldn't go alone and no one in the family would go with me. They would go berserk if I so much as mentioned it. I wouldn't dare call Jonathan again, although he would be the perfect candidate. Auntie, maybe? I could manipulate her into doing almost anything for me if I got all sad and teary-eyed and pleaded enough. I lay back, closed my eyes and tried to steady my thoughts.

The room filled with clouds of fragrant, misty vapor. I heard a soft tapping on the door. "Who is it?" I asked. No one answered. Slowly the brass door handle turned. "Is that you, Mom?" My voice trembled. The door opened with an eerie creak.

# Chapter 7

I sat up. My shaky hands gripped the sides of the tub.

From behind the door the ghostly figure of a young girl appeared. I opened my mouth to scream but nothing came out. Through the thin curtain of steam I could see that she was wearing a long black velvet dress edged with lace. Rich auburn curls dangled over her shoulders, and around her slender neck hung a heavy silver pendant. Her pale face was expressionless, her large emerald eyes vacant.

I shivered as she moved slowly toward me and stood at the foot of the tub. Then she started to disrobe, removing her dress and layers of frilly cotton undergarments. My eyes widened and my jaw dropped. Her pubescent naked body told me that she was around my age and I was sure that I had seen her face somewhere before.

She shuffled lethargically to the side of the tub, lifted her leg and proceeded to climb inside. Still cemented in the water, I bit down on my lip, tucked my feet under my bum and slid back as far as I could. Her unearthly body sat motionless at the other end of the tub. Her eyes stared unblinking, not at me but through me. My body was numb with fear and I wanted desperately to cry out, but my voice was still mute.

Suddenly her eyes moved to meet mine. My bottom lip quivered. An eerie sensation gripped me. Slowly her face started to change, turning ashen and ghostly. Her glassy eyes became deep gaunt holes with shadowy rims; her auburn hair yellowed. Oh my God, it was her!

"Colceathrar, Colceathrar," she hissed.

The water turned bitter cold and reeked. I tried desperately to force myself out of the rancid water, concentrating as hard as I could to get my limbs to move, but the force was too strong.

The specter moved toward me. I could feel her foul breath brushing my face. My stomach heaved as the stench of her ghostly form got closer and closer, penetrating my skin, through me, inside me. I squirmed franticly as her evil energy permeated my entire body and prickly dark forces devoured my flesh from within. It felt like hundreds of slimy maggots burrowing into my skin, sucking at my veins and gnawing on my bones. Sinister feelings of hate and anger consumed me as I trembled hopelessly.

Knock, knock. "Emily, are you all right?" Auntie's voice brought me back from hell. "You'll look like an old prune if ya stay in there any longer."

I pried my eyes open and gazed around the room. Everything looked normal. I breathed a sigh of relief, thinking it was only a bad dream. But the smell of rotting flesh and cat urine lingered in my nostrils and my skin was still crawling as if infested.

"Emily Anne!"

"Yes, Auntie. I'll be out in a minute." This time I was sure that it was only a dream.

Or was it?

On the floor, right where the girl had disrobed, I spotted a heavy silver pendant. How could this be? I picked it up. It was a strange piece of jewelry—a circle with an odd star in the middle.

*Put it around your neck*, the mysterious little voice inside me whispered. I draped it around my neck, wrapped my fingers around the shiny metal and prayed, "Please God, keep me safe from this evil creature. And find someone to help me solve the mystery, please."

I grabbed a towel off the chair, wrapped it around my dripping wet hair, shook off the cold creepy feeling that clung to me, threw on my house coat and scurried out the door.

Auntie was sitting in her favorite easy chair by the hearth darning a heavy brown sweater. Her stubby little legs were propped up on a crow-legged tapestry stool and covered by a patchwork blanket. "Where is everyone," I asked?

"Yer Mum and Dad went for a walk and Reg went to the neighbors; have some business to discuss, they do." She dug her needle into the ball of wool and studied me. "Bloomin' heck. Look like death warmed over. White as a ghost, you are."

I shoved her slippered feet to one side and sat down beside them. Digging into my pocket, I pulled out my brush and handed it to her. Winny jumped on my lap, kneaded her paws into the raised loops of my terry housecoat and purred contently. Auntie placed her warm motherly hand on my forehead. "No fever, but you're coming down with something, mark my words." She unwrapped the towel from around my head and rubbed my hair briskly between its soft white fibers. Then she took my brush and ran it through the damp, tangled, red strands, tugging ever so gently at the knots.

Auntie loved brushing my hair. It was a sort of bonding ritual. A silent speech that whispered, "I love you," and was in some ways more authentic than words.

The sound of Winny's purring and the warm glow from the fire had a peaceful and calming effect. I felt safe and comfortable now.

But I couldn't hide all the pent up emotions that desperately wanted to escape. Tears pricked my eyes as I held my hand over my face, trying to restrain them. But it was no use; they trickled slowly down my cheeks, unchecked and unrelenting.

"There, there, luv, what's ailing ya?"

I turned around and nuzzled my face into Auntie's lap and sobbed pitifully like a little child. She stroked my head, put her hand under the blanket and pulled out a large white hanky with the initials E A F embroidered in the corner. "'Ere, luv, 'ave a good blow." My stomach lurched at the thought of where the hanky had been and what it had been used for. I declined.

"Oh, Auntie Em, I need you to believe me. I'm not crazy, honest I'm not. All the things that I have seen are real. And just now in the bathroom I had a terrible nightmare, but I'm not sure if it was a real dream, because I found this on the floor." I pulled at the top of my housecoat and revealed the silver pendant.

Auntie let out a loud "Bloody Hell!" Her eyes grew round like marbles; the color drained from her face and out came the hanky again. "Where did you get that?"

It was obvious that she had seen it before. I explained what had happened, in detail. It was still with me, as surreal as a dream but as vivid as a true experience.

"That's a load of codswallop. Where did you find it?" Her voice was edged with anger.

"I just told you! Why won't you believe me?"

Her bottom lip quivered. "But it can't be. That was m' mum's. Wore it all the time, she did. When she died it went missing; turned the house upside down and inside out looking for it, we did." She swallowed hard. "I wanted to put it around 'er neck before I buried 'er. She found it hidden away in a little box when they moved 'ere. The name Sara was on the box. Must 'ave been Reg's grandmother's, we figured. " She held out her trembling hand and touched the silver pendant timidly, as if it were a precious jewel, and gazed at it in wonder.

"It was my great grandmother's?" I asked eagerly.

"Must 'ave been. She were the only Sara that ever lived 'ere."

"That's it! That's where I've seen that girl before, in an old photo album. The girl I saw in the bathroom was my great grandmother."

Auntie frowned. "Rubbish. Are you off your rocker? 'Er's been dead donkeys' years."

I could feel that familiar, uncontrollable urge to explode bubbling up inside me. I whisked Winny off my lap, flew to my feet, grabbed the brush out of her hand and waved it in front of her face. "How can you not believe me? Look at this." I held out the silver pendant. "Maybe it is a sign from your mom." I got closer to her face and drew my brows together in an angry frown. "I bet she's mad at you for not believing me."

Auntie flung her chubby hand over her mouth and sank back into her chair. Her old eyes looked sad and distraught. I threw the brush on the floor, knelt down beside her chair, put my hands together in a praying fashion and pleaded, "I'm sorry, Auntie Em, but I need you to believe me. I have no one else to turn to." I drew back. "I'm going back into the wood-lot, by myself if I have to."

I waited, expecting to be scolded for my rude behavior, but instead, her eyes filled with tears and her bottom lip quivered. She put her white cotton hanky to her nose and gave a hefty blow, then she dabbed her watery eyes with the embroidered corner.

I was shocked. I'd never seen Auntie cry before; seeing her so vulnerable and upset made me ashamed and sad. I flung my arms around her plump body and gave her a warm hug. Her apron smelled like grease and fried onions. Auntie always smelt of food. "I'm sorry; I didn't mean to upset you."

"It's all right, luv. Seeing ya in such a state and wearing m' mum's star has put me in a bit of a tizzy." She shoved her snotty hanky back into her apron pocket and gave me a serious look. "Truth is, luv, there's been something funny goin' on around 'ere for years, there 'as. But we keep sweeping it under the rug, hoping it will go away. Some folks say this area's cursed. Most folks are too afraid to talk about it, in case it makes things worse or whatever it is comes after them.

"Reg knows it, too, but he's too stubborn to admit it. He ain't goin' to let no ghost chase 'im out of 'is own home. 'The only way they're going to get me outta this place is in a wooden box,' is what he says. His great granddad built it, ya see. In 'is blood, it is, and there ain't no man as stubborn as my Reg, there ain't."

"Auntie Em, what have you seen?" I asked anxiously.

"I need a cuppa," she said as she lifted herself awkwardly out of the chair, which gave a squeak of relief, and hobbled toward the kitchen, scratching her bum along the way. I followed close behind, irritated that she would make such an intriguing confession and then calmly putter about, keeping me guessing.

She flipped the little brass latch on the pantry door, walked inside, brought out a box of Jammy Dodgers and set them on the table in front of me. "A little bit of what ya fancy does ya good," she said with a smile. These were my favorite English cookies. On the bottom lay a round, buttery, semi soft cookie with a hint of almond, and on top sat a fancy donut-shaped piece sprinkled with fine sugar, and in between, a layer of scrumptious strawberry jam oozed through the hole in the middle.

Normally I could eat four or five of these delectable delights, but right now I had more important things on my mind than food. I pushed them aside and asked impatiently, "Are you going to tell me what you've seen or not?"

She wagged her scolding finger at me. "Hang on, will ya?"

I noticed that her hands were slightly crooked and trembled as she lit the gas stove. Little beads of sweat glistened on her brow and her cheeks were glowing red.

"Are you okay?" I asked.

"I'm all right. It's just arthritis, the change and old age. Bloody nuisance, it is, but I ain't ready for the knackers' yard yet, I ain't."

I had no idea what that meant and I didn't care to ask.

She scooped a couple spoonfuls of loose tea into the large brown pot, wiped the perspiration from her brow with the back of her hand and sat down beside me.

I was bursting with anticipation.

Slowly she lowered her weathered hand on top of mine, leaned forward and met my eyes with a warm, reassuring smile. "I don't think you're goin' off the deep end, luv. At first I told myself you'd inherited the sickness. Then I blamed it on your queer imagination. There's always some sort of excuse or another. I do know this for sure—what you said you saw in them there woods, you saw."

"You believe me?" I gasped.

The familiar whistle of the faithful old kettle interrupted us.

Auntie lifted the bottom of her blue flowered apron, placed it over the handle of the kettle and carefully carried it to the table. "Now where were we?" she asked as she poured the steaming water into the pot.

"You said you believed what I saw in the woods."

"Ah yeah."

Her face turned grim as she lowered herself back into her chair. "When we were young'uns, me and my best mate, Martha Davis, went into them there woods in the autumn to pick chestnuts." The tone of her voice mirrored her anxious expression. "We'd take a jam sandwich, a bottle of water and a pair of our dads' old farming gloves. Prickly things to open, are chestnuts. Some said it were haunted, but that didn't bother us. It were a challenge. Prided ourselves in being fearless and brave, we did. Besides, the money we got from selling them at the farmers market was too good to let some daft old superstition bother us. A shilling a bag we got for 'em, and that were a lot of money back then."

She picked up the heavy pot and poured the tea. Her voice took on a low, alarming tone. "One day as we were tearing the thorny casings off our collection of nuts, we spotted a girl running through the thicket. We ran after 'er and followed 'er to a clearing." She hesitated, then out came the snotty hanky, straight to her mouth. I gagged.

"Then what?"

"'Er was sitting on a log by a massive oak tree." Again she hesitated.

116

"Yes, go on."

She glared into my eyes and bit into her bottom lip. "I think you know the rest, m' luv."

"Oh my God, Auntie Em, you knew I wasn't hallucinating. Why didn't you say something?"

She sighed. "I'd convinced myself it didn't happen, that it were all a bad dream, till now."

"Does anyone else know?"

She shook her head. "Never told a soul. Frightened folk would think I were making it up or I'd gone bananas. I were so scared that I peed m' knickers, I did. Martha's family immigrated to Australia not long after it happened. Funny though, I could have sworn that I saw Martha a while back, walking down the main street in Salisbury. 'You must be going off the deep end, Emy,' I told m' self. 'That can't be 'er.' I often wonder how she's doing. Good mates, we were."

I wondered if this was the Martha my grandmother's spirit had warned me about. But why would she want to hurt me? "What other strange things have you seen, Auntie?"

A deep frown set into her rugged face. "Nosey madam, ain't ya? Like I said, there's been a lot of odd goings on over the years—things disappearin', voices, noises, windows breaking, murders, and them there what-ya-ma-call-its in the hay fields."

"What-ya-ma-call-its?"

"Crop circles, I think they call 'em."

"Oh yeah, I've heard of those."

"We've learnt to live with it. What choice do we 'ave, I

ask ya? No one talks about it, except for taking the micky, and those that complain are scorned or sent to the mad house, they are."

I couldn't believe what I was hearing. *Everyone knows this place is haunted but no one will admit to it.* I thought it was ludicrous, but I didn't want to say anything that would offend her or shut her up. "Auntie, do you ever get the feeling that someone is watching you or smell lavender?"

"No, I don't, and I told ya, I wouldn't have that stuff in the house if ya paid me. There were a strong smell of it in the room where m' mum died, God rest 'er soul, and the stalks were nowhere to be seen. It's a curse, I tell ya. I used to tell yer grandmother, 'You'll be cursed if you keep wearing that stuff, you will.' And look what happened to 'er."

"My grandma wore lavender?"

"Reeked of it, 'er did."

That's interesting, I thought as I drew close to her. "Auntie Em, would you go back in the woodlot with me? I have to see what's under the log that Mary Eliss pointed to. It's the key to the mystery, I'm sure of it." Her eyes widened as her head moved back and forth in a fearful refusal. "I'm going in there with or without you. My mind won't rest until I do. There is some kind of invisible force, like a magnet, that seems to be pulling me back there and my inside voice tells me that I have to go."

"Your what?"

"My intuition. My gut."

She rolled her eyes, put her hands at the back of her wiry

gray head and scratched. "All right, all right. I ain't letting ya go into them there woods by yourself, stubborn madam. It's about time we got to the bottom of all these goings on, I suppose."

I was so relieved I almost burst into tears. "Can we go tomorrow?" I asked enthusiastically. "I heard Mom say that they were going into town." I opened the box of Jammy Dodgers and dunked a tasty biscuit into my tea. The soft, warm, buttery texture melted in my mouth, as the gooey, sweet jam squeezed between my teeth.

"We'll go in the morning as soon as they've left." She thought for a moment. "Take the bull by the horns, that's what we'll do."

I shook my head and chuckled. *Where does she come up with this stuff?*

"Must need m' head looking at, I must. And don't ya go blabbing to your dad or uncle Reg. They'd 'ave a fit, they would!" She lowered her voice. "Best go to bed now, luv, get yourself some shuteye."

\* \* \* \*

It was another restless night of tossing and turning. My mind was filled with fearful chatter, mulling over all my horrible experiences. Visions of my recurring dream flashed before me and there were doubts, lots of doubts. I couldn't believe I had talked myself into going back into the woodlot, let alone taking Auntie there too. What if the ghost came after us? Auntie wouldn't stand a chance of outrunning it. What was I thinking? But my inside voice kept prodding me. "You must go back, you must go back," its subtle whisper insisted. I wished it would shut up and leave me alone.

Twice I had to get up and nudge Dad. Mom said that's what I had to do if his snoring kept me awake; I guess she must be immune to it. And the frequent loud whoosh from across the hall of the toilet flushing was enough to wake up the dead. It sounded like Niagara Falls. I knew it was Auntie, she said that being on the change had sent her bladder "ski-wiff". Or perhaps she was just restless like me, fretting over tomorrow. I drew the warm covers around my neck and shivered, as I thought of tomorrow's pending adventure and the dread of what might happen.

When I woke, my parents were already gone. I blinked the sleep out of my eyes, threw on my house coat, staggered into the kitchen and poured myself a large glass of cold milk. Except for the repetitive tick-tock of the old grandfather clock, the cottage was hushed. The sweet smell of wood smoke from the evening fire, mingled with Uncle Reg's pipe tobacco scent, still lingered in the air. I could sense the essence of my invisible companion nearby, a subtle awareness of being watched that had become almost commonplace to me now. The air was damp and cool, which caused me to shiver and cuddle deep into my house coat. There was no central heating in the cottage; the only heat came from the fireplace.

I walked into the sitting room and pulled back the pretty lace curtains from the window. Uncle Regs' old car wasn't in its usual spot. Mom and Dad must have left already, but where was Auntie? I tapped on her bedroom door and called but there was no answer. Slipping my feet into my sandals, I opened the back door and stepped outside. Winky scurried past, almost knocking me off my feet. "Where's your mommy?" I asked.

It was a cool, damp, dreary morning. Charcoal clouds, shaped like whimsical creatures of all sorts, scurried across the gray-blue sky. I hugged my shoulders as the chilly wind blew in my face. It smelt like rain. "Auntie Em!" I shouted as loud as I could.

Then I noticed an odd looking spectacle walking up the beaten path. It was Auntie. She was wearing an oversized yellow raincoat, a red flowered head scarf with a plastic hat pulled over the top, hefty rubber boots that came up to her knees and tattered leather farming gloves. Strands of unruly gray hair stuck out from under her scarf. Over one shoulder she carried a garden shovel, over the other a large axe.

I put my hand over my mouth to stop myself from laughing. She looked hilarious. "Where you going dressed like that, Auntie Em?"

"We're goin' in them there woods. Gettin' to the bottom of this once and for all, we are." Her tone was serious and steadfast.

"Looks like you're going on a wild animal hunt," I said with a sarcastic snicker. She stood in front of me like a soldier, weapons in hand, ready for battle.

"There's more than wild animals in them there woods." Pointing to the door with her shovel, she ordered, "Go put some clothes on yourself and don't dawdle."

A twinge of apprehension grabbed at my stomach muscles as I dashed into the cottage. Rummaging through my clothes, I pulled out a pair of gray sweats, my heavy red basketball hoodie; threw them on and flew out the door. As I turned the corner of the narrow passage, I caught a glimpse of myself in the brass-framed mirror that hung between the bathroom and kitchen door. What I saw startled me.

I moved closer to get a better look. I gasped, put my hands to my throat and blinked rapidly, hoping the image would change. But it didn't. The face of the girl that was looking back at me was the same one that I'd seen in the attic room mirror, but it was much clearer now. Her pretty delicate features were similar to mine but she was perfect, with creamy, unblemished skin, blushed pink cheek bones, eyes like a clear lake of emerald and full rosy lips. Leaves and berries intertwined in a circular pattern in her silky orange hair.

She stared at me, expressionless and motionless, as I stared back at her, bewitched and wondering where I had seen this face before. Was I in some kind of time warp? *Is this how I will look in a few years?* I was sure I had visualized myself looking something like this when my ugly pubescent features evolved into maturity.

"Who are you?" I asked.

"What's keeping ya?" Auntie's voice bellowed.

I turned my head and shouted, "I'm coming!" When I looked back into the mirror, her image had gone. The reflection of an unattractive fourteen-year-old glared back at me.

"Leave me alone!" I screamed, as I bolted out the back door.

Without a word, without a gesture, Auntie turned and
off she marched into the battle zone, down the beaten track,
past the big red barn and up the zigzag path that led to the
meadow. I kept asking her if I could carry her tools but she
just shook her head, her gaze locked on our destination, her
face ablaze with steely determination. Her feet made a soft
squishing sound inside her oversized boots. "Left, right, left,
right," I mumbled.

Slender grasses and wild flowers danced franticly in the
blustery wind. Ominous dark clouds loomed over our heads
as we trudged through the rough sea of untamed vegetation.
Cool gusts rushed at us from behind, tugging at our clothes
and pushing us forcefully toward our goal.

We arrived and stood at the entrance of the foreboding
woodlot, windswept and weary. The giant trees seemed to
beckon us, daring us to come closer. I pushed the long red
strands of wispy hair off my face and swallowed hard. A tight
fist formed in the pit of my stomach.

"Are you sure you want to do this?" I asked as my bottom
lip started to tremble. I wasn't sure if I could muster up
enough courage to go in there myself, now.

"It were your idea, and ya want to solve the mystery,
don't ya?"

"Well, yes."

"Well, there ain't no time like the present." Her voice
was firm and final; her countenance displayed an air of intense
fortitude. She dropped her tools, took off her rugged gloves,
stood in front of me, and fumbled with the silver chain

around my neck, pulling the pendant out from under my hoodie. "Keep this 'ere," she said as she patted it down on the front of my sweatshirt.

Then she opened her rain coat, tugged at the inside pocket and pulled out a small bottle of what looked like whiskey. Holding it to her mouth, she whipped back her head and took a generous swig. I stood in amazement, my mouth agape. I had never seen Auntie drink hard liquor before. She wiped her mouth with the back of her hand, let out a loud gut-wrenching burp, then handed the bottle to me.

Was she serious? "I'm only fourteen, remember?"

She shook her head, shrugged her shoulders and went to put the bottle back into her pocket.

I grabbed it from her hand and took a quick gulp. "Yuck!" Like hot lava the disgusting brown liquid burnt as it flowed down my throat and into my stomach. "How can any one drink this stuff? It should have a bone and skull on the bottle."

Auntie threw back her head and let out a hearty laugh, but she quickly regained her serious, military-like composure.

"Are you ready, luv?" She bent down to pick up her weapons.

I felt a tad light-headed and more confident now. Putting on a brave smile, I took a deep breath. "I'm ready."

We marched into the gloomy thicket like soldiers on a mission, steadily advancing bit by bit toward the battlefield. "Find that there massive tree, girl," Auntie said in a solemn voice as she stepped aside, allowing me to take the lead.

With eyes wide, I searched for clues, something familiar

that would point us in the right direction. I could feel my heart going thump, thump, thump under my sweater, fully aware of the possible danger lurking behind every tree. The rich, pungent smell of pine cones, rotting wood and damp moss rose up from the ground. The wind roared and the heavy branches of the formidable giant trees flayed around like the arms of a giant octopus.

I spotted a large patch of blue bells under a chestnut tree. I was sure that I had seen them before. The profusion of delicate blue-mauve bells was alluring but I couldn't stop, not even for a quick sniff.

"It's this way," I said, pointing in the direction that looked familiar.

Like a human bulldozer, Auntie pushed in front of me and ploughed her way through the dense bush, slashing at the tangled branches furiously, using her shovel as a machete.

Everything started to look familiar, the towering evergreens, cascading chestnuts, clusters of birch, thicket, brambles and patches of wild flowers.

"Is it this way, luv? Is it this way?" Auntie's voice was breathless and bewildered.

"I don't know. Let me go in front." She moved aside as I barged past her.

The cool wind whirled and whistled around us, whipping my hair about my face. A large hawk squawked angrily overhead. More tangled bushes, more blue bells, more of the same.

"It's no use," I cried. "I can't remember." My voice echoed through the forest.

I stopped, perplexed, and took some long deep breaths to still my hammering heart. Auntie leaned against the trunk of a birch tree, her face flushed, puffing and panting like a deflating yellow blimp.

Then, out of the corner of my eye, through a screen of pines, I caught a glimpse of something moving.

"I just saw something. Come on."

I headed in its direction, waving my arms for Auntie to follow. Burdened by her heavy load, her stubby little legs struggled to keep up with my long stride.

I caught another glimpse and another. It looked like a woman in a long green dress. As we got closer, I realized that it was Mary Eliss.

# Chapter 8

"Mary Eliss, is that you?" I hollered.

Auntie gasped. The color drained from her face. "Bloody Hell! What is it?"

The girl was weaving in and out of the trees in a floating motion and giggling playfully. Rather than feeling alarmed by her appearance, I was relieved and comforted by it.

Auntie stopped, threw down her shovel, gloves and axe, then grabbed the back of my sweater and pulled. "It's 'er, the one I seen when I was a young'un'. Don't go near 'er, luv," she said in a shaky voice.

I turned around, took her trembling hand in mine and whispered in a calm, reassuring tone, "It's okay. She's not going to hurt us. She just wants us to follow her."

Auntie opened her raincoat and stuck her hand into the inside pocket. I thought she was going for the whiskey bottle, but instead she pulled out a ratty, palm-sized Bible. She raised her hand and held out the little Bible like a weapon, mumbling something about fearing no evil.

I put my hand on top of hers and lowered it gently. "That stuff only works on vampires, Auntie Em." I cupped my hands around my mouth and called out, "Show us the place where you were killed, Mary Eliss."

The giggling stopped. I narrowed my eyes and scanned the woods.

She was gone.

The wind had diminished now. We were shrouded in a cloak of unearthly silence as we stood fearfully still, cold and shivering, gazing around, perplexed, wondering if we should turn back or venture on. Then I spotted her standing by a cluster of spruce trees, her arms waving at us in a beckoning motion.

I picked up the shovel, handed it to Auntie, threw the axe over my shoulder and ran after her. Off she flew, a streak of green, orange and white, gliding through the woodlot like a great parakeet.

As I scurried through a patch of evergreens, my foot slipped on a damp carpet of pine needles, causing me to fall with a thump to the ground. I hit my head on a large jagged rock.

The woods spun dizzily around me. Blood trickled down the side of my face. Then darkness.

When I came to, I could feel the warmth of something heavy lying on top of me, something that smelt like rubber mingled with sweat. I pried my eyes open a little bit at a time; slowly they focused, then opened wide. I gasped.

Bending over me, looking right into my face, were the

glassy unblinking eyes of Mary Eliss.

Her pale complexion was brushed with soft pink, a sprinkle of freckles dotted her little pug nose, and feathery ginger curls dangled over her shoulder. She was radiant, almost angelic, and smelled like the garden. Her head tilted from side to side, like an animated porcelain doll, as she surveyed my face. Then her rosy lips parted into a sweet smile and she whispered, "Come, Emily, come."

I lifted my fuzzy head carefully from the damp ground. The bleeding had stopped but I felt a faint throb in my temple. Auntie's heavy rain coat lay on top of me and on top of that, the little Bible. She must have placed it there, thinking that it would protect me. Coarse white stuff that looked like salt was spread in a circle around me and axe and shovel lay beside my feet.

I moved the coat and Bible aside, put my hands on the ground and carefully eased myself up. Feeling a little wobbly and light-headed, I grabbed the rough bark of a nearby pine tree to steady myself and gazed around anxiously. Where did Auntie go? Where was Mary Eliss? Had I imagined her staring me in the face and calling my name?

"Auntie Em! Auntie Em!" I cried feebly, franticly.

The wind had given way to the pitter-patter of a dreary fine drizzle, the type of rain that seeps through your flesh and into your bones. The dank smell of wet wood and leaves filled the air.

Fear consumed me. I was shivery cold, lost, and all alone in the bleak, damp, haunted woodlot. My stomach growled as

I leaned my head back, opened my mouth wide and stuck out my parched tongue, catching tiny droplets of water to quench my thirst.

I climbed into Auntie's raincoat. It was dirty, weighty and smelled like wet rubber. As I bent down to pick up the Bible, I noticed a tiny trickle of blood from my skinned ankle dripping on my sock. I dabbed it with a leaf.

Trembling uncontrollably, I stood under a prickly pine tree, clutched the little Bible in my hand, drew it to my chest and sniffed back the tears of desperation. "God, please send someone to help."

"Someone will come, someone will come," I mumbled in a wishful repetitive chant. My flesh was covered with goose bumps, I could feel them popping up under the arms of the sodden rain coat. I ached with hunger, fatigue and deep gut-wrenching dread.

In the distance I heard a vague whisper, and as I listened carefully, it became closer and clearer. "Come, Emily, come."

I pushed the soggy wet strands of hair away from my face and searched, my eyes wide, scanning desperately through the thin gray curtain of rain.

I spotted her standing by a cluster of tangled trees. "Mary Eliss!"

She took off, her long green dress floating behind her, drifting just above the ground, as if a current of wind had swept her off her feet and carried her away.

My hand shook as I tucked the Bible into its pocket,

picked up my weapons and pursued her. A wave of nausea churned in my stomach and washed up into my throat, as I hobbled sluggishly through the tangled wood. *You won't throw up, you won't throw up*. I hated vomiting, the feeling of heaving, the foul taste and the smell of regurgitated food. As a child, when I felt nauseated, I would hold my breath and try to push the feeling back down inside me.

The mysterious force that had impelled me to come here and now drew me to Mary Eliss was stronger than my form. It seemed to inject a rush of energy into my veins. The sick feeling subsided. Adrenalin started to pump.

She moved more slowly than before and turned her head periodically to see if I was still behind her as she weaved around the large giants, through clusters of bushes, over brambles and into a familiar opening. I ignored the objections of my inside voice crying, "Warning, warning," and followed her tentatively.

There she was, just as I had seen her before, sitting on the log, tears trickling down her pale cheeks. I gritted my teeth and looked around suspiciously, wondering when the disgusting creature would appear. Then, as before, she dismounted, stood beside the log and pointed to the ground.

"Is there something buried there?" I asked.

She said nothing. Her vacant green eyes stared intently at the ground.

Nervously, I walked over to the log, shovel in hand. Placing my tool on the mossy covered earth, I pushed down hard on the handle, sinking the blade into the ground. It was softer and easier to penetrate than I had expected.

I dug deep with an incredible strength and determination, as if my life depended upon it.

Mary Eliss stood still, her gaze glued to the ground in a trance-like state. She had lost her warm radiant aura, and the energy that radiated from her now made me uncomfortable.

My shovel hit something hard. I bent down to get a closer look.

Then I heard a hissing sound, like that of a large cat. Slowly I turned my head and swallowed hard.

Mary Eliss was mutating.

Gradually her delicate features and pretty clothes took on a bedraggled, devilish appearance, transforming her into the horrid creature. Her disgusting odor drifted toward me as she lifted her ugly head.

My body shook with a paralyzing fear as her angry eyes met mine. Impulsively I dropped the shovel, shoved my shaky hand inside the raincoat, pulled out the little Bible and held it out, arms stretched in front of me. With the other hand I revealed the pendant. This stuff worked in the movies. I thought it was worth a try. Oh please God, let it work.

"Expel this evil spirit," I commanded as my lips quivered.

She looked at the pendent and tilted her head from side to side, as if perplexed. Then she looked into my face, her eyes smoldering with a savage inner fire.

Her dark, thin lips opened. "Colceathrar. Colceathrar," she hissed as she moved toward me.

All of a sudden I was bathed in the scent of lavender and a

strange, serene warmth enveloped me.

The creature glared at me, eyes wide. Then she snarled like an angry lion, exposing her dirty, broken teeth and tossing her head back and forth in an agitated manner. She spun around and flew into the woods, screeching like a wounded animal.

The warm scent lifted, sucking the energy from my body and leaving me in a state of utter of shock. My ankle hurt and my head throbbed. I collapsed in a heap on the ground, dizzy and overcome with a bone-weary exhaustion that rendered me numb. With my arms wrapped around my knees, my hands clutching the silver pendent and the little Bible, I curled up into a ball on the cool, damp mulch.

In the distance I could hear the terrifying sound of breaking twigs and the rustling of dry leaves, getting closer and closer. *Oh no, she's coming back.*

"Emily! Emily Anne!"

The sound of Mom's anxious voice rang like heavenly music. I managed to squeeze out a feeble "I'm over here."

Mom, Auntie and Jonathan came running toward me.

"Oh my God. What happened to you?" Mom knelt down beside me, drew me up into her arms and sobbed like a baby.

"Calm yerself, Penny. We've found 'er now," Auntie said, looking at me pitifully. "Didn't wanna leave ya, luv, alone in these 'ere woods, but you were out for the count and I couldn't carry ya. Went to get help, I did. Uncle Reg, your dad, and John went one way and we went the other. Followed m' inside voice, I did." She gave me a wink.

I forced a smile. "Good for you, Auntie."

I gazed up at Jonathan. He was standing beside a huge slab of rock and wearing a long, green, hooded raincoat, similar to Auntie's. His thick black hair was damp and windswept. His mysterious dark brown eyes met mine as his lips drew up in a sweet sensual smile. I turned my head quickly, not wanting him to see me so bedraggled and ugly. *Oh no. I'm becoming vain and superficial.*

"Been digging for treasure, 'ave ya?" Auntie peered down the hole.

"There's something in there."

I turned my head and looked into Jonathan's face, realizing that this was more important than my vanity. "Take a look down there, please."

He gave a slight nod, flashed an agreeable smile and walked over to take a look.

"Dig!" I shouted in an authoritative tone. "Please," I added hastily.

He undid his raincoat, grabbed the shovel and shoved the blade into the ground. Auntie stood by his side.

My head rested comfortably on Mom's lap as she stroked my scraggy, damp hair with her long slender fingers. Her mascara had run, leaving dirty black smudges under her eyes. It was only at times like this, desperate times, when my need to be nurtured and comforted was greater than my teenage pride, that I allowed her to baby me.

"Looks like bones of some sort," Jonathan called out. He knelt down, bent over the hole and dug into the muddy earth with his bare hands. We watched him intently.

His brow arched in disbelief. "It's a skeleton!" he shouted. Mom gasped, put the back of her hand over her forehead and swayed. I thought she was going to pass out.

"Flipping heck," Auntie mumbled as she shook her head and fumbled up her sleeve for her hanky. "Leave it alone, lad. Don't touch it."

Jonathan stood back and stared at his gruesome discovery with a stern expression. "We will have to contact the police." His voice was dull and troubled.

"All right, that's what we'll do. Let's be off, then," Auntie said in a hasty voice.

Mom stood on one side of me, Auntie on the other. They put their arms around my back, cupped my elbows with their hands and heaved me up. I felt woozy, and my legs gave way and buckled under me.

"Jonny, you bring them there tools," Auntie ordered as she struggled to hold me up.

Jonathan placed the axe and shovel by our feet, ran his strong muddy hands down his raincoat and said with authority, "You two take them. I'll take her."

My eyes widened. My pulse started to race in anticipation. He drew close to me and put one muscular arm behind my legs and the other around my back. I swooned. Gently he lifted me up and cradled me in his arms.

Even though my ankle and head hurt and the events of the day had been numbing, the warm feeling of being carried in his sturdy arms and the heat from his body, so close to mine, was heavenly. I rested my damp face against his soft woolen sweater and breathed in his manly scent. My whole body tingled. Ecstasy is the only way I could describe it. Pure ecstasy.

On they trudged through the tangled woodlot. Auntie was leading the way with Mom following close behind us, a cigarette dangling from her lips. She was fussing with her clothes and hair and grumbling about the thorny bushes. Every once in a while she let out a squeal as the bushes that Auntie was pushing aside for Jonathan sprung back to hit her in the face. Auntie was oblivious to her actions; she just marched on purposely, in a fearful trance.

Jonathan's strong arms were steady and unwavering; they never flinched once or strained under the heavy load. *He must be immensely strong.* I closed my eyes and imagined that I was a beautiful princess being carried to an enchanted kingdom by a handsome prince who had just rescued me from an evil wood witch. I wallowed in my fantasy.

"You found her. Is she hurt?" Dads' voice brought me back to reality.

As Jonathan placed me carefully into my father's arms, I looked into his face.

"Thank you," I whispered.

He gave me a charming smile. It was only a courteous one, but it left me weak, and again I felt that uncanny feeling that I'd seen him before, somewhere, someplace in time. The pleasurable sensation I felt being so close to his body stayed with me for the rest of that day and lingered in a corner of my heart for years after that. This was the last time I'd see the gorgeous Jonathan McArthur through the eyes of a fourteen-year-old girl.

As soon as we got back to the cottage, Uncle Reg contacted the authorities. Two skeletons were found—one of a middle-aged man and one of a young girl, later to be identified as Preston and Mary Eliss. Their remains were taken away for a proper burial. Elizabeth Eliss's remains were never found.

I insisted that they take a look to see if they could find the cubby-hole in the attic room. They found the skeletons of two cats there. I looked for the note in Annabella's dress, but it was gone.

Mom and Dad begged my aunt and uncle to leave Merryweather Lodge, but they insisted on staying. "It's our home; besides, Mary Eliss is at peace now. She won't be bothering us again," Auntie Em said.

I knew one thing for sure: even though Merryweather Lodge had an air of magic and fairytale charm, and even though I'd found my prince charming here, I never wanted to come back again.

On the day of our leaving, I was surprised to find myself so distressed. I'd been looking forward to this day and had been anxious to leave. I had missed my home, my computer, my dog and my friends. But a nagging need to stay gnawed at the pit of my stomach like a hunger, and the warm fragrant shadow that had followed me around seemed to cast an embrace, hugging me tight like an old friend, reluctant to say goodbye.

It was here that I had learned to face insurmountable

fear, recognize my intuition and step outside into the adult world. It was here that I had witnessed hell, found magic in ordinary things, glimpsed my vocation, and met my soul mate—someone, I was sure, I had met before and with whom I had a profound spiritual connection, too deep to define.

As we drove away from the cottage along the winding dirt road and out into the enchanting countryside, the hunger grew. Then I heard it, deep inside, the unspoken sound of my inside voice. A soft reassuring whisper, "You'll be back."

Five years later, because of my uncle's untimely death, I was forced to do just that.

# Chapter 9

"Do you need a hand up there, Emily?" The sound of my dad's voice brought me back from the past.

"No, I think I'll leave everything the way it is. We might have to seal it off. The stairs are not safe and I'm afraid someone might get hurt." I shivered as I closed the heavy wooden door and descended the creaky attic stairs.

"Whatever you say. It's your place now."

"Dad!" I protested. "Auntie Em isn't dead yet. She will pull through this, you know."

"Perhaps. She's a tough old girl, that's for sure." Dad was sitting at the kitchen table, flipping through a pile of papers. He removed his reading glasses and forced a smile. "If she does pull through this, she's going to need a lot of care, and there's no one around here to look after her."

I thought for a moment. "Maybe we can talk her into coming back home with us." Although I couldn't see my aunt wanting to do that, since she was very independent and loved this little cottage dearly. I knew that if anyone was going to talk her into doing anything, it would be me. But I was no longer a spoiled, selfish child and I really wouldn't want to coerce my aunt into doing anything against her wishes.

Dad sighed and slid the arms of his glasses over his ears. "I don't think that would work. How would we manage with two sick women in the house? Anyway, I haven't had time to think about it. All that I can think about right now," he swallowed hard, "is giving my brother a proper funeral."

It had been three days since John McArthur found my uncle's lifeless body sprawled out on the sitting room floor. And my aunt curled up in her chair, pale, mute and glassy eyed, clutching her handkerchief and rocking back and forth like a frightened child. They had determined that my uncle had been dead for twelve hours. Massive heart attack, the coroner said. Maud McArthur was the last one to see him alive. She had walked over to the cottage that evening to deliver a loaf of her homemade bread. She said that they were both fine when she left.

Auntie was in Salisbury General Hospital. There had been no change in her condition since they found her.

Dad and I took the first available flight out of Edmonton when we found out what had happened. My mom had breast cancer and was too weak to travel.

My aunt and uncle had informed my parents some time ago that if anything happened to them, Merryweather Lodge would be left to me. If I'd known, I would have protested. I didn't want to leave Canada or live in such a creepy place, but the thought of selling it saddened me deeply. Now my dad and I had the painful task of arranging Uncle Reg's funeral, getting the farm business in order and deciding what to do with Auntie.

"What time are the McArthurs coming over?" I asked.

"About seven, I think," Dad answered drowsily, as he wandered into the kitchen, stretching his arms and yawning loudly. "Would you like some tea?"

"Is there anything stronger?" I needed something to steady my nerves. This was all so sudden, and the memories of what happened here five years ago still resonated within me, loud and clear as if it were only yesterday.

"There are a couple of warm beers, Emy's sherry and something labeled black current brandy–homemade by the looks of it."

"That'll do." I said, anxious to get anything down me that would relieve the tension and dull the pain.

Dad had lit the fire as soon as we arrived, bright red and orange flames crackled and danced franticly in the hearth but it still felt cold and damp. I shivered and huddled into my fleecy sweater. "It's so cold in here, Dad."

"It takes a while to heat this drafty old place. Should be nice and toasty by this evening though."

He handed me a small crystal glass glowing with the homemade concoction. Then he blew into his large mug of steamy hot tea, spiked, I assumed, with a dash of scotch, and headed for the door. "I'm going outside to chop some wood before the McArthurs arrive."

He lifted Uncle Reg's hefty plaid jacket from the coat

stand and pulled it over his shoulders. I noticed him taking a quick sniff of the collar, and then lowering his head and biting down on his lip to stop it from trembling.

"Are you okay, Dad?" I asked sympathetically.

He sniffed and straightened his back. "I'm fine. No conferring with ghosts while I'm outside, okay?"

"That's not funny!"

"Sorry, Princess." Joking and pretending that everything was fine was my dad's way of covering up his grief. I knew that losing his only brother had hurt him deeply. I could tell by the way his eyes kept filling up with tears and the way he had swallowed hard when we walked into the cottage.

I snuggled down into Auntie's well-worn comfy chair, put the glass to my lips and sipped slowly. The fruity dark-red liquid flowed down my throat, smooth, warm and comforting. Auntie's personal aroma emanated from the cushions around me. As I breathed it in my heart sank and a lump formed inside my throat. Poor Auntie Em, lying there in that sterile hospital room all alone. No one seemed to know how long it would take for her to regain her sanity, if she regained it at all.

The last time I saw my aunt and uncle was two years ago when they came over to Canada for my eighteenth birthday. Auntie seemed a little despondent then, but I thought that was because my mom had just been diagnosed with breast cancer. I kept asking her if everything was okay at Merryweather Lodge; all she would say was "Right as rain, m' luv, right as rain." But the tone in her voice said something different.

Her letters had become brief and dull. A year ago she had written to tell me that Wooky had passed away. "Wooky's dead," she wrote. "Found him in the barn, we did. Something fishy about it, there were, something not quite right." I sent her my condolences and asked her what was fishy about his death. In her next letter she wrote, "Let sleeping cats lie. All right, luv?" As if she was telling me to mind my own business. It was just like Auntie to offer me a tasty tidbit of information then pull back the morsel before giving me a bite. I still wondered what happened to Wooky.

It was no surprise that my Uncle Reg had a heart attack. He'd been told to give up his pipe and cut back on fatty foods, but he refused to do either. His blood cholesterol level was extremely high.

But why was Auntie in such a state? It was the shock of seeing her husband dying in front of her, they said. Why didn't she phone someone or go for help? Even though she didn't have her license, she drove the old car around the farm and wouldn't hesitate to use it in an emergency. No, this wasn't like Auntie. She was a strong woman, a fighter. Unless something diabolical happened, something so terrifying that it incapacitated her and scared her half to death.

I could hear a car slowly approaching outside, gravel crunching under its tires, brakes squeaking, a door slamming, then the sound of muffled voices. I lowered my glass onto the little table beside me and eased out of the chair.

"Hi, it's so nice to see you again." I said, extending my hand.

Maud McArthur placed her cold limp hand in mine and

shook it feebly. Her lip turned up ever so slightly into a sour grin. Her eyes scanned me with a disapproving look. She hadn't changed a bit, I thought. She was still the stout, miserable, stern-faced woman I remembered. A navy blue cardigan hung over her shoulders and underneath a plain black dress flowed down to her ankles, met by a pair of brown laced boots. On her head she wore a black scarf that she promptly untied and handed to me.

John strolled in behind her, took off his tartan cap, shoved it under his arm and took my hand. "So sorry for your loss, luv."

His voice was genuine and compassionate. I looked down at his shiny bald head; graying hair formed a thin semicircle around it and brown age spots dotted the top. He was dressed in baggy black trousers and a thick, navy sweater. His neck was wrapped in a long dark green, hand-knitted scarf. The shadows under his eyes and the gloomy expression portrayed a sad and despondent man. It was evident that the death of his boss and good friend had hit him hard.

Dad walked in behind John, carrying an arm full of wood.

I paused for a moment before closing the door. I had hoped to see Jonathan, just out of curiosity, I told myself, but the deep surge of disappointment I felt signified it was more than that.

"You guys sit down and make yourselves at home; I'll make us a nice cup of tea," I said, trying to add a little cheeriness to the solemn air.

"Thanks, honey," Dad replied in a phony optimistic tone.

· John's face lit up. "That would be nice, luv. Milk and two sugars, if you don't mind."

Maud slipped off her cardigan, plunked herself down in Auntie's chair and folded her pale flabby arms under her ample breasts. She glanced at the wine glass on the little table beside her and tossed her head in a haughty manner.

"Miserable old bitch!" I whispered under my breath.

My cold hands shook a little as I fumbled with the matches and lit the gas stove. I could feel Auntie's presence here more than anywhere else in the cottage. This was the hub of the home and her domain. She'd spend hours scrapping and cutting vegetables on the wooden draining board, kneading bread dough and rolling pastry on the rough kitchen table. Her hands would get red and sore from rubbing socks and delicates up and down the corrugated washing board in the large enamel sink. And making tea, she was always making tea. I could almost smell the delicious aromas of fried onions, gravy simmering in the pot and apple pie sprinkled with cinnamon and brown sugar, and hear her jolly voice singing happily, "I've got a lovely bunch of coconuts..." Dear Auntie. It wouldn't be the same here without her.

"Tea's up," I announced.

Maud straightened her back and gave me a stern look as she nudged at Winny with her elbow. The cat was perched on the arm of her chair, looking for a comfy lap to curl up in. Maud was doing her best to make sure it wasn't hers.

I placed the tray on the vintage chest that was used as a coffee table and lifted Winny's soft, warm body off the chair. I couldn't resist giving Maud a quick critical glance. Then I placed the cat down gently on the fireside rug beside Winky, who gave me an indignant "this is my rug" look.

"Cookies anyone?" I asked as I poured their tea into Auntie's best china cups.

"I'll have a biscuit—if they're not stale, that is."

I held out a plate of assorted cookies: Digestives, Custard Creams, Jammy Dodgers and Ginger Snaps. "I'm sure they're not stale, Mrs. McArthur. My Aunt wouldn't have anything stale in her pantry. She was very particular about her food."

She took one custard cream. "Is!" she snapped.

"Pardon me?"

"Is. Emy isn't dead yet!"

I spit back at her in an angry tone, "I know that. It was just a slip of the tongue, that's all!"

Dad cleared his throat. "Emy's a strong woman. There's a good chance she'll come around."

"Will you be taking her to the funeral?" John asked meekly as he dunked his cookie into his tea.

Dad shrugged his shoulders. "We'll have to see what she's like by then."

"She can't go like that," Maud piped up. "She doesn't speak or recognize anyone. Just stares into space, gormless-like. Lost her marbles, she has, and if she doesn't come out of it they'll be putting her in the nut house, mark my words."

Her callous words pierced my heart and made me angry. I wanted to slap her. "My Aunt is not going to any nut house."

John pulled a crumpled blue hanky out of his trouser pocket and gave a hefty blow. "I'll do anything I can to help."

Dad tipped his head and smiled. "Thanks, I'll need all the

help I can get. We will be going to see Emy in the morning, and the funeral director is coming in the afternoon. I'd appreciate it if you'd continue to tend the sheep and look after the dog while we're getting things sorted."

Before John could open his mouth, Maud spoke up. "That, he will, and we'll get our lad to help."

"How is Jonathan?" I asked eagerly. Too eagerly, I thought, right after the words came out of my mouth.

He was the first boy I'd had a real crush on and the only one that I have ever felt a true connection with. After I had returned home, his smell, his voice, his very essence had stayed with me for a long time. It faded after a while but never disappeared completely. Even when I started dating one of the hottest guys in high school, thoughts of Jonathan would subtly intrude on our most intimate moments.

John squared his round shoulders, his thin lips turned slightly upward. "He's got a good job. Draws pictures for magazines and books, earns good money doing it, too. And he's got himself a flat in Salisbury, on a real posh street." There was an air of pride in his voice.

"He's happy, and it's a living, I suppose," Maud said in a disapproving tone.

"An illustrator! That's an exciting career, and one that seems perfect for Jonathan." Maud raised her eyebrows and gave me a look that seemed to say *How would you know?* "From what I can remember of his personality, that is."

"You wanted him to farm, Maud?" Dad asked.

"Good grief. No."

John cleared his throat. "She wanted him to be a vet." He looked pitifully at his wife. "Didn't you, dear?"

"Always had a soft spot for animals, did our Jonny, and he's very smart. His teachers thought he was marvelous. Could have done anything with his brain, they said."

Dad leaned back in his chair and stretched out his long legs. "A vet, now there's a booming profession. It's a sin how people pamper their pets these days."

I shook my head. "You don't have to be a doctor or a lawyer to be successful. You're successful when you're happy and content; find inner peace and your authentic self, no matter what that might be." They looked at me with blank expressions as if I were speaking in a foreign language. But what did I expect? They were just simple folk, as Auntie would say.

"Success is when you have enough money in the bank for an early retirement." Dad walked over to the fireplace and shuffled the embers around with the iron poker. He loved to contradict me and I was always up for a challenge. But this wasn't the time or the place.

"How's Belinda?" I asked, changing the subject.

They glanced at each other suspiciously. John ran his hand over the stubble on his chin in a contemplative manner. "She's going through a bit of a stage right now."

"Oh, really?" I tried to sound compassionate. "What sort of stage?"

"Just a stage," Maud pronounced as she heaved her bulky body out of the chair and brushed the cookie crumbs off her dress. She gathered the tea cups, put them on the tray and proceeded into the kitchen. Just before she got to the door she stopped, glanced over her shoulder and said in a bossy tone, "Come on girl; leave the men to discuss business."

*Who does she think she is?* I grabbed the wine glass and followed her. If I was going to be alone with Maud McArthur, I'd need another drink.

With a brazen air of authority, Maud grabbed Auntie's apron off the hook on the pantry door, tied it around her waist, rolled up her sleeves and handed me the dish towel. We stood in silence as she squeezed the liquid soap into the hot water and swished it around with the back of her hand.

"Never touched my bread, they didn't. It was here on the draining board, still wrapped in my best tea towel." She sniffed. "To think of her lying there half dead, while her man is being buried. It don't seem right." Her soapy hand slid across her face, leaving tiny white bubbles glistening on her cheek. She looked mournful and I pitied her.

*She really does have feelings.* I put my arm around her tentatively and gave her a gentle squeeze. "Emy will recover. I just know she will."

She pulled away from me sharply and screwed up her nose in distaste, as if I had some contagious disease. "And what if she don't and they put her away? You'll be selling the farm then, I suppose?" She lowered her head. "It'll be worth a bob or two."

I suddenly remembered that my aunt and uncle owned the cottage that the McArthurs lived in and that the wages John earned on the farm were probably their only source of income. Perhaps this was why she was being so nasty. She might be worried sick about their situation.

"Don't worry, we have no intention of selling the farm, and your husband's job is secure. We'll need him more than ever now."

Maud yanked the rubber plug out of the sink, grabbed the kitchen towel and wiped her hands vigorously on its terry fibers. Then she turned and glared at me with a scornful scowl. "I'm not worried about that." She drew close to my face. "This place should be mine by rights. It belonged to my great granddad. My granny inherited it when the Elisses disappeared, but she didn't want it. So she sold it to Emy's folks, of all people. Outsiders, they were. Her dad was a Londoner and her mom came from Yorkshire. A right bloody mixture, that was." The angry words spewed out of her mouth accompanied by a sour smell of bad breath.

*Is this woman for real?*

"Kept all the money to herself, she did; squandered the lot. Stingy old sod. Should be mine, not some foreigners."

That did it! I stepped back but refused to be intimidated. "Ah, so that's why you're being so rude! If you think my aunt and uncle should have left this farm to you, you're crazy!" My voice was loud and firm but it trembled slightly. There was something about this woman that scared me and made me uncomfortable.

Her mouth was agape and her face flushed. But before she could lay into me, the kitchen door crept open steadily, with a long alarming creak. I gasped as the memories of what happened here five years ago came flooding back.

# Chapter 10

John's bald head peered timidly around the kitchen door. "Is everything all right, ladies? We thought we heard some squabbling?"

Maud whipped off her apron, threw it on the table and stormed out the door. As she passed her husband, she gave him a quick disapproving glance and muttered, "Mind your own business."

When the McArthurs left, I wandered into Auntie's bedroom to finish unpacking my suitcase. A bulky brass bed occupied most of the room. It was draped in a handsome, well-worn patchwork blanket, with an assortment of pillows and cushions piled on top. An old-fashioned wardrobe sat tall and proud against one wall. A rich cherry wood dressing table displaying framed black and white photos, a silver jewelry box and a china cat sat against the other. It was flanked by a small window dressed in simple net curtains. At the foot of the bed an intriguing wooden chest whispered at me to look inside.

*Later*, I told myself, as I switched off the main light and turned on the bedside lamp. Its shade had a beautiful rose pink pattern, with a long silk fringe that tickled my fingers when I flicked on the switch. Next to the lamp sat an old Toby mug with some sort of murky liquid inside and something pink lurking at the bottom. I stuck my pen inside and fished around. "Yuck!" A pair of pale pink gums with stubby off-white teeth perched on the nib of my ballpoint pen. I dropped them back into the mug and pushed it behind the lamp. *I'll have to take those with me tomorrow,* I thought. *Auntie doesn't like anyone but family seeing her without her teeth. "It's not proper," she'd say.*

I climbed into my flannel pajamas and burrowed beneath the crisp, linen sheets. They were clean and smelt outdoorsy-fresh, but I could still smell my aunt's scent buried in the fibers of the old quilt.

I swallowed the lump in my throat and sniffed back the tears as I gazed around the dimly lit room suspiciously. The memories of what had happened here five years ago kept sneaking into my mind even though I was trying hard not to let them. *Why have I come back to this scary, ancient place with its simple, narrow-minded people?*

Dad had told me not to come. "It will be too painful for you," he kept saying. I was sure that what he really wanted was for me to stay at home and look after Mom, but I had to come. I couldn't let him go through this alone, and my inside voice was louder and clearer than it had ever been before. "You must go back," it kept insisting.

And there was something else, something I couldn't quite put my finger on.

My mom's sister had flown down from Toronto to look after her while we were away. Aunt Pam is a registered nurse and better able to take care of Mom than I was. At least, that's what I kept telling myself. She promised to phone us if Mom's condition got worse.

I couldn't bring myself to turn off the light and was too afraid to close my eyes. So I just lay there—tired, frazzled and nervous, trying hard to force my mind to think positive thoughts and visualize beautiful things. My eyes became heavy.

I could hear Celtic music playing in the background as I twirled round and round, tossing my head, waving my arms and swaying my hips to the intoxicating sound. My long red hair caressed my naked body, sending tiny ripples of pleasure all over my skin. Other young women danced around me, giggling and shaking their bare, voluptuous bodies passionately. The smiling, enthusiastic faces of men in white robes looked on. I felt no shame. It was liberating, exciting and devilishly erotic.

Suddenly the music stopped and the scene changed. I was surrounded by enormous gray stones. I shivered and huddled deep into the hooded robe that was covering my naked form, as the cool wind moaned and whistled through the huge slabs.

Then I heard a voice, coming from behind me: "Colrea, Colrea."

I turned. In front of me stood the most beautiful woman I had ever seen. Wavy, blonde hair with wisps of red flowed over her shoulders and trickled down her back. It was crowned by a wreath of red berries. Her heart-shaped face held mysterious green eyes that bore into me and made me shudder. She smiled mischievously, then turned and ran. Her cloak of deep purple fluttered behind her in the wind. "Catch me if you can, cousin," she called playfully.

I chased after her, laughing and frolicking as the brisk wind whipped my hair about my face. In and out of the giant stones we flew Cool gusts tugged at our cloaks, pulling us back and pushing us forward.

The sound of a young man's voice interrupted us. "Merthia, Merthia," he called. My playmate opened her arms and ran to greet him.

As she embraced the dark-clad figure, a surge of jealousy welled up inside me. Anger stirred in the pit of my stomach. I put my hands over my face and sobbed.

The howling wind stopped. A pungent smell of pine and damp moss filled my nostrils. Slowly, I drew my hands away from my face. I was now standing in a forest shrouded by a bleak fog. Lofty evergreens towered above me, capped by low lying gray clouds. I gazed around, scared and perplexed.

Suddenly, wailing and bloodcurdling screams came rushing toward me like a blast of wind. I gasped as a hand from behind grabbed me and pulled me forward.

It was the mysterious man that my playmate had embraced.

"Stop!" I screamed as I tried to free my hand from his grip. He squeezed it harder, dragging me along forcefully. His black cape flapped behind him, like the wings of a giant raven.

We reached a small clearing. He slowed down and advanced cautiously into the opening. I froze, shocked and repulsed by the gruesome sight in front of me.

Beneath the branches of a sturdy oak tree sat a large slab of gray rock. Sprawled out on top lay the pale mutilated flesh of a woman. Parts of her arms and legs had been hacked off and her head was split open, exposing her skull. Blood was everywhere.

I trembled. The strange figure drew me on. I pulled back.

"Colrea," he whispered in a soft, comforting, familiar voice. Then he turned to face me and pushed back his black hood. His face was stunningly handsome, with ebony eyes that looked down on me lovingly.

I swooned as a deep connection resonated in my heart. This was not the face of a stranger but someone I knew, someone I loved.

Instantly I was whisked away by some strange force and pulled into a vortex of dismembered bodies. Heads of young girls, hands, legs and severed cat parts—tails, ears, paws—whirled around me, blood soaked and gory. "Help me!" I screamed.

The gruesome scene vanished. I was back in the gloomy forest. My handsome friend stood by my side. In between us lay an axe. Its blade was stained crimson. We were covered in blood. It dripped from my clothes and trickled down my face. The putrid stench of fear, sweat and death hung in the air. Gagging at the taste of iron in the back of my throat, I shook uncontrollably.

155

I bolted upright, eyes wide, heart racing, clenching the covers under my neck. The bed was damp with sweat and the taste of blood was still on my breath. It didn't feel like I had just been dreaming. It was as if my soul had drifted back in time and re-lived some horrible experience.

I pushed back the covers and moved my legs slowly, one at a time, from under the sheets. A dull pain throbbed inside my head; the rays of early morning light that filtered through the net curtains hurt my eyes. It felt like I had a terrible hangover.

I reached for my purse beside the night stand, fumbled inside for the bottle of pain killers and threw a couple of capsules to the back of my throat. Then I grabbed the mug from behind the lamp and put it to my lips. A sour medicinal smell flew up my nostrils. I dropped the mug without drinking and swallowed hard, sending the pills rushing down my gullet.

A sick feeling churned inside my stomach. It moved into my throat, causing me to heave. I looked down at the false teeth sitting in a pool of discolored water and thought about what I had almost done. Carefully I stepped over the mess and dragged my bare feet across the wooden floor.

"Ow!" Something had pierced the skin on the sole of my foot. It was the cat ornament, broken into three pieces. A shiny black and white china feline, with a pink bow that looked a lot like Winky. *How did that get knocked off the dresser?*

Maybe Dad had come into the room to check on me and accidentally bumped into it.

Or maybe? No, I wasn't going to think about that!

I picked up the pieces and cleaned up the mess, wrapped

Auntie's teeth in a large white hanky and hobbled to the bathroom.

* * * *

The air was nippy, but the sky was a clear celestial blue and the sunshine lit the countryside, enhancing its glorious autumn hues. But the flamboyant view could not compensate for the gloominess I felt inside.

Dad hadn't said a word since we left the cottage. His long fingers were wrapped tightly around the steering wheel of our rented Buick. His worried eyes fixed firmly on the windy road ahead. I knew he was anxious and scared of seeing his sister-in-law in such an incapacitated state, not knowing what to expect or what to do. These past few years had been hard on my dad. After Mom's diagnosis and partial mastectomy, he buried himself in a deep pit of depression. Slowly, he'd burrowed his way out, using his work, love for golf and a new thirst for scotch as tools. I was hoping that this tragedy wouldn't push him back down the hole.

I was still living at home. I hadn't had the heart to move out while Mom was so sick, but we did hire a part-time home-care assistant to relieve Dad and help with the housework.

"This must be it," Dad said with a sigh as we drove through an open ornamental cast-iron gate and onto a wide, gravel driveway. Manicured lawns and groomed trees embellished each side. We pulled up to a stately brick building with rows of tiny windows and a brown slate roof dotted with chimneys. The sign above the main doors read Salisbury General Hospital.

"Can you tell me which room Emily Fletcher is in, please?" Dad asked the stern faced nurse at the front desk.

"Just a moment." She shuffled over to the computer on the other side of the window. "Ward 4, room 5. You'll need permission to go in there."

Dad looked at me and wrinkled his forehead. I shrugged my shoulders. "Permission?" we asked in unison.

She glared at us over her dark-rimmed glasses. "It's the psych ward."

My jaw dropped. "Why is she in the psych ward?"

"Well, it's not because she's psychic, that I can tell you."

I was shocked. "Excuse me, was that supposed to be funny?"

"Sorry if I offended you." She sniffed. "I was just joking."

Dad grabbed my arm and pulled me away from the window. "Let's go before you make a scene."

"She's supposed to be a professional," I grumbled.

"Blinking Americans," I heard her mumble as we walked away.

"I'm Canadian. Pompous English," I mumbled back, just loud enough for her to hear. That wasn't called for. *You've got to think before you open your mouth,* I told myself, just like I had a million times before.

We filled out the necessary forms, then spoke briefly with Auntie's doctor and received permission to visit her in her room.

A pretty young nurse led us through a long dimly lit corridor painted stark white. A sickening smell of disinfectant hung in the air. Cries, whimpers and giggles echoed from behind closed doors. "This is the original part of the hospital," the nurse said in an apologetic tone.

"It reminds me of a penitentiary," I whispered to Dad.

"She's by the window. You can stay as long as you want."

The room was dreary with bare gray walls and a faint musky smell and something worse—vomit, perhaps? A tacky arborite table with four chrome-legged chairs sat in the middle of the room. In the corner, a dated television rested on top of a hospital trolley, and by the window two shabby arm chairs with flowery slip covers embraced a couple of elderly ladies.

I walked over to the one that most resembled my aunt. Dad followed tentatively. My heart sank, and tears of utter shock and disbelief welled up inside me as I crouched beside her.

She looked like an old rag doll, slumped between the arms of the chair. Her hair was white, her face pale and thin; above her hollow cheeks two sad bewildered eyes with dark rims stared vacantly out of the undraped window. A dribble of dry saliva rested on the corner of her mouth. I dabbed it with a tissue from my pocket. Then I took hold of her limp hand and rubbed it gently with my finger tips. It felt dry and rubbery. "Auntie Em, can you hear me?"

She didn't move. "It's your niece, Emily." Nothing, not even a blink.

I looked back at Dad. He just shrugged his shoulders and shook his head feebly. I pulled her teeth out of my purse and put them in her housecoat pocket. Then I put my arm around her torso, heaved her up, fluffed the pillow behind her back and propped her against it.

"What are you doing?" Dad asked anxiously. "You might hurt her."

"Dad, there's nothing wrong with her physically. I just wanted to make her comfortable and see if I could get a response."

"What's the use? You can see that she's mute."

"No, she ain't!" a gruff voice yelled.

The woman in the other chair was sitting up, back straight, eyes wide, and grinning like a Cheshire cat. She had scruffy yellow hair, bad teeth and a face that was netted with wrinkles.

"Hi. I'm her niece and this is my dad. You've heard her speak?"

The woman rose steadily from her seat and shuffled toward us. She was wearing a long blue fleecy housecoat that was stained and carried the distinct smell of urine. Dad backed away. I put my hand over my nose.

She pointed her boney finger at Auntie. "She talks in 'er sleep. Keeps going on about someone named Hag all night long. Bugger Hag, Bugger Hag, babble, babble, babble. Can't get any sleep, and there is always one geezer or another comin' in the room kicking up a hullaballoo."

She was standing right in front of me, pointing her finger in my face; the smell was churning my stomach and making my eyes water. Dad walked over to the emergency button by the door and pushed it discreetly.

"If it bothers you so much, why don't you ask to be moved?" I said to her.

She threw her head back, a roar of laughter exploding from deep in her belly, accompanied by a blast of gas and another foul smell. "Don't you think I've tried?"

The door sprang open. Two large nurses in white coats grabbed her by the arms. "Come on, Bertha, it's time for your bath."

She left without a struggle, mumbling. "I'll 'ave 'er if she keeps it up, I will."

I pulled a bottle of cologne out of my purse and sprayed it around the room. Dad waved his hand in front of his face.

"We have to get her out of here," I said.

He touched my arm gently, signifying that he wanted to leave. "I agree, but we'll talk about it later."

I yanked my arm away. "No, Dad, we have to get her out of here today."

"Emily, that's impossible. There's all kinds of procedures we'd have to go through."

"Why? We are her next of kin now and we have a right to remove her from this dreadful place if we want to."

Dad sighed. "And what would we do with her? She's totally incapacitated and needs constant care."

"We could hire a nurse or put her in a private hospital until she comes around."

"It's extremely costly. Like I said, we'll talk about it later. Today I have to plan my brother's funeral, remember?"

I nodded my head as he put his hands on my shoulders

and looked into my eyes compassionately. "You do realize she might never come out of this?"

I held his glance. "She will. I know she will."

After pulling the plaid blanket that lay over Auntie's lap up around her neck, I leaned over and kissed her cheek gently. Then I put my mouth close to her ear and whispered, "Auntie Em, I know you're in there. You will recover; my inside voice told me so. And I really need your help; the mystery isn't solved yet." She flinched and turned her head ever so slightly in my direction, then she turned it back toward the window and resumed her vacant stare. "I'll be back and we will get you out of this place, I promise."

It was as if she had been pushed inside a clumsy piece of equipment that had malfunctioned and was only able to perform the simplest tasks. Perhaps she was just sitting there, waiting for the mechanisms to shut down.

*No, I won't allow her to give up. I'll find a way to bring her out of that shell, no matter how long it takes.*

Just as we were about to leave the building, I noticed a man standing by the reception desk who looked awfully familiar. He was wearing a tailored blue jacket, blue jeans and from where I stood, looked incredibly handsome. I nudged Dad's arm, pointed in his direction and asked, "See that man who's standing over there?" Dad nodded. "Do we know him?"

He looked, drew his brows together, then grinned. "We sure do," he said as he strolled toward the familiar figure. "Well, hi there. It's been awhile," Dad said as he extended his hand.

My stomach fluttered as if invaded by a swarm of butter-flies. It was him, the gorgeous Jonathan McArthur. He was taller than I remembered. Dark hair touched his collar, gleaming with ebony lights, and his handsome face was etched with perfect, manly features.

"Mr. Fletcher. How nice to see you again." His eyes swept over my body quickly but subtly. "Emily?"

I held out my hand. "Jonathan?" There was a quiver in my voice, and when our hands touched, my heart skipped as if suddenly elated.

# Chapter 11

It had only been five years but we had both changed considerably, shedding our youthful appearances and taking on the fully developed bodies of a man and a woman.

I had been dating a colleague named Kyle Stedman for almost six months. He was the editor of our daily newspaper, *The Edmonton Reporter*, and I was a staff writer. His father was English and his mother was Cree Indian. They celebrated both the British and Native cultures and I found it fascinating. Besides his intellect, wit and charm, Kyle had a body to die for.

But he wasn't the man of my dreams, the one whose essence had stayed with me all these years, the one who now stood in front of me.

"It was a devastating blow to my family and to the community. Mr. Fletcher was like an uncle to me."

"He was very fond of you, too. Are you here visiting my aunt?"

"Yes, I come here as often as I can. My flat's just down

the road. She doesn't acknowledge me, but I'm sure she knows I'm there."

"I'm sure she does." His brown eyes clung to mine, revealing his approval, and once again I felt that same uncanny feeling that I had felt as a young girl—a deep recognition, as if I was looking into the eyes of dear old friend.

As he turned to walk away I caught a whiff of his succulent scent. It sent my heart off on a tangent. Desire, longing, and lust beat inside me, like the drum of a hungry lover. There was something about this man, something profound, a mysterious connection too complex, too intense for words. I had to have him. I just had to.

On the day of my uncle's funeral, the vicar, Dad and I stood at the arched wooden doorway, greeting people as they walked in. One by one they came, dressed in black with their heads bowed, shading their solemn faces and muttering statements of "my condolences... He was a good chap... A fine neighbor and friend, was Reg... He'd never be beholding to anyone."

I felt like a heavy weight was hanging from my heart. My eyes were watering, and no matter how hard I tried I couldn't swallow the lump in my throat. I kept thinking about poor Auntie stuck in that awful place, unaware that the man she had spent almost forty years with was being put to rest. Part of me was mad at Uncle Reg for not looking after himself and following doctor's orders. The guilt that I felt for having those thoughts added to my anguish. I had lost the only uncle that I had ever known—a kind, simple, hardworking man, unpretentious and conscientious. He was a devoted shepherd, "a man of the land" as the locals would say.

The musty damp smell of the old church made it feel cold and dismal. Loud somber music bellowed from the organ. Mournful sobs echoed and pitiful eyes watched as I wandered down the aisle and took my place in the front pew. Maud McArthur sat across the aisle. A tub-shaped black hat was perched on top of her head. A net veil hung from its brim, covering her snooty face.

Beside her sat an attractive teenager with long blonde hair that was cut in a jagged fashion. Studded silver jewellery embellished her nose and lips. This was, I assumed, the disagreeable Belinda, all grown up. Her arms were folded tightly across her chest and her face wore an expression of utter boredom. She wore a jean jacket and matching skirt, which was hardly visible below her heavy studded belt. High laced boots embraced her long slender legs. She turned her head slowly in my direction and grimaced.

I felt my stomach clench as I frowned and looked away. It was if she'd sensed my gaze on her. She knew who I was; I could tell by the icy look she gave me. It felt like she was sending me some sort of threatening message, telepathically. But why did this girl despise me so? She hardly knew me. It was so bizarre. And why would a pompous old-fashioned woman like Maud McArthur allow her daughter to dress in such a sleazy manner, especially to a funeral? They did say that Belinda was going through a bad stage but still, it did seem odd.

"Psst. Emily," a voice from behind me whispered. I turned around. It was the peculiar Mrs. Tilly. Her face was shaded by a wide-rimmed black hat laden with artificial fruit and feathers. "I need a word with you. After the funeral, if that's all right, dear?"

I nodded my head and wondered what she had to tell me.

The organ music stopped. A petite middle-aged lady in a black pleated skirt and navy blue blouse scurried to the front of the church like a timid little mouse. The organist commenced with a rendition of my uncle's favorite hymn: "Amazing Grace." The woman's eyes darted around the room nervously as she cleared her throat. Then she opened her mouth wide, and to my amazement, the most robust and compelling sound poured out. She sang with such power, such passion, it was if she was auditioning for the main part in a Broadway musical.

I listened intently, captivated by the rich tone of her voice and moved by the words. I closed my eyes and pictured Uncle Reg walking through the lush green pasture, whistling "Amazing Grace," with his precious sheep grazing contently and his faithful dog by his side. I sniffed and reached into my purse for a tissue.

Heads and eyes turned to the back of the church. Uncle Reg's casket was being carried down the aisle. My stomach tightened and the tears that I had been trying to hold back started to flow.

One side of the wooden box was held up by my dad, Mr. McArthur and Jonathan, the other side by Bob Thomas, Ted

White and an elderly gentleman I didn't recognize.

The casket was draped in a worn patchwork blanket that his mother had made for him when he was a little boy. She had meticulously sewn tufts of wheat, sheep and border collies with fine embroidery silk into the patches. In the corner she'd written in tiny gold stitches: "Reggie, may you always have food on your table, sheep in your field, and the companionship of a good dog." It used to cover his favorite chair in the sitting room. I remember thinking the first time I read this verse that her wishes for him had come true.

On top of the blanket, Uncle Reg's old cap, pipe and his walking stick sat proudly, displaying their respect for the man who had depended on them for so many years.

Suddenly, the subtle scent of lavender drifted past my nose, like floral petals floating by. I recognized the smell. *Could this be her—the elusive ghost that had followed me around the last time I was here?* I shrugged it off and told myself not to be so silly.

My dad walked straight and tall, his head held high, as he carried the coffin of his only brother to the altar. His eyes were distant and red, his mouth tight and grim. I could tell that he had been crying and felt his sorrow deep within my heart, a hollow sadness that only the death of a loved one can bring.

Jonathan's groomed hair, smart black suit, tie and starched white shirt made him look like an Italian prince. And even under those miserable circumstances, my pulse started to race at the sight of him. What was it about this guy that captivated me so?

After the funeral, the congregation came back to the cottage for tea and light refreshments. I had spent the morning and evening before making sandwiches, cakes and tarts. I'd searched Auntie's well-stocked pantry for anything that might be deemed appropriate for a funeral tea, although I hadn't any idea what that would be. Back home, practically anything edible would have done, but here things have to be "proper," as Auntie would say.

John McArthur had delivered a basket of his wife's homemade bread and buns. I was surprised that she had even bothered, after our little tiff the other day. I was convinced that she had no use for us and that she would do anything to manipulate my aunt into leaving the farm to her instead of a "foreigner". That thought made me nervous. Nevertheless, I still needed to thank her for her trouble.

I rubbed my eyes, gazed around the smoke-filled sitting room, and asked myself why I hadn't insisted they go outside to smoke. Auntie would have. The only one who was allowed to smoke in her domain was Uncle Reg with his pipe, and she complained habitually about that.

Jonathan and his dad sat by the hearth on a pair of tapestry foot stools. Jonathan's long fingers were wrapped around a hefty beer mug that rested on his lap. His bent knees came up to his chest and he looked terribly uncomfortable. I wanted so very much to relieve him from his unnatural position, but every chair, stool, nook and cranny in the cottage was occupied. Every once in a while, I'd catch him looking at me through the clouds of cigarette smoke. His dad was perfectly perched next to him like a forlorn little elf on a toad stool. They didn't look at all like father and son.

Maud sat in Auntie's chair, her elbow resting on Aunties cardigan, her back straight and her chin raised. She was holding my aunt's favorite cup and saucer in her clumsy hands, her little finger stretched straight out. She had a snobbish look on her face that seemed to imply that she was the lady of the manor. It annoyed me to no end, but I bit down on my lip, took a swig of wine, swallowed my pride and walked over to thank her.

"Hi, Mrs. McArthur. I just wanted to thank you for the bread and buns. They were delicious."

"They were rolls, not buns."

"Sorry, we call them buns back home."

She glanced at the large glass of red wine in my hand and raised her eyebrows. I felt like a little girl with a piece of stolen candy.

"Glad you liked them," she said with a sniff.

I felt a gentle tap on my shoulder. "Ah, Mrs. Tilly, I've been looking for you."

She tugged on my shirt and pulled me down to her level. Then she whispered in my ear, "She can be a cantankerous old bitty, that one."

"You're not kidding," I whispered back.

I thought it was comical that she would refer to Maud McArthur as an "old bitty" when she was at least twenty years her senior.

"Let's go somewhere private," she said, grabbing hold of my arm. She guided me into the passage and plunked me down on the bottom step of the attic stairs. My back straightened as my spine tingled. Panic rose within me. It was if I had been led to an old cemetery, sat on a grave and left amongst the tomb stones.

"That was her room, you know," she said as she pointed up the stairs.

"Whose?"

"Mary Eliss'."

I turned my head ever so slowly and drew my eyes up to the portal at the top of the stairs. I shivered and quickly looked away. "I know it was."

In a low voice she said, "Do you suppose she is still up there?" Then she grinned mischievously.

I looked into her strange glassy eyes. "She was the last time I was here, and I have a feeling she hasn't left."

Her face took on a more serious expression. "If you feel it, child, it is true for you."

"Mrs. Tilly, wasn't there something you wanted to talk to me about?"

"Move over, child." She squeezed her soft round bottom on the stair next to mine and gently took my hand. She smelt of mixed herbs and spices and her hand was warm and silky soft. There was something about this strange little lady. I remembered what my dad said about her: "'Old witch Tilly,' we used to call her." I could feel the wisdom and mystery that seemed to emanate from her soul. It was like being in the presence of a wise old oracle.

"It wasn't a natural death that your uncle had. It happened on the night of the Autumn Equinox."

"You think that same person who's been committing all those murders killed my uncle?"

"Could be."

"But he had a heart attack and there was no evidence of foul play. Are those murders still going on?"

"That they are."

"I can't believe that they haven't caught anyone yet. It's obviously a serial killer."

"The local bobbies are baffled. Problem is, they're barking up the wrong tree."

"What do you mean?"

"They are looking for someone of flesh and blood."

"You think it was something supernatural?"

She raised her eyebrows and squeezed my hand. "I do and so do you."

I sighed. "Yes, but I thought she'd been put to rest."

"Who?"

"Oh, never mind. I thought all the murders around here were brutal, people being chopped up, beheaded and such." I winced as I spoke.

"Not all of them. Some were suicides or so-called natural causes, and some people have just disappeared, wiped off the face of the earth."

"Then how do you know that those deaths or disappearances were caused by something supernatural?"

"Because they all happen on a pagan holiday. Take Lizzy Lunn, for instance. She was mutilated in her own parlor on the eve of Spring Equinox, and all the doors were locked from the inside and there was no sign of anyone being there but her. They did find blood under her finger nails and when they tested it they found it was from a female relative. But when they went back to re-examine it, all the information had disappeared from the files, the computer and even the blood itself. Disappeared into thin air, all of it. Happy and contented people killing themselves for no reason doesn't make sense. Happens every pagan Sabbath, so it's likely an offering of some sort."

"An offering to whom?"

"A goddess, of course."

"Perhaps it's someone from the British Druid Order, then."

She shook her head, then turned it slightly and looked up to the top of the stairs.

"You think it was Mary Eliss?"

She nodded. "Perhaps."

"You're wrong. It's a foul smelling ghost that haunts this place and I'm sure it's her who's doing all the killings."

She squinted as she looked into my eyes. "Listen to me, child. This whole area as far out as Chillsbury is cursed. Whether it be by the Elisses or by something else, I don't know." Her voice took on a soft compassionate tone. "Your uncle was scared to death and poor Emy; it sent her off her rocker. She came to see me a few times after you left. Said she wanted something to help her sleep and calm her nerves, told me she was still on the change, but I knew different. I could tell by the fear in her eyes that something diabolical was going on. I gave her a bag of sea salt."

"Sea salt?"

"It wards off evil spirits. Works wonders, it does. If you rub it over your body with a little dill, nothing, not even the devil himself, can get near you. She kept searching for that old pendant of her mothers, said it had gone missing again."

"She gave it to me. I took it home. She must have forgotten."

"Do you have it here?"

"Yes, for some odd reason I felt compelled to bring it with me."

"Well, you better wear it, child, and don't take it off while you're in this cottage."

All of a sudden I felt a sharp cold draft on my back. Mrs. Tilly must have felt it too, as we both quivered and turned our heads at the same time.

The door to the attic room was ajar. A frigid gust of air oozed out of its cavity. I gasped.

We looked at each other wide eyed and moved with tremendous speed off the steps and into the smoke-filled sitting room.

I spotted my glass of wine sitting on the buffet where I had left it. My trembling fingers grabbed it. I brought it to my lips and gulped hungrily until every drop was gone. *That helped.* At least I wasn't shaking any more. Then I noticed the scornful eyes of Maud McArthur burning into me from across the room like red hot pokers. I wanted to storm over there and give her a piece of my mind, but I resisted and settled for a vicious glare.

I looked around for Mrs. Tilly. Where had she wandered off to? I needed to ask her to help me survive this haunted cottage for another six days. Dad and I had decided to stay for another week. The funeral arrangements had been so time consuming, we hadn't had time to discuss the farm issues and what we were going to do about Auntie.

I caught sight of Mrs. Tilly standing in the corner talking to the vicar's wife. What an odd couple, I thought: Mrs. Tilly in her bohemian gear and Wiccan ways, Mrs. Finsbury in her conservative attire and stiff-upper-lip attitude.

"Mrs. Tilly, can I have a word with you please?" I grinned at Mrs. Finsbury politely. "If you'll excuse us?" She nodded her head.

I grabbed hold of Mrs. Tilly's arm and took her aside. "Can you help me make this cottage safe by doing some sort of exorcism or something?"

Her eyebrows arched impishly. "Good heavens, child, I'm not a priest."

"Oh please, Mrs. Tilly, I have to stay here for another week, and if my aunt recovers enough to be sent home, I have to know that the cottage is safe for her. Terrifying things happened to me the last time I was here. I saw that ghost I mentioned, in the attic room and in the woodlot. I think she is still here and I think it's me she's after." My heart started beating rapidly. I struggled to catch my breath.

She put her soft little hand on my arm and rubbed it gently. "Calm down, dear, don't fret. I won't let anything happen to you, I promise." She dug inside the pocket of her long black skirt and brought out a small plastic bag marked Sea Salt. "Use this and wear your aunt's pendant. It might have protective powers."

*Might?* "But I need to make this place safe. Are you sure there isn't anything you can do?"

She pulled on my sleeve and drew my ear down to her mouth. "Come and see me. I'll see what I can do. Bring Maud's boy with you. I know you fancy him."

How did she know that? I wondered as I looked over to where Jonathan had been sitting. He had gone. Oh no, I had wanted so much to speak with him before he left.

"He's outside," Mrs. Tilly whispered, as if she had just read my mind.

The noise and smoke were polluting my senses; *I need to get outside for some fresh air anyway*, I told myself.

I filled my wine glass and grabbed my warm fuzzy jacket from the coat stand and stepped outside. Closing my eyes, I inhaled the cold damp air deeply to clear my lungs and took a hefty sip of my wine to steady my nerves. I gazed up in awe at the splendid sight above me. A steely gray sea, with waves of blue, white, amber and magenta spread out from a giant ball of orange that was slipping slowly beyond the horizon. It was not a majestic masterpiece like the Northern Lights we see back home but a tranquil still life, vast and vivid in color. I looked around for Jonathan but he was nowhere in sight. She must have been mistaken, I concluded. A feeling of bitter disappointment welled up inside me as I turned to go back inside.

"Boo!"

I jumped as a burst of fear caught in my throat, then I looked around nervously and spotted the silhouette of a man peering from behind the old cherry tree. It was Jonathan. He was grinning playfully.

"Are you crazy? You almost scared me to death!"

"I couldn't resist, sorry." He moved toward me with an air of confidence. His long legs and muscular body clothed in black moved with panther-like grace. "Do you remember the last time I did that to you?"

"By the old barn?"

"That's right."

"We were just kids back then."

He raised his eyebrows.

"Well, at least I was," I admitted.

Slowly, seductively, his dark eyes wandered all over my body. A subtle, sensual wave of passion washed over me as I felt their desire.

"You're not a kid anymore." He paused. "You've turned into a beautiful woman, Emily."

I felt giddy, thrilled, like someone had just told me I'd won a million dollars, but I kept the excitement inside and gave him a modest grin. "Thank you. You haven't turned out so bad yourself."

The gorgeous Jonathan McArthur—the guy I had pined for, for over a year, the one who kept wandering into my dreams and interfering in my relationships—was telling me that he thought I was beautiful. I had never considered myself beautiful. Oh, I had come a long way since my pubescent years. My freckles had faded. My teeth were perfectly straight and white, thanks to my dentist. I had come to terms with my red hair, even appreciating it at times. And my long legs were now what I considered my best feature. But I still didn't care for my cabbage-green eyes that were too big for my face, broad shoulders that were too heavy for my slender torso, and small breasts that my mom once told me would blossom with implants. In spite of my imperfections, I did consider myself to be moderately attractive. I was definitely not beautiful.

There was a moment of awkward silence. Jonathan lowered his head and moved his feet slightly from side to side.

"Isn't that stunning?" I said, breaking the silence as I starred up at the evening sky, now splashed with crimson.

"Red sky at night, shepherd's delight," he said.

"Red sky in the morning, shepherd's warning," I replied.

"That's right. I suppose you learned that from your uncle."

"Yes, he would always predict the weather by watching celestial activity. With my aunt it was her aching knees, elbows, bones or lumbago that gave us the forecast."

All of a sudden the reality of his death and my aunt's situation, together with the wine, kicked in. My eyes filled with tears. I put my hands over my face and sniffed, but I couldn't stop them. The pent-up tears of utter sorrow trickled down my cheeks, unchecked and unrelenting.

Jonathan wrapped his strong arms around my form and pulled me gently into his fold. His natural smell and the warmth from his muscular body comforted me and triggered a slight, erotic sensation. I wanted to rip open his shirt and bury my face in his naked chest.

"It's all right. It's all right," he whispered as he ran his hands up and down my back gently, pressing his body firmly against mine. I was wrapped in a compassionate cloak of pure sensuality. It felt so familiar, like a faithful security blanket that had comforted me all of my life.

I had to keep reminding myself that I was already in a relationship and to have those feelings for Jonathan was not fair to Kyle. But it was such a deep, uncontrollable feeling of infatuation and lust, how it could be wrong? And Kyle was such a ladies' man. *He's probably going to cheat on me anyway.*

# Chapter 12

Jonathan reached into the breast pocket of his jacket, pulled out a starched white handkerchief and handed it to me. I dabbed my eyes and thanked my inside voice for reminding me to wear water-proof mascara.

"I'm sorry. It's just so hard, being here without them. I'm the closest thing they had to a daughter and they adored me, as I did them. And this cottage," I swallowed hard, "it terrifies me at times and then there are other times when I feel so at home here, I think I could never leave. I don't know if this place is Heaven or Hell."

"Why does it terrify you?" he asked.

"You do remember all the awful things that happened to me the last time I was here, don't you?"

He sighed. "I remember you telling me that awful things were happening to you."

*He's changed. Turned into a skeptic, a conformist like the rest of them.* I lifted my chin and glared into his dark eyes. "I wasn't making it up. And furthermore, I think that the entity that was here then is still here. My uncle Reg died on the night of the Autumn Equinox." I held his stare boldly. "Strange, don't you think?"

He shrugged his shoulders.

"And my aunt indicated to Mrs. Tilly that she was being haunted."

He scoffed and said in a patronizing tone, "Ahh, the strange Mrs. Tilly. It's best, perhaps, we try not to believe anything she tells us."

Now I was mad. My eyes widened as I held out my finger and pointed it close to his face. He moved back and grinned as if amused. "An eighteen-year-old guy telling a fourteen-year-old girl that he used to play with a ghost. And one day this ghost lured him into the woods, then disappeared into thin air. Now, that's strange!"

His right eyebrow rose slightly as he bit down on his lip to prevent a smile. "Maybe it was just the overactive imagination of a lonely young lad."

My mouth twisted into a scowl.

"I'm glad to see you're still as feisty as you used to be, Emily Fletcher."

I could tell this was amusing him. Perhaps he was too intoxicated to reason, I told myself as I turned to go back inside. "You've changed, Jonathan, and you're just sweeping it under the rug like the rest of them."

He grabbed my arm and turned me around. "I'm sorry, Emily. I was just teasing you, just pushing your buttons. It was inappropriate, especially at a time like this. I do believe you." He tipped his head and nodded grimly. "For a while it seemed that all the strange occurrences around here had been laid to rest with the Elisses."

Before he could finish, the back door opened and Mr. McArthur stepped out. His cheeks were bright red but his face wore a glum expression. "I'm sorry to disturb you but your mum's ready to go home, all right." He tipped his head and gave me a courteous smile, then he scurried back inside and closed the door behind him.

Jonathan stared into my face; a strange eager look flashed from his eyes. "Would you like to have dinner with me?"

I was surprised and excited by his sudden invitation. Then I thought about Kyle. But I couldn't say no, I just couldn't. "Hmmm, I guess so."

"How about my place? I'm a brilliant cook." His mouth twitched with humor.

"And modest, too."

"Of course. Will seven o'clock tomorrow be all right? I can pick you up here."

"That's fine."

He turned to leave, then stopped. "By the way, I popped in to see your aunt this morning. She's showing some signs of recovery."

"Really! How?"

"She smiled when she saw me and nodded her head when I spoke to her. A definite improvement, I'd say."

"That's great!"

"She'll come around, slowly but surely, you'll see.

Cheerio. I'll see you tomorrow."

"'Bye for now."

This was good news. *I'll go see her first thing in the morning.*

"Oh no!" I suddenly remembered that I'd forgotten to ask Jonathan what he was about to tell me before we were interrupted. He seemed to indicate that there were still some strange things happening around here. It would have to wait until tomorrow now.

That night, after writing in my journal, I rubbed sea salt all over my body, sprinkled it around my bed and dabbed a little on the door knob. Then I draped Auntie's pendant around my neck. I felt a strong urge to wear it even though it made me feel a tad uncomfortable, now that I knew what it was.

Auntie associated it with good fortune and protection. She'd said, "My mum swore by it, she did. Called it 'er good luck charm, she did. She lost it just before she died, might 'ave still been alive today if she'd ad it on." That was enough to convince me that no matter what it represented to me, it held some sort of protective power.

I slept in a deep sound sleep, like that of my early childhood. There was no recurring dream or nightmarish visions, no restless chitter-chatter from the blabberer inside my head. Just a still, quiet slumber.

I rose early, wide-eyed and surprisingly clear headed. I made myself a breakfast of lemon tea, fresh fruit and a couple of poppy seed bagels that I had bought at a bakery in Chillsbury. I'd found them in a glass case under the catchy phrase of

"America's favorite breakfast bagels." I wondered at first how they could make such a claim when the bagels were made in the shop daily. Then I realized that this small family baker had caught on to the clichés of slick advertising. Commercialism is seeping into this simple culture. *How sad*, I thought. I squeezed the juice out of a couple of oranges into a glass. Fresh juice helps to detoxify you, or so I had read, after an evening of too much junk food and wine.

After downing the juice, I proceeded to tidy up the mess we had neglected the night before. I couldn't stomach the ash trays, so I left those for Dad who was still fast asleep on the pullout couch in the parlor. His snoring was a familiar, commonplace sound along with the ticking of the old grandfather clock. I decided I'd wait until he got up for a fire, since I could never seem to get the darned thing lit and it didn't feel quite as chilly this morning. I had to open some of the windows; the acrid smell of cigarette smoke still polluted the air and made my stomach churn.

Winny was curled up in Auntie's chair, snuggled deep into the fibers of her thread bare woolen cardigan. Happy, it seemed, to have the chair to herself after yesterday's influx of people and contented to be enveloped in her mother's scent. Winky was in her usual spot on the fluffy fireside rug. When I was here before, the cats would follow Auntie Em and Uncle Reg into their bedroom when they retired for the evening and make nests in the rumpled bed covers at the foot of the bed. But now I couldn't get them into the bedroom. It was as if they refused to sleep with anyone else but their parents, or that they sensed something sinister about the room.

I put that thought out of my head in a hurry.

Opening the back door, I stepped outside for a breath of fresh air. The promise of "red sky at night" had been fulfilled. It was a delightful morning, bright and sunny with a gentle autumn breeze. The lawn was littered with colorful leaves that had been touched by an early frost. Little drops of dew lay on them like tiny tear drops, transparent yet filled with a range of color. Withering vegetable heads in the garden waited for the reaper. Auntie had harvested most of the vegetables but the potatoes, carrots and turnips were still in the ground. "I'll put that on my list of things to do," I said to myself.

One of Sam's old bones was lying under the wooden table. I wondered how he was doing at the McArthur's. John had taken him home after they'd discovered Uncle Reg's body, and he had been there ever since. I imagined by now he would be wondering where his old friend and master was, poor thing.

They had been together for ten years. Uncle Reg had bought him from a local breeder when he was four months old. There were four puppies in the litter but Uncle Reg said Sam had that certain look in his eye that said "Pick me, I won't let you down." And apparently, he never did. "The best dog I've ever had. Listens well, learns quick, has good stamina, and loves his job; as faithful a companion as any man could ask for," Uncle had said. My heart ached as I visualized Sam's sad brown eyes searching hopelessly for his master. I sniffed back the tears, pushed back the sorrow and went back inside.

I could hear Dad moving around in the parlor. "Full English breakfast, Dad?" I asked as I tapped on the door.

"Sure. Thanks, honey."

I wasn't accustomed to making his breakfast but I was anxious to get going this morning and visit Auntie. Every morning since we'd been here, Dad had gotten up and cooked himself a huge breakfast of bacon, eggs, sausage, beans, fried bread and canned tomatoes, which usually took him a good hour to prepare. They call it a full English breakfast here, but I call it toxic. My Dad never ate like that at home. I wondered if food had replaced work, golf and other activities he had used to numb his pain, and I worried about him having high cholesterol like his brother.

On our way to the hospital I said, "I think we should talk about bringing her home and getting a nurse to look after her."

Dad's face wore a vacant, sad expression as his eyes focused on the winding road ahead. "That's very costly."

"But I remember you saying at some time that Uncle Reg was quite well off."

"Yes, but most of it is tied up in his land and stock."

"Then we will have to sell some of it off, won't we? I'm not going to have her stay in that awful place too much longer."

"It's not an awful place, it's a hospital." He sighed. "Let's see how she is today and go from there, okay?"

"Okay."

We spoke to Auntie's doctor first, and he said that there was a definite improvement. She hadn't spoken yet but she was responding with gestures, moans and facial expressions.

A tartan blanket was draped over her pale little legs. Two wrinkled hands laced with purple veins were folded neatly on her lap and her eyes stared at the stark white wall as she sat slouched to one side on a cushioned high-backed chair.

I crouched down beside her. "Auntie Em, it's your niece, Emily." Her tired old eyes moved slowly to meet mine and the corners of her mouth turned up ever so slightly.

I looked at Dad and nodded my head as a glimmer of hope flickered inside my heart. Then I met her eyes boldly and said in a kind but firm voice, "I know you're in there, Auntie. You must fight to come out of that shell. If you want to go home you must prove to them that you're capable of taking care of yourself. Say this over and over to yourself: 'I will recover, I will recover.'"

Dad cleared his throat and gave me a disapproving gesture. Then Auntie's eyes moved away from mine and they regained their fixated stare. It was as if I had offended her, or she'd simply slipped back into the cocoon she had spun for herself.

I had to do something; I wasn't going to let her slip away again.

"Feel this, Auntie Em," I said as I grabbed her hand, placed it on the pendent around my neck and rubbed her fingers over the star. "It was your mother's, remember? She wore it all the time." I pulled it over my head and draped it around her neck. "It will protect you, keep you safe."

She didn't respond. I was desperate to get a reaction. "If you don't come out of this, we will have to sell the farm." I wanted to take the words back as soon as they came out of my mouth.

She tilted her head ever so slightly, as if she was trying to hear a distant sound—her mother's voice, perhaps. Then she drew her pale limp hand up slowly and grasped the silver pendant. Tears glistened in her eyes then trickled pitifully down her dear old face.

A deep sadness tightened across my chest. This was not the type of reaction I wanted. *How could you have made her cry?* With my arms around her neck, I hugged her tenderly. She felt cool and clammy and smelt like musky old bed clothes. "I'm sorry. I didn't mean to make you cry. I just want you to get better and come home where you belong."

*She knows*, the mysterious voice inside me whispered.

"I'm going to get you a wheel chair and take you outside for some fresh air," I told her. "I'll be right back."

"Are you sure that's a good idea? It's not exactly summer weather out there, and you might need permission, you know," Dad said as we walked toward the door.

"She needs some fresh air and I don't need permission."

"Don't ya go sellin' that there farm!"

We stopped and turned, our mouths agape. It was Auntie's voice clear as a bell.

I ran to her side. "I won't sell it, not if you don't want

me to. I promise."

Nothing. Just a blank, emotionless expression. It was almost as if she was up to her old tricks of offering me tidbits then pulling them back.

Dad couldn't stand it; he left with a disappointed and confused expression on his face while mumbling, "Just call me when you're ready and I'll come back to pick you up."

I took her outside for a while and stayed until they fed her supper. But she didn't venture out of her shell until the moment I said goodbye. Then she gave me a silent toothless grin that reminded me that her false teeth were still in her house coat pocket. I pulled them out and placed them on her lap. As I did, she put her hand on mine and stroked it ever so gently. I kissed her pale wrinkled cheek.

"I love you, Auntie, and I will get you out of here, I promise." I knew at that moment that she was on the road to recovery. It was just a matter of time.

* * * *

Dad had gone to have a few drinks with an old friend in Chillsbury. Just before he left my Aunt Pam phoned to tell us that Mom's cancer was in remission. The black shadow of looming death had been lifted. Mom was going to be okay.

I felt a little uneasy about being alone, but I was glad to have some time to myself. I needed some time and space to think and collect the thoughts that had been buzzing inside my head like a swarm of bees.

It was five o'clock. I had two hours to prepare this untidy body for the lovely Jonathan McArthur. I kept telling myself that it wasn't a date, just a meal with an old friend. I washed the mud off my hands and dried them on Auntie's red gingham apron. I'd grown accustomed to wearing her aprons, or pinnies, as she called them. They smelt like Auntie and I felt close to her when I wore them. I shoved one of her crisp white hankys, ironed and starched, into one of the deep pockets.

Auntie was seldom seen without her pinny and she was never without her hanky. The pinny was supposed to protect her dress, but her dress was seldom exposed and her hanky was rarely used for blowing her nose. Instead, they were used for other practical purposes like carrying eggs from the chicken coup, removing baking from the oven, wiping a sweaty brow, cleaning reading glasses, concealing false teeth, and after being moistened with a bit of spit, polishing the cutlery.

I sighed and hung the pinny up inside the pantry door. Then I put the tin bucket full of potatoes, carrots and turnips beside the back door, ready for Dad to take down to the root cellar. I had enjoyed my time digging in the garden, smelling the fresh earth and feeling its moist consistency between my fingers. It gave me a feeling of the simple life which I had dreamt of living one day. Tucked away in a secluded cottage, far away from the hustle and bustle of today's world, with a vegetable patch, lots of animals and an antique desk tucked under a scenic window, where I would weave my fantasies into wonderful words. Mother Nature had always fed my imagination and nurtured my soul.

I went into the sitting room, picked up the iron poker that leaned purposely against the stone hearth and stoked the fire. It would be late when Dad or I returned and we needed the fire to burn as long as possible, otherwise there would be no hot water. I poured myself a glass of blackberry brandy, sank deep into the depths of Auntie's arm chair and sipped the succulent elixir. *I'll have about half an hour to relax and a drink or two will help steady my nerves.*

The fire crackled; its bright flames danced busily like flamboyant little pixies. This was the only room in the cottage where I felt completely safe, untroubled by the subtle sense of an unearthly presence. I pulled the woolen blanket off the arm of the chair and draped it over my legs. It was mushy soft from years of wear and hand washing. As I basked in the quiet relaxing warmth of the fire, brandy and homey feel of this peaceful little room, I drifted off. Off on a nostalgic trip, pondering the past—high school graduation, family picnics, Christmases, my private spot at home—they were comfy, wistful thoughts I snuggled up to in times of stress.

Suddenly, I heard a noise and sat up sharply. It sounded like someone walking on the stairs with hard-soled shoes: click, click, creak.

My sense of bliss evaporated quickly and was replaced with an intense feeling of dread. "But we haven't any stairs."

"*Oh yes, you do,*" my inner voice whispered.

The attic stairs!

My chest tightened as panic rose in my throat. I flew off the chair. The sound stopped. I stood still, listening fearfully, wondering if I should go and check it out or stay in the safety of this room and wait for Jonathan to arrive. "No, I can't let him see me like this; I haven't even got any makeup on." But I had to pass the attic stairs to get to the bedroom. I had to be brave; I had to go.

Slowly, I opened the sitting room door and edged myself into the passage that led past the attic stairs. My legs were shaky and my bare feet that stuck to the hardwood floor hesitated with every step. Then I felt a familiar scent drifting toward me. Perhaps it was the unseen angel that protected me the last time I was here.

The smell got stronger. I peered around the corner of the passage wall and gulped.

It was Mary Eliss.

She was sitting on the attic stairs. She looked the same as she did five years ago, except this time her form was translucent; I could see right through her. It was like looking at a hologram trapped in a time warp, not really here nor there. I wasn't afraid of her, only of what she might become.

"What do you want?" I asked.

Her eyes, like tiny twinkling emeralds flickering on and off, glared into mine. Her angelic voice faded in and out as she whispered. "Leave this place, Emily. She's after you."

"Who, Mary Eliss? Who?" I moved a little closer. "Tell me, please."

Then she turned abruptly and scurried up the stairs. The attic door opened as if on command.

She stopped before entering and turned around to face

me. "Come, Emily. Come." Her voice was deeper, more abrasive and her form was becoming more solid.

My gut twisted and turned as I shook my head back and forth.

"Come, Emily. Now!" she demanded. There was an eerie quality about her now and the more solid she became, the more her appearance changed. The beautiful scent of lavender was slowly becoming a rancid odor. I knew what was happening but I was consumed by a strange urgent feeling that I had to follow her.

# Chapter13

Just in time, the magnetic pull subsided. Fear and bold determination mounted inside me. I clenched my teeth, made a tight fist and drove my sharp nails deep into the palm of my hand.

"I'm not going. I'm not going. No!" I screamed at her.

The silent voice inside me rose up. "*Move. Move.*"

I pried my feet from the floor, dashed through the passage, into the sitting room and slammed the door. Quickly, I dragged the heavy chest, which was used as a coffee table, across the floor and pushed it in front of the door.

Drained, I sank into Auntie's chair and wrapped her comforting blanket around me. I could hear the rapid thump, thump, thump of my heart and feel the moist heat of sweat on my brow.

I slipped my arm out from under the cover and reached for my little glass of courage. There was only a mouthful left. I threw it down my throat, shoved my arm back under the cover and I sat fearfully still, afraid to move, afraid to be heard.

I thought about Mary Eliss. *How does she turn into this horrid creature and why? Does it possess her? It must. But how can that be, if she is herself an apparition? It's all so utterly confusing.* And the scent that emanated from Mary Ellis was the same lavender perfume that was a source of comfort to me last time I was here. It had made me a feel calm and protected, as if I were being enveloped in motherly love. I had concluded in my own mind that it was the spirit of my Grandmother Fletcher, but now I wasn't so sure.

Mary Eliss was warning me to leave this place because someone was after me. It was, I assumed, the ghostly creature. But why? Who was she? What had I done to her? I remembered when Skye and her mom unintentionally conjured up my grandmother's spirit, she warned me about someone named Martha. But I still didn't know anyone named Martha, except for Auntie's school friend. *Perhaps she is the creature?*

I shivered as the all-consuming, ever so conflicting emotions of fear, grief, commitments, sadness, enchantment and passion whirled around inside my head like a tornado. *I'm too young to have all these responsibilities and worries.* I just wanted to be back in college, hanging out with my friends, going to the mall, playing games on my computer, sending text messages to Skye on my cell phone and conversing with Mother Nature in my own safe, private spot back home. I didn't want to have to think about what to do with Auntie or the farm. I didn't want to have to worry about my mom dying and I especially didn't want to be tormented by some ghost.

Part of me wanted to escape, dash outside into the fresh

evening air and run, as far as I could from the stress and mysteries of Merryweather Lodge. But where would I go? Dad had taken the car and in a little while it would be pitch black out there. I couldn't imagine being out there by myself in the dark. If only Dad had left me his friend's phone number. I would have called him and made up some phony excuse about why he needed to come home right away. It was possible though, in these parts, that his friend didn't even have a phone. If I had Jonathan's number, I wouldn't hesitate to phone him.

Jonathan! I had momentarily forgotten. How could I have forgotten? The clock on the mantel read six-twenty. In forty minutes, my Prince Charming would arrive to carry me away to his palace. Running the back of my hand over my sweaty brow, I thought how horrible it would be if he saw me like this. But how was I going to venture out of this safe room? *What are you more afraid of. Something lurking in the corridor or Jonathan seeing you like this?*

I stood up, squeezed my eyes tight and took two deep breaths. "I'm not afraid. There's nothing out there, there's nothing out there," I chanted. Then I visualized myself walking through the empty corridor, opening the bedroom door and making it safely inside.

I opened my eyes, marched bravely to the door and put my ear against the rough wood.

Nothing.

Slowly I moved the old chest away from the door. My hand quivered ever so slightly as I grasped the brass knob, turned it and opened the door. Poking my head out, I sniffed the air and listened carefully, surveying the empty passage.

No smell, no sound, just an empty ominous hallway waiting for its victim.

I sucked one long deep breath into my lungs, let it out slowly, then dashed out of the door, through the passage and into my bedroom as fast as I could, my eyes fixed straight ahead, not daring to look around. I closed the door and leaned against its hard surface, panting heavily. *Was this room safe?* But I couldn't think about that now, I had a mission: to transform this lanky body and ordinary face into something alluring. I had to move fast.

Opening the wardrobe, I pulled out my only dress. English women would never be seen on a first date in a pair of pants. "But you're not English or going on a date," I mumbled to myself.

The dress was black rayon with thin shoulder straps and a v-neck—not too low, not too high. An emerald belt wound its way through the middle, which made me look like I had a waist. The dark green tailored jacket that I had borrowed from my mom's closet matched perfectly and enhanced the color of my eyes. I'd wondered at that time why I felt the need to bring these clothes, but now I knew.

I grabbed my brush and makeup case, drew the padded stool up to the dressing table and sat in front of the mirror. There were smudges of dirt on my face and under my finger nails. I'd planned to take a bath and spend some time primping myself, but all I wanted to do now was to make myself presentable as quickly as I could and get out of here. My red hair fell loosely about my shoulders as I removed the elastic band from my pony tail and shook my head.

I didn't usually wear a lot of makeup but today my face needed all the help it could get. Luckily, when I was sixteen, my mom had insisted on showing me the right way to apply makeup. It seemed frivolous then, but now I was glad she did. Poor Mom. She tried desperately to retain her looks after her surgery and even while she was on chemo. As a little girl I adored and imitated her—the way she dressed, did her hair ever so neatly and applied her makeup from an oval pink case stuffed with cosmetics.

When I was in my early teens, I decided that trying to be like her or admiring her was not cool, so I rebelled against everything she said or did. Secretly though, I have always longed for her approval. Oh, I knew she loved me, even doted on me at times; but I always felt that I wasn't quite what she wanted in a daughter. Not pretty enough, not popular enough, not enough like her. Putting all that aside, I wished now that I had spent more time with her and told her more often that I loved her.

I applied a little raspberry lip gloss, silver-gray eye shadow, very black mascara to hide my gingery lashes and enough foundation to add color to my pale complexion. Then I brushed my hair vigorously from the parting down and sprayed it with instant shine. I really needed my straightener, but it was in the bathroom and I didn't have the time or the courage to go there right now. The slight pressure I felt in my bladder told me that I would have to go soon. *I'll go as soon as we get to Jonathan's apartment. I like snooping in people's bathrooms; it tells you a lot about them, especially guys'.*

I took one last look in the mirror, pressed my lips together and smoothed down my hair with my finger tips. I wasn't really happy with what I saw. There were times when I had wished for natural blonde hair, blue eyes, voluptuous breasts, a straight nose and tanned complexion. But whenever I had those thoughts, I quickly told myself that it was a condition of our society, my mother's influence and the voice of my ego, not the real me. If only I could be totally content with the way I am. "You'll have to do," I said to my reflection.

Then to my horror, just like it had done five years ago, my image started to change. Slowly it took on the appearance of the woman I had seen in the mirror when I was here before. Her face was much more like mine now, but she was still more beautiful—with a smooth flawless complexion, high cheek bones that were touched with pink, and full rosy lips. Our almost identical green eyes locked. My stomach fluttered as I felt an overwhelming attachment, as if we were connected to each other by some magical link. "Who are you?" I yelled.

Knock. Knock.

I jumped.

Someone was at the door. Surely it couldn't be Jonathan. It was too early. A gush of fear rose up inside me. "Don't be silly," I mumbled to myself. "Ghosts don't knock."

I opened the bedroom door and stepped out into the dimly lit corridor. All seemed well.

Tentatively, but with haste, I walked to the front door. What if it wasn't him? Then I took a deep breath, said a silent prayer and opened the door ever so slightly, just enough to see a tall figure standing on the door step.

"Oh, Jonathan!" I swung open the door and flung my arms around his broad shoulders.

He backed up, his eyes wide as if he had just been attacked by a vicious dog.

"Oh, I'm so sorry." What was I thinking? *What will he think of me now?* A warm glow spread to my cheeks. *Stop it. You're too old to blush.*

His gorgeous face split into a wide grin. "Don't apologize. I like a woman who's enthusiastic."

"Don't flatter yourself. I wasn't throwing myself at you. I was scared, that's all. Come on in." I moved out of the doorway and ushered him inside.

He held out a dark blue box of Milk Tray chocolates and a single long-stemmed rose wrapped in white tissue paper. "I wasn't sure if you liked flowers or sweets."

*How romantic. What a gentleman.* But I had to stop myself from appearing too eager. "I love them both." I took the rose, put it up to my nose and gently inhaled its sweet perfume. "Ahh, heavenly. And how did you know that Milk Tray are my favorite English candies?"

"I didn't, but I have heard that Canadian and American women are turned on by gentlemen bearing gifts of

Merryweather Lodge

chocolates and roses."

My illusion of a romantic Prince Charming evaporated. I rolled my eyes. *He's just like the rest of them, out for what he can get.*

"The key word there, Jonathan, is gentleman!"

His mouth twitched with humor. "I'm just teasing. Truth is, I know very little about Canadian women."

"And you're not likely to if you get too cocky."

"I'll behave myself from now on, I promise."

"You'd better," I said with a playful smile and a reprimanding tip of my head. "I hope you don't mind waiting for a few minutes. I'm not quite ready. You're a little early."

"No problem." He plunked himself down in Uncle Reg's armchair and stretched his long legs lazily in front of him. "By the way, you look ravishing."

"Thank you."

Ravishing? What kind of word was that to use on a girl? It made me feel like a bowl of strawberries and cream, waiting to be devoured. *Will I ever get used to this English lingo?*

"Would you like a drink while you wait?"

"Yes, please. Beer, if you have one."

I walked into the kitchen, found a delicate vase for the rose at the back of the pantry and poured us both a drink. I felt safer and protected now with Jonathan here.

"Here you go." I handed him a tall glass of beer. The tips of his fingers touched mine as he took the glass. It sent a tingle right up my arm, as if I'd been touched by a magic wand. His dark brown eyes were full of desire as they swept over my body.

"I'm sorry about being early. I popped in to see my parents and forgot that they like to keep their clocks at least a quarter of an hour fast."

"Oh really? Why?"

"They have a thing about being punctual, and they think that it helps to put their clocks ahead. I've never quite understood it myself."

"I don't understand a lot of things that you English do. Or say, for that matter."

"I suppose we do seem like a rather peculiar bunch to foreigners."

I smiled. "Peculiar in a nice way. Listen, I really must finish getting ready. Won't be long." The nagging pressure in my bladder told me I couldn't wait any longer and I needed to put on some jewelry and a dab of perfume, just in case we got really close. But I couldn't let that happen before I broke up with Kyle. Could I?

I managed to maneuver my way through the passage into the bedroom and over to the bathroom without distress or incident. The cottage had regained its warm, homey atmosphere.

"I'm ready if you are," I announced a few minutes later.

Jonathan held out his half empty glass. "Not quite." In a quiet serious tone he asked, "Why don't you sit for a minute and finish your wine. There's something I want to ask you."

I grabbed the glass of wine I'd left on the makeshift coffee table and sat poised on the edge of Auntie's chair.

"What happened just before I got here? You looked petrified when you opened the door and pounced on me."

"Oh, it was nothing."

He furrowed his brow. "Emily."

I took a sip of my wine, a deep breath, and told him what I had just seen. He sat still, his face devoid of any emotion or expression.

When I had finished, he ran his fingertips through stray locks of black hair that had fallen across his brow. Then he straightened his back, sighed and glanced at the clock. It was as if he had just sat through a long, boring lecture.

I glared at him. "I'm not making this up."

He flopped back into the chair and sighed. "I know you're not. I've tried to put the strange things that go on here to the back of my mind. It's been a lot easier since I moved away, to forget or pretend that it was all in my imagination. But no matter how much I try to rid myself of those creepy memories, every so often they crawl back and bother me like pesky little bugs. It wasn't all bad though, growing up here. At times it was so peaceful...almost magical, I suppose. I still feel that way when I come back. It's a paradox. Hard to explain, really."

"That's exactly how it feels to me. It's a sort of fairy tale kingdom with a sinister twist."

"Exactly."

Our eyes met and we exchanged warm, tender smiles that echoed a deep spiritual connection and promise—lots of promise.

Winny had found a cozy resting place in the crotch of

Jonathan's lap. She scolded him with a dirty look and a disapproving meow as he lifted her off his lap and placed her gently on the floor. Then he downed the rest of his beer and glanced at the clock. "If we don't leave here soon, there'll be burnt offerings in my kingdom." He stood and took my jacket from the arm of the chair and held it by the shoulders, ready for me to slip into.

*He does have that unique British humor and some gentlemanly ways,* I thought with an inner sigh of approval.

Jonathan's flat was in a stately old Victorian building. A prestigious wrought iron gate complemented the entrance, followed by concrete steps leading to a shiny black door with a brass knocker in the shape of a lion's head. Under the tall windows, wooden boxes overflowed with dying flowers.

He fumbled inside his pocket for the key. The door groaned as he pushed it open. We were greeted by the smell of lemon polish and the musky-oily scent of old wood as we stepped inside the door.

"Follow me. I'm afraid it's quite a ways up," he said as we trudged up three flights of narrow stairs. At the top stood a door painted bright cobalt blue with a little brass plaque that read "Mr. McArthur."

Inside was a compact but interesting room, filled to the brim with an eclectic array of things conducive to the artistically inclined. Colorful landscapes and portraits, both old and contemporary, hung from the wall beneath a majestic molded ceiling. Volumes of books, maps and stuffed envelopes were piled in a corner. Potted plants fought for sunlight on a shelf close to the window. Antiques and odd ornaments were scattered about the room. An old desk with an ink well was littered with sketches. Next to the desk sat a little round table filled with paints, and beside that an easel displayed a half finished painting of a bowl of fruit. There was a retro-style two seat sofa in the middle of the room and by the window a rough wooden table, accompanied by a couple of ladder-back chairs, was set for two. The room smelt a little like fried onions mixed with old paint.

Jonathan said, "The flat also has a boxy little bedroom, a galley kitchen designed for one, and a bathroom with a toilet and a pedestal sink. The main bathroom is on the second floor and is shared by all the tenants."

"It's quaint," I said, gazing around the room. I was quite surprised that it was so bohemian. I expected his apartment to be a lot more traditional. Perhaps this was his true self, emerging from the trappings of its stylish, well-groomed exterior and expressing itself.

"It's a small bed-sitter, but it suits me," he said as he scurried about the kitchen.

"Can I help?"

"No, thanks. I've got it all under control. You just relax."

I wandered around, intrigued by all the unusual knick knacks. A pile of paintings with a thin white sheet draped over the top lay stacked against an unlit, white brick fireplace. Curious, I moved the sheet ever so slightly to take a peek.

My eyes widened as I slowly pulled the cover away from the canvas. I gulped. My hand shot to my mouth as I glared with shock and amazement at the images in front of me.

# Chapter 14

It was a picture of my recurring dream—naked ladies dancing in a circle, men in white robes, with large boulders in the background. I flipped through the other paintings and saw more of the same: the woods, the black cloaked man, the blood stained altar, and at the back of the pile, a vivid portrait of Mary Eliss.

"Ah, I see your curiosity has not dwindled with your youth."

I was too stunned to feel guilty. "Jonathan, where did you get these?"

"It's my own work, I'm afraid. Not the most professional, I must admit."

"No, they're good, but where did these images come from?"

"They've been with me for a long time, in a dream. It's like an old movie rerun. My mind keeps playing it over and over again. It's downright annoying and confusing."

I stood staring at him, my mouth gaping.

"What's wrong?" he asked.

"I have the same dream." I could barely lift my voice above a whisper. "I've had it since I was a child."

He looked at me in disbelief. "Are you sure?"

"Of course I'm sure. It was vague when I was very young, but it's quite vivid now. Almost as if I'm really living it."

"Wow. That's how it is for me."

I glanced back at the paintings and pointed to the red-headed girl. "I was her. My name was Colrea." I wasn't sure how I remembered that; it just popped out of my mouth without me even thinking.

He drew his brows together in a puzzled expression. "Colrea?"

"You've heard that name before?"

"Yes. It was the name of my sister's imaginary friend when she was little. We used to wonder why she picked such a strange name."

Then I remembered the vision I'd had when I was here before. Jonathan and I were on our honeymoon, when he called out the name Colrea. This was getting weirder and weirder.

"It's all very intriguing, but I have no idea what it means." He walked over to the supper table, bowed courteously and pulled out a chair. "Sit, my mysterious damsel."

I tucked my dress under my seat as I lowered myself gracefully into the chair. He lit the candles and poured the wine. Then he went to the kitchen and brought out a bowl of salad, a little clay plate of tomatoes, a basket of buns and a meatless casserole that looked dried out and unappetizing. I couldn't wait to taste the wine, my courage-enhancing elixir, but I had to control myself, hold back and sip slowly. I didn't want him to think I was a lush.

The flickering flames from the candles gave his ebony eyes a sensuous glow and his light brown complexion a luscious sheen. He was so irresistibly handsome that it was hard not to stare. "There must be a reason for all this," I said, breaking the awkward silence.

"Baffling, isn't it?"

"We must have some sort of connection… subconsciously, I mean."

"Like two strangers that feel like they've known each other all their lives."

"Yes, that's right." I stared into his bright eyes, my gaze searching for clues. "You've felt it too, haven't you?"

He stretched his arm across the table. His long tender fingers gently fell over my hand. The sensation of his touch sent an erotic current all the way up my arm like an electric shock. Everything about this man aroused me.

"I have felt it from the moment I saw you, a sort of recognition as if we'd met before—but not as friends, Emily, as lovers. It was an uncanny feeling, of affection and longing, and I wanted to reach out and pull you into my arms. But I fought it and thought, 'This is ridiculous. I must be a pervert.' You were only a kid. I've never stopped thinking of you, though, and have always longed to see you again."

My heart leaped, but I restrained my exhilaration, flashed him a cordial smile and said in a humble voice, "I felt the same way."

Lightly, the tips of his warm, smooth fingers traced feathery patterns on the back of my hand. Before I lost control of myself, grabbed him, ripped his clothes off and ran my fingers all over his naked body, I pulled my hand from under his, picked up my utensils and started to saw through the leathery potatoes. *This guy is special. He's to be savored, not guzzled.*

"I didn't put any meat in it, just in case you were still a vegetarian."

"I am. Thanks for remembering." The bland taste of overcooked, unseasoned vegetables mingled with wine-flavored saliva and was hard to swallow. "It's delicious," I lied.

"You're joshing. It's as tough as old nails and totally tasteless."

I put my hand over my mouth and chuckled. "I thought you said you were a brilliant cook."

"I fibbed. The salad should be okay, though, the rolls are fresh, and those tomatoes are out of my mum's greenhouse."

"It's fine. Really." I lowered my knife and fork and leaned against the high-backed chair. "Jonathan, will you help me find out what really happened to my aunt and uncle at their cottage? And who this entity is that's haunting me there? I have a feeling it's all tied together: the murders, Mary Eliss, the thing that's out to get me, us and our mysterious dream."

He shrugged his shoulders. "I don't know what I can do. How much longer are you staying here?"

"I was supposed to go back in three days with my dad. But I've decided to stay for a while. I phoned the office yesterday and told them I'd need another couple of weeks off. My aunt is coming around but her doctors advised us to wait another week before bringing her home. I need to get her settled and find a live-in nurse to look after her...if she'll have one, that is. I'm hoping she'll come around enough to make some decisions for herself, but as you know, she's pretty withdrawn right now. And she doesn't remember anything about that dreadful night."

"She's definitely getting better. I popped in to see her yesterday and heard her telling one of the old ladies to 'Shut her cake hole.' And just before I left she said 'Stop gawking at me. I'm not ready for the knackers' yard yet. There's a good lad.'"

I shook my head and grinned. "That's my Auntie Em."

He poured me another glass of wine. "What do you have in mind?"

"I think we should go see Mrs. Tilly and ask her for some suggestions. She told me to come visit her and bring you with me."

"Really? That woman scares me."

"I think she's sweet."

The alcohol was starting to take effect and all I could think of was how much I wanted to kiss his irresistible face and touch his firm, muscular body. But I didn't want him to think I was easy. I had learned that most guys like to think that they made the first move. It sits well with their male egos. I would have to do as I've done in the past: lure him innocently and playfully into my web. But first I must phone Kyle and tell him it's over. I just had to think of what to say and how to say it.

I took a warm bun and ripped open its crusty brown shell; inside the soft dough was pale and yeast-scented. I took a knife and smeared the dough in thick, golden butter. Then I picked a tomato from the clay plate. It was perfectly round and smelled fresh like the outdoors. I fondled it for a moment, then slowly brought the rosy red ball to my mouth and savored it between my lips. Jonathan's longing eyes gazed at me lustfully. Then I sank my teeth into its ripe skin and through its soft meaty flesh. I moaned seductively as a shower of juice with tiny seeds squirted into my mouth and trickled down my chin. Aware of his eagerness, I ran my tongue around my wet lips, licking at the juice slowly.

Jonathan reached across the table and dabbed the corner of my mouth with his napkin. Our eyes met. "These are delicious," I whispered in a soft, sensual voice.

"Are you teasing me, Emily Fletcher, or trying to seduce me?"

Suddenly I felt a little silly and turned my head quickly as I felt my cheeks starting to light up. "Neither. I'm just enjoying the food."

"I think you're theatrical and a bit of a temptress—a tantalizing temptress. You're a true Leo, Emily." His tone was provocative.

"Aren't you a Leo, too?"

"Yep, Leo the Lion, that's me." He made a flirtatious roaring sound.

My cheeks were getting hotter. I prayed that he wouldn't notice under this dim candle light.

A feeling of awkwardness swept over me. It was time to change the subject. "Your apartment isn't at all what I expected it to be."

"What did you expect?"

"Something more traditional and subdued, I guess."

He laughed. "I'm not traditional or subdued."

"You look so conservative, the way you dress and conduct yourself."

He seemed abashed as he stiffened and lowered his eyes. "Looks can be deceiving, Emily. I've never really thought of it before, but perhaps unconsciously I have suppressed the off-beat side of me—afraid, maybe, of all the ridicule I suffered as a young boy for being different. The strange sensitive little lad whom everyone assumed was 'Not quite all there, or gay.'"

I gave him a sympathetic smile. "I was also chastised as a child—for always having my head in the clouds, for my over-active imagination, for being too bold or too old for my age. One of my teacher's would say, 'You are an enigma, Emily Fletcher.' I shrugged it off and told myself that I'd take it as a compliment, but I never really did."

"Being an enigma is better than being strange," he said teasingly.

"You think so, eh?"

I gave him a cheeky grin, reached across the table and took his hand in mine. "I like the strange sensitive little lad inside you. I wish he'd come out and play more often."

His gaze raked over my face. "I can play if you like."

I smiled coyly, withdrew my hand and started to clear the table. He walked up to me, took the plate out of my hand and gathered me in his arms. His manly scent and the feel of his powerful body pressing against mine made me quiver. I dismissed all thought of Kyle and tilted my head back to receive his luscious mouth.

He drew back and cocked his ear. Someone was coming. The tap, tap, tap of high-heeled shoes walking toward the door gave me a strange, uneasy feeling. As if it was the footsteps of a rapist or something unearthly.

*Knock knock.*

"I wonder who that could be. I wasn't expecting anyone," Jonathan mumbled as he went to answer the door. "Belinda, what are you doing here?"

"That's no way to greet your little sister." She pushed him out of the way and barged in.

"Great timing," I mumbled. Her hazel eyes widened and her face turned grim when she saw me.

A full-length, red layered skirt with a tasseled belt drawn to the side covered her shapely hips and long legs. A tiny white t-shirt exposed her diamond-studded belly button. She had become a strikingly attractive young woman, but still she held no resemblance to her brother. She threw her large canvas shoulder bag on the sofa and eyed me up and down.

"You remember Emily Fletcher, Mrs. Fletcher's niece."

"Hi, Belinda," I said, offering her my hand.

She took it and shook loosely, and then pulled away quickly as if it were contaminated. Her eyes scanned my face with an air of arrogance and distaste. "I remember her."

There was something about this girl, something I couldn't put my finger on. It wasn't just that she had made her loathing for me so obvious, or her rude disposition. It was more like a feeling of panic and dread. Similar to the feeling I had for her mother but worse, much worse.

"Would you like a drink?" Jonathan asked her.

"No thanks, darling." She tossed her bag off the sofa, threw herself down and dangled her legs over the arm.

Jonathon rolled his eyes. "Are you already drunk?"

"Of course not!"

"How about tea?" He turned to me. "Would you like a cup of tea or coffee, Emily?"

"No thank you. I really must be going."

"But you can't go yet."

I glanced at Belinda; she had a smirk on her face and her hand was moving back and forth, bidding me goodbye. I took a deep breath to stop myself from responding. "I really have to go. Would you call me a cab?"

"I'll do no such thing. A taxi would cost you a small fortune from here. I'll drive you." He glanced at Belinda. "You don't mind, do you?"

"Not at all. I'll be waiting for you." She was using that

same flirty tone. I thought how strange it was for someone to talk to her brother in that manner.

Jonathan grabbed his jacket from the brass coat stand and dug into his pocket for his keys. Then he turned to his sister. "I won't be long."

"'Bye," I said just to be polite. "Bitch!" I whispered under my breath.

"Hey, when are you going back to Canada?" she called abruptly.

"Maybe never!" I fired back at her in an equally abrupt tone.

She raised her torso from the sofa in a contemptuous way and scowled at me; her mouth tight, her cold eyes pinned to me like a viper waiting to strike. I shivered. *What kind of ugly soul lives inside that form,* I asked myself as I closed the door.

"I apologize for my sister's rude behavior. She's got in with an unruly crowd and they are having a bad influence on her. My parents are worried sick about her."

"I'm sorry to hear that." He took my hand with gentle authority and wrapped his long fingers around mine like a velvet glove. It was comforting and so familiar.

"I'm afraid she despises me. She has from the moment she first set eyes on me. I wish I knew why." *I think she fancies you and is viciously jealous of me. Sick bitch!*

"Nonsense, who could despise you?"

"Jonathan, she makes it obvious."

"She's just fickle at the moment, that's all."

I decided there was no point in going on about it. "Will

215

you come and see Mrs. Tilly with me?"

"I suppose I could."

"I'd appreciate it. How would we contact her to let her know we were coming? My aunt said that she doesn't have a phone."

"I'm sure her crystal ball will tell her we're on our way." He winked playfully as he gave my hand a gentle squeeze.

\* \* \* \*

Uncle Reg's weathered old car was parked on the gravel driveway of the cottage. Light beamed like yellow gems from the diamond framed windows. Dad was home, thank goodness.

I expected Jonathan to pick up where we left off and I anticipated it eagerly, but there was no kiss or warm embrace. He just lifted my hand, drew it to his mouth and touched it tenderly with his soft lips. *Never mind*, I thought, *tonight I will have him again in the privacy of my own imagination, as my unruly mind wanders into his room, under his covers and satisfies the longing between my legs.*

"Tomorrow, my beautiful lady."

"Tomorrow?"

"Mrs. Tilly's. I don't work on Saturdays. Is that convenient for you?"

"Oh, of course."

"Will half past three be all right?"

"Yes, that's fine."

"Good. I'll pick you up here."

"Thanks for the lovely evening," I called as he drove away. I stood for a moment and gazed at the charming little cottage. It was bathed in a radiant glow from the setting sun. I sighed deeply as I felt its snug comforts beckoning me. It seemed to open its arms and whisper, "Come in, sit down, put your feet up. You're home now."

"You perplex me, Merryweather Lodge," I mumbled.

As I swung open the garden gate, a great huge crow swooped down and landed right in front of me. I flinched and stepped back, shocked by its sudden appearance. On large clawed feet, it strutted back and forth across my path like a pompous old schoolmarm dressed in black. Its beady eyes fixed on my feet as if warning me not to move. Its smooth ebony head shone like pure silk as it nodded in a scolding fashion and squawked at me in a harsh repetitive shrill.

I stood perfectly still, and only the tips of my fingers twitched nervously. *This bird's an omen*, I thought, *a dark omen.*

All at once it spread its majestic wings and flew up, up and onto the ledge of the attic room window. Then the silhouette of what looked like a woman appeared behind the lace curtains.

I gasped and ran into the house.

"Dad, Dad," I screamed. He had fallen asleep on the sofa and shot up, startled. His eyes were wide. "What's wrong?"

"There's someone in the attic room."

"What?"

"The attic room. Someone's up there!"

He staggered to his feet. "How do you know that someone's up there?"

"I saw a woman in the window."

"You stay here. I'll go take a look."

"Just a minute." I pulled the little bag of sea salt out of my purse. "Rub this on yourself before you go up there."

He looked into the bag and screwed up his nose. "What's that?"

"Sea salt. It'll protect you."

He pushed it away. "Practicing witchcraft now, are we?"

"Well, at least take this with you." I gave him my bottle of mace.

He shook his head. "Save that for the real monsters."

I stood by the sitting room door, listening anxiously with my arms tightly folded, taking long deep breaths to steady my nerves.

## Chapter 15

I heard his footsteps going up the stairs, then the ominous creak of the heavy wooden door.

When he came down he gave me a cold look and shook his head from side to side. "There's no one up there. You're starting to hallucinate again. It must be this place."

I should have expected it. It was as if some devious entity was playing tricks on me. "I can't believe that after all that happened to me the last time I was here, you still don't believe me. And why do you think that it's only here that I supposedly hallucinate?"

"Stress, I would imagine. Now, how was your evening?" he asked, changing the subject to avoid the question.

I raised my hands. "I give up! My evening was fine." Not wanting to get into any sort of confrontation, I turned to leave the room.

Dad wasn't giving up. "Jonathan's a nice guy, but how do you think Kyle would feel if he knew you'd been out on a date?"

Immediately, I felt awfully guilty. I'd almost forgotten about Kyle. My dad was very fond of him, especially the fact that he had a bright future and earned a substantial income. "It wasn't a date. Jonathan and I are just friends."

His lips twitched in a cynical smile. "Oh, really?"

"Yes, really!" I lied.

"Okay, if you say so. I'm going to make myself a cup of tea. Would you like one?"

"No, thanks, I'm going to have an early night." I kissed him lightly on his cheek. "Good night, Dad." Then I turned at the door. "By the way, there was someone or something at the window."

"Sure, Princess." It was frustrating to hear him patronize me. But when I considered the fact that my dad has always been extremely pragmatic, I understood why he was so skeptical.

I spread some sea salt along the crack at the bottom of the door, sprinkled a little around the bed and dabbed the rest on my flannel pajamas. *I'll have to ask Mrs. Tilly for more.* I had no idea where to purchase it myself and wasn't really sure that the sea salt would protect me. But it gave me a sense of security, even if it was false.

I fluffed up the pillow, propped it behind my back and balanced my laptop on top of the quilt. Thank goodness my dad got me this new cell phone that I can connect to my laptop. Now, at least I had some link with the civilized world. I had three emails—one from my mom, one from Skye and one from Kyle.

Mom was feeling much better. She'd sent her sister home and was thinking about going back to work. It was a great relief for Dad and me. "Can you pick me up one of those pure wool sweaters that they sell in that quaint hand-crafters market?" she asked. *She must be feeling better if she's thinking about clothes.*

Kyle was going to some convention in Colorado. His email was cold and formal. "I'll see you soon. Don't try to contact me; I'll contact you." Why didn't he want me to contact him? He was probably seeing someone else and taking her with him. I wouldn't put it past him; I've always known he was prone to fooling around. I could hear Auntie's chastising voice inside my head: "That's the pot calling the kettle black." Part of me was hoping that it was another woman, and then perhaps he'd break up with me and save me the trouble. It was all physical with Kyle. There was no depth to our relationship and I always knew it wouldn't last. I scratched my head while I chewed on my bottom lip. What was I going to say to him? After a few minutes of picking my brain, I couldn't come up with anything—anything that had a tad of truth to it, that is. So I said nothing and put it off for another day.

Skye sent her condolences and asked me how my aunt was doing. She was still my best friend and the only one in the world who really understood me. She was going to university, studying the paranormal in all its elements. On the weekends she worked in her mother's New Age store. I often helped out when they were really busy. "Don't forget to meditate and keep up with your yoga. It will help alleviate the stress." Then as if she couldn't help herself, she went on a rant. "Have you had any encounters? Is Mary Eliss' spirit still there? Feeling any strange vibes?" I wished she could have come with me. It would have been so beneficial to have an expert and a kindred spirit here.

I sent her an email explaining everything that had happened and asked for her advice. Then I lay back on the pillow and drifted off.

I awoke suddenly to the sound of footsteps and muffled voices. I looked around the room as I listened carefully. At first I couldn't make out where the sound was coming from. My stomach tightened with alarm when I realized it was coming from above me.

The attic room.

I pulled the blankets up to my chin and swallowed hard.

There were heavy footsteps and lighter ones and voices of a woman and a child. The woman's voice was gruff and frightfully angry. "You'll do as I say or else!"

The child's voice was a shrill scream. "No, mummy, no!" The pleading cries of a tortured child echoed through the walls.

I couldn't stand it. I threw off the covers and sat up. As I was about to put my hands over my ears the sound stopped. The only thing I could hear now was the steely wind rattling the window panes and the distant tick-tock of the old grandfather clock.

It was Mary Eliss; I was sure of that. But what was her

mother doing that terrified her so? Why won't her spirit leave this place? It's all so creepy. I'd helped her to reveal her remains and that of her father. Now what did she want? For me to find her mother's skeleton perhaps? Or to uncover some other unearthly mystery that only I can solve? How was I going to stay in this haunted cottage by myself?

I crawled out of bed and peeked at the bottom of the door to make sure the sea salt was still there and left the light on for comfort.

The next morning Dad and I went to visit Auntie. She smiled when she saw us, exposing her false teeth and mumbling something about us being late. It was the first time she had worn her teeth since being in the hospital.

I caught glimpses, throughout our visit, of her old self emerging from the dark cocoon she had wrapped herself in. Her doctor told us she would be able to come home in a couple of days. The same day as my dad was flying back home.

I was excited, and it was such a relief to know that I wouldn't have to spend a night in the cottage alone. Before we left, I told her that she was coming home in two days. She simply nodded her head and said solemnly, "About bloody time, it is."

\* \* \* \*

Mrs. Tilly's cottage grew out of a grove of wild grasses and untamed bushes. I looked around with interest. Moss, ivy and clematis gently touched with autumn hues clung to the stone walls. A rustic wooden porch had been added to the front of the cottage. It was furnished with baskets, pots, rusty watering cans and a large straw broom. A white wicker rocking chair with a multicolored blanket draped over its arm coaxed visitors to come sit for a while. An assortment of wind chimes hung off the roof and tinkled joyfully in the breeze. This was the cottage that my dad had grown up in.

The door opened. "Come in. I've been expecting you."

Jonathan and I looked at each other, brows raised and mouths agape. He drew close to my ear and whispered, "I told you she'd know we were coming."

"She's psychic," I whispered back with an air of delight.

Our noses were greeted by a delightful aroma of fresh herbs and warm ginger bread. She led us into a whimsical little kitchen which was painted three shades of purple.

"Sit down. I have the kettle on."

*She's amazing. A real soothsayer.*

Jonathon shook his head while gnawing on his bottom lip. It was obvious that he was uncomfortable, even a little scared, perhaps.

Quirky, bright-colored knick knacks cluttered the floor, cupboards and counters. Bundles of dried lavender and grasses hung from the low-beamed ceiling. It was like being in a gypsy caravan.

Mrs. Tilly plunked a plate of homemade ginger bread in front of us and poured tea into brightly painted china cups. "Don't drink it all," she warned. "Leave a spoonful at the bottom, give it a minute and let the leaves settle. Then hold it in your left hand, swish it around three times and pour the liquid into the saucer. The leaves that remain will reveal your future."

Jonathan rolled his eyes. I could almost hear his thoughts. *It will be the same old predictable stuff when young couples go to get their fortunes read: love, ring, wedding, baby booties.*

But her brows raised and her lips narrowed as she gazed into my cup. Without a word she pushed it aside and picked up Jonathan's.

"Ah, small stems means there's a woman in your life, and there's an M, as clear as a bell. The woman's name starts with M." Her eyes met mine. "Sorry dear." Then her lips twitched in a sneering sort of way that made me uncomfortable. "And there's a number nine. Means good times are coming." She gave him a nod. "It's all good."

My heart sank. *How can it be good if the name of the girl in his life doesn't start with E?*

She picked up the tea pot and walked back to the stove.

"Mrs. Tilly, what about mine?"

She looked at me pitifully. "It's not good."

Her expression made me anxious. Was I going to contract some terrible illness or get into a bad accident and die? "I have to know."

"All right, if you must." She shook her head slowly back and forth as she stared into the cup. "Another M and all around it jumbled stalks, lots of them. Means trouble, big trouble."

I could feel my insides constricting as her words and abrupt tone of voice chewed at my gut. "Could you be more specific?"

"Can't. That's as clear as it gets." In a kinder tone, "Sorry, dear."

Jonathan cleared his throat. "I'm certain that whatever it is, we can handle it." His dark brows arched impishly as he flashed me a reassuring smile.

I was comforted by the light-hearted tone of his voice and the word "we".

"Emily and I have come for your help, not to have our fortunes read. She thinks that someone or something is after her." He hesitated and cleared his throat. "Something not human."

"I don't think, Jonathan. I know."

I told her everything—my first encounter with the hideous ghost, the woodlot, Mary Eliss and our identical recurring dreams. It spewed out of me like vomit from undigested food that had sat in my gut for far too long. She listened intently, tilting her head back and forth as if she were trying to read my expression and interpret my thoughts. After I'd finished I asked, "You do believe me, don't you?"

She put her wrinkled little hand on top of mine. "Of course I do, dear." She said it with such poise. Her voice echoed integrity. Her sincerity was unquestionable.

My bottom lip quivered; a fountain of emotion rose up inside me, flooding my eyes with tears. No one had totally believed me before. Even though Skye said she did and was fascinated by my experiences, I knew she had her doubts. And Jonathan was ambiguous, to say the least. It was such a relief to tell someone who didn't doubt me, especially someone who might be able to help me.

I put Auntie's large white hanky to my nose and blew as

gently and ladylike as I could.

Mrs. Tilly poured me another cup of tea. "Drink this. It will do you good. And don't fret; we'll get to the bottom of this."

Jonathan was devouring a thick piece of dark ginger bread smeared with melting butter and now seemed oblivious to what was being said. I cleared my throat and shot him a disapproving glare.

"What do you think it all means?" he asked, trying to sound concerned as he brushed the crumbs from the corner of his mouth.

"Well, let's see. It's obvious that Mary Eliss is trying to tell you something and she's not going to leave you alone until it becomes clear to you. I think you should go back to the attic room and look around a bit; you might find another note or some other clue."

A sudden surge of anxiety rose inside as I thought about it.

"They never found her mum's remains. Perhaps she wants to show you where they are so she can have a proper burial like the other two."

"Yes, I've thought of that." *But I'd rather not know.*

"The dream you both keep having can mean only one thing." Her mouth turned up into a mischievous grin and her eyes grew wide.

"What?" I asked anxiously.

"You're soul mates. You've been together in another life. Maybe you were lovers."

When she turned, Jonathan looked at me and shook his head.

Skeptic, I thought. It made perfect sense to me and would explain why I've always had the feeling that we'd met before. "Don't you believe in reincarnation, Jonathan?" I asked.

He shrugged his shoulders. "I'm open to the theory."

Mrs. Tilly lifted her chin and gave him a filthy look. "It ain't no theory, lad!"

"What about the hideous creature and the M in my tea? My grandmother's spirit warned me about someone named Martha when I was here last time. She told my friend Skye to tell me, 'Martha's out for revenge'. But Skye wasn't really sure if it was Martha she said or something that sounded like Martha. And this hideous creature is somehow able to possess someone else's body, even the unearthly bodies of ghosts. I know that for sure."

"They're the worst type," she said, in a matter of fact way.

"But how do I get rid of these apparitions?"

"First we have to find out what they want. It's all tied with the same rope, you can be sure of that. And this woman whose name starts with M has something to do with it."

She glared at Jonathan. "Your reading seems to suggest that this M woman has something to do with you."

Jonathan bit off a piece of ginger bread, popped it into his mouth and chewed thoughtfully. "I don't know any woman whose name starts with M, except my mum." He sounded disinterested and annoyed, as if it was all too dreary and far-fetched.

Mrs. Tilly scratched the side of her head with her long red fingernails. "Martha or something that sounds like Martha. The only name that comes to mind is Merthia."

I flinched. The name instantly triggered a sense of fear and dread inside of me. A cold shiver ran down my spine, as if someone had poured icy water down my back.

Mrs. Tilly noticed my reaction. "You've heard of her?"

"That name gives me the creeps, but I don't know when or where I've heard it."

"She was a Druid priestess. Maybe you've heard someone mention the Legend of Merthia."

"It's probably just another tale," Jonathan said as he eased himself out of the chair, brushing the crumbs form his lap. "I think we've heard enough. It's time for us to leave." I was shocked by his bold presumption.

"Speak for yourself! I haven't heard enough." He stiffened, eyes agape as though I had just struck him. "You can go if you like. I want to hear what she has to say."

He lowered himself back into the chair. "No, I apologize. Go on, Mrs. Tilly."

"He's right. It is only a tale, but behind every tale hides a smidgen of truth." She lowered her voice. Her strange eyes peered at me over the top of her granny glasses.

"Merthia, it's said, was a beautiful but devious druid priestess. She sacrificed virgins to the goddess Odina in exchange for her immortal youth. The young priest that she was betrothed to found out about her evil ways, killed her and then fell in love with her cousin. She's said to roam the earth looking for revenge." There was a slight smirk on her face and her eyes held a mischievous sparkle. It made me nervous. "Of course there's more to it than that. But that's the gist of it."

"Mrs. Tilly, are you suggesting that Merthia is the one who is after me?"

"It's possible."

"But highly unlikely," Jonathan said mockingly. "Emily, it's just a myth, a legend like all the others, made up by the locals. Next she'll be telling you to believe in fairies."

I drew my eyebrows together and glared at him. "I do believe in fairies."

Mrs. Tilly looked equally annoyed at Jonathan's sarcasm and rude comments. She took off her round rimmed glasses, lifted a piece of her brown ruffled skirt and started wiping the lens. Her fingers moved hastily as she lifted her eyes to meet mine. "Skeptics are full of fear, fear of the unknown. As you know, child, there is more to this world than meets the eye." She held out her glasses, examined the lenses, then set them back on her nose.

"That's so true," I said, giving Jonathan a hostile glare. "What about the other local legends and tales? Could you tell me about them?"

She rested her elbow on the table and rubbed her wrinkled fingers over her chin in a contemplative manner. "Well, let's see. There's the one about the lonely old wood witch who was supposed to have taken the Elisses to keep her company. Then there's the one about the Elisses having twin daughters. One they kept, the other was killed at birth. The spirit of the dead girl is said to roam around, searching for her family.

"The B.D.O. gets blamed for some of the strange happenings around here. That's the British Druid Order. Folks call them the devil's children. Good pagan worshippers is all they are, really. Some say that the souls of the ancient Celts come back every Sabbath to reclaim one of their own and others think it's aliens, the same ones that make those crop circles. They think they're abducting folks and taking them away for experiments."

Jonathan put his hand over his mouth and stifled a cough, or was it a snicker?

She took off her glasses and placed them on the table. "Like I said, there's probably a smidgen of truth to all of them."

"I'm sure there is." But none of them resonated so clearly as the one about the Druid priestess. "Mrs. Tilly, my aunt is coming home and I need to make the cottage safe for her. Can't you just come over and do something to get rid of it? Whatever it is?"

"I don't do exorcisms. Like I said, I'm not a priest, my dear."

A priest. I hadn't thought of that. But none of us were Catholic. I'd keep that in mind if all else failed.

"However, I can offer you some protection."

"Like what?"

"Sea salt for scattering about and for rubbing on yourself. A pinch under the tongue will stop you from getting possessed. Dill is good for warding off witches." She snickered. "The bad ones that is. You'll need holly for your windows and doors and a little lavender with a touch of sage, to burn. That will protect you if nothing else will. And don't forget to keep that amulet around your neck. And wear red; it will give you courage. Once we find out what we're up against, I'll mix you a potion."

She ran her boney fingers down the side of my head, stroking my hair gently. "Redheads make the best witches. They have the gift. There's something in their blood."

"Really!" I must remember to tell that to Skye. On second thought, I'd better not; she'd try to persuade me to join a coven or cast some spells. "How will we find out what we're up against?"

"Ask your invisible friend, the one that protects you. Or your dead grandmother; she was a gifted seer in her time. And there's always Mary Eliss. It's obvious she's trying to tell you something. But be careful; I have my doubts about her. Some spirits can be crafty."

"But they're all so unpredictable and elusive."

"Call for them and they will come."

The very thought of calling out to ghosts in that cottage gave me goose bumps. And which one of my unearthly friends should I summon? What would I say? And what if I summoned the wrong spirit and "she" came?

It was all too scary, too dreadful to imagine.

## Chapter 16

Mrs. Tilly reached for one of her wicker baskets that hung from the low wooden ceiling beams, packed it with herbs and draped a colorful linen cloth over the top. "There you go, dear; all you need now are some bat wings."

"Bat wings?"

She giggled. "Holly, of course. That's the proper name for it. You'll find some in your aunt's garden."

"Well, you learn something new every day," Jonathan said as he grabbed the basket out of my hand and hurried toward the door. *There he goes again, with that condescending tone.*

I felt more confident now. I had someone who believed me and was willing to help. I kissed her rosy red cheek softly. "Thank you for listening."

"You take care of your aunt. You're all she's got now."

"I will. Thank you."

"She's eccentric," Jonathan said as we got into the car.

"She's sweet and very gifted."

"I don't know. There is something about her that makes

me really uncomfortable. And what she was saying, well, it all seems so far-fetched."

"Don't you think that having a ghost as a playmate is far-fetched?"

"Yes, it is, as you keep reminding me. I wish I hadn't told you now."

"I'm glad you did." He glanced in the rear view mirror, brushed a lose strand of hair away from his eyes then turned the ignition. "What do you plan to do now?"

"I'm going to do exactly as she said."

"What, ask the friendly ghosts for help?"

I could hear the whispers of sarcasm in his voice again and it was starting to tick me off. But he had said that he believed me, I reassured myself. And he had admitted that besides his ghostly playmate, other strange, unexplainable things had happened to him here.

I thought it better not to say anything and restrained the urge to assert myself. This wasn't the time or place, and I wasn't confident enough in our friendship to run the risk of annoying him. I'd done that too many times already. He just wasn't as open-minded as he used to be. He's become pragmatic like my dad, I concluded bitterly. But if he had, why would he go along with any of this? Why not just tell me he thought it was crazy?

*Because he wants you,* my inside voice murmured.

His head turned slightly in my direction as if he'd sensed my silent words. A twinkle of desire flickered in the depth of his dark eyes as they met mine, and the corners of his mouth turned up in a warm, sensual smile. I felt that familiar tinge of desire between my legs as I asked myself if he read my mind. Oh, what did it matter, who or what he believed? He was the ever so gorgeous Jonathan McArthur, he was by my side, and I wanted him badly—all over me and inside me. That erotic thought made me quiver.

Dad was outside chopping wood when we drove up. He put down his axe, strolled over to the car to greet us and gave me a disapproving look. Then he asked Jonathan why he hadn't found a nice girl friend yet and hinted that I was already taken.

I wanted to tell him about Kyle's questionable business trip and the fact that I was going to end our relationship. But what would be the point? He would blame Jonathan for coming between us and tell me how stupid I was to give up such a suitable suitor. Dad used to tell me that I was very lucky to have caught such a prize. As if I'd dangled my lure into the water and snatched the biggest fish in the sea.

I didn't blame my dad. He only wanted what he thought was best for me. Kyle was a very likable person and came from a wealthy family. He knew that financially I wouldn't want for anything if I married Kyle. I was going to disappoint him again.

*Tomorrow Auntie comes home and Dad goes home. A welcome exchange.*

* * * *

Auntie sat on the foot of the bed, clutching the handle of the tartan suitcase that rested on her lap. The bed was stripped, and the white sheets and worn woolen blankets were folded neatly on top. A spark of enthusiasm lit her tired old eyes when she saw us and her mouth opened into a small smile, just big enough to reveal her false teeth.

I felt a lump swelling in my throat. "I see you're all ready to go, Auntie Em." She nodded. I sniffed back the tears.

Finally she was going home to her beloved Merryweather Lodge. But I wasn't at all sure how she was going to react once she got there. Would the memories of that dreadful evening come rushing back? Would she look for Uncle Reg? We had told her about his passing as gently as we could, but she hadn't shown any emotion. We weren't quite sure she understood.

At the cottage I undid Auntie's seat belt and tucked my hand under her arm to help her out of the car. She held out her hand, slapped my fingers and pushed me away. I stood back a little, shocked at her newfound boldness. Slowly she straightened her back, brushed herself off and gazed at the cottage as if seeing it for the very first time.

"Your home," I whispered.

She showed no expression as she moved steadily toward the door. Suddenly she stopped and lifted her gaze up to the attic room window. My hand shot to my chest as I felt my heart starting to race. What was she looking up there for? What did she know? What had she seen?

Her eyes lowered slowly, sadly, then she proceeded toward the door. I hurried past her, placed the large iron key inside the lock and pushed open the door. She barged in front of me and entered the hallway, her eyes moving back and forth as if searching for something.

"She's looking for Reg," Dad whispered in my ear.

When she walked into the sitting room and spotted Winny snoozing in the comfy chair, her face lit up. The cat seemed to sense her presence, opened its big blue eyes and gazed up at Auntie in an "Oh, you're home" sort of way. Auntie picked her up gently and nuzzled her face into Winny's soft white fur. Then she walked over to the fire side rug, bent down and stroked Winky. Her face beamed like a loving mother who had just been reunited with her children. "I'm home, luvs." she murmured softly.

Tears filled my eyes; I couldn't hold them back. Warm and wet, they trickled down my cheeks uncontrollably. I knew from that moment, as long as my Auntie was alive, I could never sell Merryweather Lodge.

After her blissful reunion with her kids, she marched into the kitchen, strapped on her apron and put the kettle on the stove. Then she took out her false teeth, rinsed them under the tap and plopped them back in her mouth. It was as if she'd all at once snapped out of a deep sleep.

But my inside voice told me it was too good to be true. Something about her demeanor wasn't right.

My dad had insisted on getting a cab to the airport, even though John McArthur and Bob White had offered him a ride. Like his brother, Dad was stubborn and wouldn't be beholden to anyone. "You'll phone and e-mail, let me know how the two of you are doing, won't you, Princess?"

"Of course. Every day, I promise."

Dad sighed deeply as he took one last look around. His eyes filled with tears. It was as if he was saying goodbye, not only to his brother but also to the cottage. Perhaps he thought that it would be too painful to ever return. I could feel his pain. The deep void he must have felt, knowing that he would never see his older brother again, the one with whom he had shared his childhood and looked up to in his own respectful way.

He walked over to Auntie and gave her a peck on the cheek. "'Bye, Emy. Look after your niece and yourself."

"If ya can't be good, be careful," she said with authority. "And tell that girlfriend of yours to stop smoking. Those fags will kill 'er."

Dad gave me a sympathetic look and shook his head. Auntie's memory was fickle, but for now I regarded that as a blessing. She had forgotten about that dreadful evening and her husband's death, or so it seemed.

"'Bye, Dad. Tell Mom that I love her and I'll be home as soon as things have settled."

Jonathan phoned that evening to ask how we were doing. I told him that Auntie's mind was still out there somewhere but physically she was fine. She'd spent the day puttering about the cottage, dusting, refolding laundry while shaking her head, rearranging her pantry and making numerous cups of tea. She had even been down to the coop and fed the chickens. She said that they looked like they were half starved.

I asked Jonathan if he'd take me to the library tomorrow

evening. I wanted to get some information on the history of this area and its legends, especially the one about the Druid Priestess, Merthia. I kept hearing her name, like the whisper of an angry ghost inside my head. He said that he had tomorrow afternoon off work and could take me then, and asked if I'd like to have his Mom come over and sit with Auntie while we were gone.

But as soon as the words came out of his mouth my inside voice rose up inside me, like a sort of Morse code. *No! No! No!* it tapped.

"Is there any way of contacting Mrs. Tilly and asking her to come over? My aunt's been asking about her," I lied. "She'll know what to do if anything strange happens while we are gone."

"You can contact her telepathically."

"Very funny."

Jonathan said that he'd pop in and see Mrs. Tilly that evening, as he had to drop something off at his parents' house and it was close by. He would phone me after he'd spoken to her, but if she wasn't available, he'd ask his mom.

I whispered a prayer: "Please let her be available." I wasn't sure why I felt so uncomfortable about leaving her with Maud. Perhaps it was because I still wasn't sure about her intentions. Or was it something else? I couldn't quite put my finger on it.

That night I slept on the pull-out couch in the parlor. Before retiring, I'd mixed the herbs and spices, spread them discreetly around the cottage and hung sprigs of holly above the doors. I sprinkled sea salt under Auntie's bedroom door, rubbed a little on her bedroom slippers and dropped some in the pocket of her housecoat. For an extra precaution, I draped her lucky pendant over the headboard.

I kept waking up, expecting to hear footsteps on the ceiling, cries from Auntie's room or worse. Finally I fell into a deep sound sleep only to be awakened at five a.m. by the click of cups and saucers and the shrill sound of the whistling kettle.

Bug-eyed and half asleep, I slipped into my terry housecoat and hurried into the kitchen. Auntie was sitting at the table. A china cup, the one she always used, sat in front of her. A large glass of orange juice waited for me across the table.

Uncle Reg's chipped mug full of warm tea, with cream and sugar and a side plate with thick white bread toasted and smothered in butter sat hopefully in its regular spot.

Auntie's hands were resting, one on top of the other, in her lap. She didn't move when I walked into the room. She just sat there calmly, expectantly, in a sort of nostalgic trance.

I put my hand to my heart and swallowed hard as I sat down beside her. "Good morning, Auntie Em. You're up early."

She flinched as if she had just been woken up from a deep sleep. Without a word she rose from her seat, walked over to the stove, picked up a vintage spoon and started stirring her homemade porridge in the cast iron pot. "This new fangled stove ain't like my old Aga, it ain't. Don't cook worth a darn, it don't." A warm oaty smell wafted through the kitchen as she spooned the creamy thick mixture into two earthenware bowls.

"Did you remember that Mrs. Tilly is coming over to visit you this afternoon, while Jonathan and I go to the library?"

She plunked the steaming bowl of porridge in front of me and rolled her eyes. "I don't need a babysitter, our Emily. I'm quite capable of looking after m'self, I am."

"I thought you liked Mrs. Tilly and would enjoy her company."

"Rubbish. You didn't want to leave me alone."

*How can she be so senile one moment then completely sane and perceptive the next?*

"Nutty as a fruit cake, she is. Not quite right in the head. But the devil ya know is better than the devil ya don't, I suppose."

I wondered what she meant by that. And why was she so angry and bitter? Auntie had always been critical and somewhat tactless, but never cruel and miserable. I longed to see her laughing and singing again, back to her jolly old self.

"He never touched it, not even a smidgen," she mumbled. Then she sighed, shook her head and cleared away the dishes.

"Would you like some help with that, Auntie?"

"Stop yer fussing girl. I ain't an invalid."

"Sorry I asked." I strolled into the parlor and left her alone.

After slipping out of my night clothes, I got out my lap top. There was an e-mail from Skye:

*Thanks for sharing. It's all so fascinating. I've done a little research, conversed with my spirit guides and come up with a theory. I believe that your old friend was right. And you, my dear Fletch, were, in a past life, a Druid maiden. You and Jonathan were passionate lovers and you've come back to be reunited. How romantic is that!*

I smiled as I pictured the eager and enthusiastic look on Skye's face as she typed and wondered what she would have said if I'd told her more about the legend of Merthia.

*That thing that you call the hideous creature is probably Jonathan's jilted chick. She'll need to possess a human form before she can kill you, and she's likely to have an accomplice.*

I shivered.

*Don't know how Mary Eliss fits into all of this but I'm sure you'll figure it out. Have fun, Fletch!*

Fun? Was she kidding? It all made sense though, no matter how crazy it sounded.

I sent an email to Kyle. Although it was hard, I knew that I had to be honest. I couldn't live with myself if I lied, and he deserved to know the truth. I simply told him that I had met someone else and fallen in love. As I lowered the lid of my lap top I said a silent prayer, that his feelings would not be hurt and that he would find the girl of his dreams. I knew that wasn't me.

A flurry of excitement fluttered in my stomach when I heard the screech of tires pulling up on the gravel driveway. I recognized the sound of Jonathan's car as if it were a faithful old friend.

I glanced out of the window. Mrs. Tilly was wearing a multicolored knitted shawl and a full skirt in a cabbage rose print. Her white hair was braided and twirled around her head like a snake.

Auntie strolled to the door, wiping her hands on her apron. "Come in, come in. Don't stand there gawking." Her weathered old face crinkled into a warm smile as she gazed up at Jonathan. It was obvious that she was extremely fond of him. "Come for my niece, 'ave ya, little Jonny?"

"If that's all right with you, Mrs. Fletcher."

Mrs. Tilly took off her heavy shawl and handed it to Auntie, who scowled and threw it over the umbrella stand beside the door.

"Well, Emy, you look as right as rain."

Auntie's eyes rolled up and down Mrs. Tilly's odd little form and peculiar attire. "That's more than I can say for you."

Her blatant rudeness made me cringe.

"Cheeky, madam," Mrs. Tilly replied in an endearing manner, adding a girlish giggle. She knew, I was sure, that Auntie wasn't joking but politely pretended that she was.

With a puckered and tight expression, Auntie pointed to

the sofa. "Sit there. I'll make a cupper."

We left the two of them in the sitting room exchanging gossip. Just before we walked out the door, I heard my aunt say, "You can't stay for long. Reg will be home for his dinner soon."

"All right, Emy, I won't stay long."

I was happy that Mrs. Tilly hadn't corrected her but saddened by the fact that she was still waiting for Uncle Reg to come home. I thought that her memory lapse was perhaps her mind's way of shielding itself from whatever had happened, because the reality was too painful to bear.

It was a gloomy afternoon. The air smelt damp, and low gray clouds scurried across the sky, threatening rain.

Jonathan was dressed in brown corduroy pants that hugged his firm thighs, and a tailored jacket to match. Under his jacket a white shirt unbuttoned at the neck revealed hints of wispy black hair. His stylish attire shamed my worn jeans and plain sweater and I was kicking myself for not being more selective.

"Thank you for taking me," I said as he opened the car door and motioned me inside.

"My pleasure." His face beamed with that cheeky, lusty smile that filled me with passion.

The mingled scents of pine, leather, spicy aftershave and peppermint gum hung in the air. I inhaled discreetly. It was delicious, all of it.

"She looks good today," he said as he turned the ignition.

"Who?"

"Your aunt."

"Yes, she is improving but her mind is still in another world. I'm wondering if she'll ever come back down to earth. I'd really like to ask her what she remembers about the evening my uncle died. But I'm so afraid of what it might do to her or how she'll react."

"There's probably a good reason why her memory has erased it."

"I'm sure there is. She didn't like the idea of Mrs. Tilly coming over to sit with her. 'I don't need a baby sitter,' she said."

He laughed. "I thought they were friends."

"So did I."

"I don't blame her for being anxious around Mrs. Tilly; she's a bit of a creepy old girl."

"So is my aunt at times." He chuckled. "Why does everyone call her Mrs. Tilly? Doesn't she have a first name?"

"If she does, I've never heard it. She's always been old Mrs. Tilly to me. My mum said that when she was a young girl they called her old witch Tilly, and she looked just the same then as she does now."

"So I heard. Doesn't anyone find that odd, or do they just sweep it under the rug with all the other obscure dust mites?"

He smiled and shrugged his shoulders. "I suppose it is rather odd, come to think of it. When I was a young lad, there was a rumor going around that she had given birth to a baby girl and that the child was so ugly that she killed it and buried it at the bottom of her garden."

"What an awful thing to say about someone. Seems like the kids are as bad as the adults for making up stories around here."

"Yes, but remember what she said. There is usually a smidgen of truth in every tale."

He paused, then cleared his throat. "Emily, are you in a relationship?"

It came so unexpectedly, just out of the blue. I struggled for words. "No! Well, not really. Not now, anyway."

He gave me a quick glance while twisting his mouth into a dubious smirk. "It's okay. I just wish you had told me."

"I'm sorry. I should have said something. I was dating this guy back home but I've just broken off our relationship. It wasn't going anywhere and my feelings for him were just superficial."

"And his feelings for you?"

"Don't think he had any. True feelings, I mean. What about you? Bet there's been lots of girls in your life," I said quickly, trying to deflect the attention from me.

"A few but only one that was serious"

Serious? I was curious but thought it would be best to leave it at that. At least for now.

# Chapter 17

Depressing, low-lying clouds loomed overhead as I gazed out the window, contemplating the legends, secrets and unearthly shadows that shrouded this mysterious place.

The road was so narrow that Jonathan had to pull onto the verge and stop when another car approached. On both sides, towering trees with sturdy old trunks grew out of the hard ground. Flaming branches shook erratically, sending leaves adrift like confetti in the gusty wind. On and on we drove through a maze of endless winding roads darkened by the shadows of squally trees.

Then suddenly, as if emerging from a long, gloomy tunnel, we were out in the open. Fields of ripe golden hay, quaint farm houses, pastures of cows and sheep. Rich vegetation touched with brush strokes of yellow, russet and brown stretched out in front of us. It was a masterpiece.

"I don't remember coming this way before."

"It's the scenic route. I know how much you love the countryside."

The dark clouds had lifted but it was still quite breezy. We traveled up a steep hill. At the top we could see for miles.

I wound the window down and looked out at the wind-swept variety of scenic terrain. Salisbury, with its stately old buildings and tall steeple, towered in the distance. To the right the great monoliths of Stonehenge stood erect and fore-boding in the middle of an open field, as if dropped there by a giant bird. Not far from there, grassy burial mounds disguised as gentle rolling hills covered their dead. I felt like a queen looking out over her kingdom.

"Can we stop here for a moment?" I asked. He pulled over onto a small grassy approach. "It's mysterious and beau-tifully captivating."

"Like you," he said, as his eyes swept over my body. Then he gave me one of his crafty, sensual smiles.

"I wish I was beautiful." *Oh my God, Emily, why did you say that?* It sounded weak and coy. I was cross at myself for not exuding more confidence.

"Trust me, you are a very attractive woman."

I could feel myself starting to blush now. I turned my face to the window, hoping the cool breeze would stop it.

"I've heard that Canada is a beautiful country."

"It is. It's majestic, rugged and vast. But this place is magical and enchanting. It has a strange, mystical energy, as if it were holy ground."

"It's just this area. There are parts of England that look more hellish than holy."

"What is it about this area that's so mystical?"

"I've often wondered that myself. Perhaps it has something to do with Stonehenge and the ancient Celts. Maybe this whole area was consecrated ground, one big pagan church."

An interesting theory, I thought as I turned and gazed into his gorgeous face.

His smooth, slightly tanned complexion was perfect, his dark brown eyes deeply compelling, his nose straight and distinguished, his cleft chin irresistibly sexy, and his lips, full, velvety and so very tempting. He lifted his slender finger and caressed my cheek as he stared longingly into my eyes. My body quivered with a lusty sensation more pleasurable and more intense than I had ever known A soft, blissful sigh slipped from between my lips as I felt a hunger throbbing inside my groin. I needed him badly.

His warm hand cupped my chin and drew me closer and closer to his lips.

*Beep! Beep!* We jumped.

A red sports car pulled up beside us. The driver beeped his horn repeatedly.

"What does he want?" I asked anxiously.

Jonathan sighed. "It's Posh and Beck."

"Who?"

A young woman wearing a tight jean skirt and skimpy nylon sweater got out of the passenger seat. "Oh no, it's her," I mumbled.

Jonathan rolled down his window.

"Hi ya, brother. Have you run out of petrol or something?"

"No, just enjoying the view."

She lowered her head and glared at me through the open window, emitting a strong scent of expensive perfume and locking her eyes onto mine in a hypnotic stare. Like that of a spider immobilizing its prey. She sniffed. "Not much of a view."

I bit down on my lip and took a deep breath to restrain myself. I wanted so much to say something, something clever and nasty, or slap her around the face and tell her what a bitch she was. This girl pricked every vengeful nerve in my body.

A handsome young man with a fair complexion and curly blond hair waved at us from the driver's seat of the red car.

"I see you've brought your puppet along," Jonathan said.

Belinda twisted her face. "Very funny."

"I thought you were working today."

"I'm on the evening shift this week." She stuck her hand in the car and flicked a piece of lint from Jonathan's jacket while she flashed him a warm, mischievous smile. It wasn't the kind of smile a sister gives her brother. "Come to the pub this evening and have a drink on me."

"Thanks, but I have things to do."

She shot me another nasty glare as she brushed her wind-blown hair away from her face. "I bet you do."

The young man in the red car was getting impatient. He kept glaring at us through the open window and clearing his throat. Then he gave two quick beeps of the horn.

Belinda turned around and snarled at him. "Hold your bloody horses!"

"You'd better go. He's getting restless."

"Sod him."

"Still out of work, living off his parents and catering to your every whim, is he? You know, you really could do better. There's plenty of fish in the sea."

"It's not a tadpole I want, it's a whale." Her eyes met mine. "A sperm whale."

*This chick is sick,* I thought. And there was no doubt in my mind now that her hatred for me was out of pure jealousy.

Jonathan shook his head and started the ignition. "Well, sis, it's been nice talking to you, but we have to be off now. Emily wants to do some research at the library."

"How thrilling, I'm sure," she said with a smirk as she tossed her head and strutted back to the red car.

The young man immediately slammed his foot on the gas and accelerated at a tremendous speed, sending a cloud of grit from the dusty road swirling around behind him.

"Moron," Jonathan said angrily.

"I assume that you don't like the boyfriend."

"You assumed right. He's arrogant, lazy and spoiled rotten."

*Sounds like they make a good pair.*

"Has Belinda finished school? A little young to be working in a pub, isn't she?"

"She just turned eighteen, got accepted into the local college and was supposed to start her classes two weeks ago, but she decided to take a job as a barmaid instead. She'll just live on love, I suppose. The new boyfriend can afford to keep her, along with her bad habits. His parents are loaded."

"Bad habits?"

"Booze, sex, clothes, and drugs, I suspect."

"You must be worried about her."

"Yes, I wonder what's going to become of her. She was a lovely child."

I remembered my aunt saying the same thing, but I couldn't imagine Belinda being lovely, at any age.

"She's very fond of you, Jonathan." *Too fond.*

He fondled the steering wheel and sniffed as he glanced at me out of the corner of his eye. It was as if I had touched a nerve or discovered a dark, hidden secret.

"She changed after she found Lizzy Lunn's body. Seeing such a gory scene at such a young age affected her mind. She hasn't been right in the head since then." *You're not kidding,* I said to myself. "My dad wanted her to go for therapy but my mum wouldn't have it."

"It must have been awful. And they still haven't found out who did it?"

"No, I don't think so. The police were at our home a few times, questioning my mum and Belinda. I assumed it was because Mum was the last person to see her alive and my sister found her body."

"I thought I heard someone say that your mom was away when it happened?"

"She was in Chillsbury visiting a sick friend, just down the road from where Lizzy lived."

*Now that's interesting,* I thought. "I can see why they

would want to question her, then. Did they take DNA from them?"

"Why would they do that?"

"For evidence."

"Of course not! It was obvious that they didn't have anything to do with it. They were pretty sure it was a man, with a female accomplice. The blood they found under her nails was from a female but it would have taken a lot of strength to hack someone up like that."

I shuddered. "I'm sure it would have."

The library was in an imposing, colonial, red brick building, with layers of steps leading up to a majestic arched door. Inside, there was a massive room with wood panel shelving, high beamed ceilings, alcoves and a few polished, reading tables. I inhaled deeply. I have always been fond of libraries, with their musky sweet scent of old leather and paper, and their timeless treasure troves of books with dog ears and gilded pages, waiting patiently, on deep shelves to be discovered and reveal their secrets.

I strolled down the corridor, not really sure of where to look or what to look for. The aisles were not marked and the librarian was nowhere in sight. I remembered what Skye had told me to do when I was lost or unsure. "Close your eyes and ask your guardian angel to show the way."

I stood still, shut my eyes and whispered, "Lead me to a book that will help me to solve the mystery." Then I felt a presence, as if someone was standing next to me, and with it, the familiar floral fragrance of my unearthly companion.

I opened my eyes slowly. No one was there.

I wandered up and down the gloomy aisles scanning the hard backs, soft covers, books with appealing colors and interesting titles, listening ever so carefully for a clue from my inside voice.

A sunbeam streamed though one of the tall windows at the back of the library. It was alive with dust motes that floated like tiny fairies within its luminance. Through the slanted ray my eyes caught sight of a large black book with bold gold lettering.

*This one,* my inside voice nudged in a soft knowing whisper. It was titled, *Local Legends, Tales and Fables.*

I pulled down the heavy volume and carried it to a table. Flipping through the pages, I discovered that 'local' meant the whole county of Wiltshire. There were numerous stories and theories about Stonehenge. I found the Legend of Mary Eliss in much the same way as Auntie had told it. The tales that Mrs. Tilly had mentioned were there, too.

When I turned the page to the Legend of Merthia, I gasped and blinked my eyes to make sure they weren't playing tricks on me. There, in full color, were the scenes from my recurring dream. Could I have seen this picture before, when I was a child perhaps, and dreamt about it? I was sure that I hadn't, but how could I keep dreaming about something from a book that I had never seen?

I examined the pictures. One of the women in the picture looked a lot like me but more beautiful, just like the face I saw in the mirror. The young man in the black cloak could have been a photograph of Jonathan, and there was something very familiar about the stunning woman who was standing by a slab of stone, holding an axe, drenched in blood.

I read the legend.

"Loki, the high Druid priest, was seduced by a beautiful but evil sorceress named Hagmanis. A child was conceived in her sordid womb. When the infant was born, Loki took her and banished Hagmanis to the end of the earth. He called the child Merthia. She was graceful and alluring, with exquisite features and hair like spun gold. But in her heart she carried the evil seed of her mother. As a young girl, for amusement, she would torture the village cats. All the other children feared her. As she grew, she became more alluring and seductive. Her lust for blood also grew. The young men in the village could not refuse her. She conceived two illegitimate babies, whom she tried to kill at birth.

"Merthia was obsessed with her youth and beauty and feared growing old. One day she made a pact with Odina, the Goddess of Immortal Youth. If she sacrificed a young virgin every Sabbath, Odina would in turn bestow upon her immortal youth. Merthia kept her promise."

Loki was desperate to change his daughter's ways. At the age of eighteen she was betrothed to a handsome young priest named Golwin Just before her wedding day, Golwin discovered her evil deeds. He called off the wedding and gave his attention to her cousin, Colrea. Merthia was furious and vowed revenge. On the day of the Autumn Equinox, she took her cousin into the forest and tied her to the altar of sacrifice. She

255

was just about to cut off her head when Golwin arrived. He grabbed the axe out of her hand and buried the blade deep into Merthia's skull. As the evil life force drained from her body, she screamed, "I will be back, and revenge will be mine." Her spirit is said to roam the earth in search of revenge. Before she died, she was given a gift by Odina: the power to possess the bodies of her female descendents. But only the ones with evil hearts could kill for her.

I jumped at the touch of a hand on my shoulder.

"Found something interesting?"

"Jonathan, look at this." I pointed to the picture.

His eyes grew wide. "Looks like bits of our dream."

"Look closely at the faces."

He put his hand on the table and leaned over my shoulder. "They look a little bit like us."

"Don't you see? They *are* us!"

He straightened his back and raised his brows. "Emily. That's ludicrous."

I scowled at him, lifted the book and pushed it into his chest. "Read this." He sniffed and stood back as if I had struck him.

"I'm sorry, Jonathan, but your skepticism ticks me off. It's all so obvious—at least to me—no matter how crazy it sounds. Don't you see? Our dream. The feeling that we'd met before. They are remnants of memory from another life, buried deep in our subconscious minds. As I look at these pictures and read the words, something resonates inside me—a stirring, an echo from the past.

"I am Colrea and you are Golwin. Merthia is after us, for revenge. It all makes sense now. Merthia sounds like Martha, the M in our tea leaves, the murders. Every Sabbath she takes a life, or her human host does."

"Brilliant. I have a jilted maniac lover, who's been dead for thousands of years and is after me. How am I supposed to believe that, Emily?"

I stood up, grabbed his jacket and pulled him roughly against me. I tilted my chin and gazed into his eyes. "Look into these eyes. Don't tell me you don't recognize them. Did they not stir your soul the first time you saw them? Dig deep, Jonathan, way down past all the layers of debris into your subconscious, and unearth that past life. Put aside your ego and rational thoughts. Please."

His soft moist lips gently touched my forehead. Then he smiled. "All right, I can't deny it. The first time I saw you, it was like being reunited with a long lost little sister."

"Little sister!"

He laughed and drew me in. "You were just a kid back then." His lips wandered to the back of my ear and around my neck, each caress more tender and more luscious than before. "But you're all grown up now and still strangely, stimulatingly, familiar."

I smiled and moved my hungry lips to meet his.

All of a sudden a foul-smelling, icy cold gust of wind swirled around us. I gasped, flung my arms around Jonathan's neck and pressed my face in his jacket.

# Chapter 18

Jonathan looked around, baffled. "What on earth was that?"

"I don't know." I tried to swallow the lump in my throat. "Maybe it was her."

We were being watched, somewhat discreetly, by two women in frumpy tweed suits who were pretending to browse the shelves. They kept glancing over at us and whispering to each other.

I pulled away from Jonathan and asked, "Do you have your library card?"

"Yes."

I picked up the heavy book and plunked it into his arms. "Good. Let's get out of here."

On the way home, the logical, babbling debater inside my head wouldn't shut up. It kept contradicting my inside voice and spurting out things I didn't want to hear.

*Do you really believe that you're the reincarnation of a Druid maiden? How can that be possible? There must be a rational explana-*

*tion for all of this. It's too bizarre. Maybe you're going crazy like your grandmother.*

I've always tried to repress these negative thoughts but today I couldn't stop their constant nagging.

Jonathan didn't help. He kept going on about how the mind can play tricks on us and how there's often a logical explanation for things that appear supernatural. But I did manage to convince him that we should show the book I had found to Mrs. Tilly.

When we arrived back at the cottage, the heavens had opened up. Rain lashed against the car windows. A steely wind blew forcefully across the yard, stirring up leaves and all kinds of debris.

I didn't bother to linger for that long awaited kiss. "Let's get inside. Quickly! And don't get that book wet," I ordered.

"All right, your majesty," Jonathan teased. He tucked the book inside his coat and drew up his collar. Then he slammed the car door and dashed toward the cottage.

"Last one inside is a rotten egg," I called.

He barged past me, giggling like a school boy, and flung open the garden gate. He slowed down just before we got to the door and bowed gracefully. "Ladies before gentlemen."

I enjoyed his tomfoolery. After all I'd been through, it felt good to be silly and let myself go.

We shook the rain out of our hair and hung our wet jackets on the coat stand beside the door. A damp strand of hair fell over Jonathan's eyes. I brushed it away gently, letting my finger slip across his forehead.

"Thank you," he whispered as his mouth eased into a warm sensual grin—one of those grins that stirred my groin. Oh, how much I wanted to feel those sensuous lips on mine. Just one kiss. One gentle touch, mouth to mouth.

Auntie was sitting in her favorite chair, her slippered feet propped up on the tapestry stool, darning one of Uncle Reg's heavy woolen socks. She had her hair net on, but there were no curlers underneath. Mrs. Tilly was slouched in the wingback chair, her head crooked, mouth agape. Short, quick snorting sounds were coming out of her nose. She was such a comical sight. I could hardly keep myself from laughing.

"Leave 'er sleep. I've 'ad enough for 'er chin-wagging, I 'ave."

"I thought you liked a good chin-wag, Auntie Em."

She ran her eyes over us and sniffed. "Looks like the two of you 'ave been pulled through a bush backwards. Go get some dry clothes on. I'll make us a cupper."

Jonathan's pants were stained with wet patches. "Would you like to wear a pair of my uncle's pants while those dry?"

His eyebrows raised "Pants?"

"Pardon my lingo. I mean trousers." I had forgotten that the English do not use the word pants for trousers. We laughed.

"No, I'm all right. I'll just stay close to the fire." He walked over to the hearth, squatted on the little wooden stool and stretched out his long legs.

I went to my make-shift bedroom to change my clothes. A bushy bunch of stalks with bright green leaves and plump white berries was sitting on the coffee table in a large brown jug. It looked like mistletoe, but where did it come from? Auntie must have put it there to cheer up the room, mistaking them for something more pleasing to the eye. She got so mixed up at times, poor thing. Or, maybe it was Mrs. Tilly, adding more magical foliage to the room to protect us. But where would they have found mistletoe at this time of year?

We sat in front of a blazing fire. Auntie was sipping tea and nibbling a custard tart in her comfy chair. Mrs. Tilly, still fast asleep, had her hands folded demurely on top of her lap and her mouth, closed now, was wearing a contented little grin. Jonathan and I snuggled close on the sofa.

Outside a harsh wind rattled the window panes, gushed through the cracks under the doors and whirred around the cottage ferociously, like a wild beast trying to get inside.

I felt a deep sense of cozy contentment. It was as if I had just returned home after a long and tiresome journey. *Could I live like this? This laid-back, humble, slower-paced life style—it's so isolated from commercialism, consumption, trends and the need to race against the clock. How would it feel to greet each day with a warm cup of tea, through a tiny, open, lace-covered window? And the English countryside is like a smorgasbord for the artistically inclined, with its deep history and exquisite array of hues, views, textures and scents.* This simple, unsophisticated way of life was seeping into me.

If this place didn't have its dark side, I'd definitely be tempted to stay, especially now. I glanced at Jonathan. *I have found my soul mate.* I squeezed his arm and snuggled closer, inhaling his natural scent.

Mrs. Tilly opened her eyes slowly. Then she yawned and stretched. "Oh dear, I must have fallen asleep."

Auntie snickered. "Ya don't say."

Mrs. Tilly ignored her and gave me a funny little grin. "Did you have a nice afternoon?" she asked.

"Yes, thank you."

"We found something of interest in the library. Something Emily would like you to take a look at." I gave him a sharp prod with my elbow. "It's about herbs," he said, realizing that I didn't want to stir my aunt's curiosity.

Auntie frowned. Mrs. Tilly winked and nodded her head as she heaved herself out of the chair and pinned a stray strand of white hair back into its tight braid. "I have to be going now."

Jonathan stood up and brushed the crumbs off his lap. "I'll drive you."

"Why don't ya wait till this bloody rain's stopped? Ain't fit for man nor beast out there, it ain't."

"I'm sure that if Maud can walk here and back again, I can."

"My mum was here?"

"We told 'er she was barmy, we did."

"Why did she come here?" I asked. The tone of my voice must have echoed my distrust, as Jonathan drew his brows down in a frown.

"She came to bring me a loaf of 'er bread. My Reg loves it, he does. But she must be going off the deep end to walk all the way down 'ere in this weather. I told 'er so as well."

I was glad she had left before we returned.

Jonathan grabbed his jacket from the coat stand. "Are you sure I can't give you a ride, Mrs. Tilly? I'm leaving now anyway, and your place is on my way. It seems silly to get drenched when I can drop you off."

"Oh well, all right dear, if you insist." She pulled her colorful shawl over her head and wrapped it tight around her arms and chest. "So long for now, Emy. It's been nice to see you again, in such good health and all."

Auntie just grunted and nodded her head.

*Why is she being so stand-offish? I will have to speak to her about that.*

"Goodbye, Mrs. Fletcher." He gave her a peck on the cheek. "I'm happy to see that you're getting back into the swing of things."

My heart sank. I didn't want him to leave.

Auntie must have sensed it. She tugged on his sleeve and drew his ear down to her mouth. "Don't you go driving on that there motorway in this. Drop 'er off and come back and stay the night. We'll 'ave a nice tea waiting for ya." She looked at me and grinned mischievously. "Won't we, our Emily?"

I was stunned and a little embarrassed by her bold invitation. I didn't know what to say. His dark eyes met mine, waiting, it seemed, for approval. I gave him a coy smile and a consenting nod, then turned away quickly as I felt my cheeks starting to flush.

"Thank you. I'd love to," he said softly.

*Yes! Yes!* my silent, inner voice yelled. A rush of excitement sprang up inside me, and it was hard to restrain it. Then I noticed him looking at me out of the corner of his eye with a cocky, seductive smirk on his face, which told me what he was thinking. How dare he *presume*, I said to myself. Part of me wanted to give him a swift kick on the butt, but the other part of me was titillated and wanted to play along. I just turned my head and walked away.

"Cheerio, dears. Have a nice evening." Mrs. Tilly flashed me a quick wink through the lenses of her spectacles.

"We'll visit you soon with that book," I called as they ventured out into the wet, blustery, autumn evening gloom.

By the time Jonathan returned, Auntie and I had prepared a delectable tea. On top of a crisp linen tablecloth sat a plate full of cheese and tomato sandwiches cut into tiny triangles, a dish of pickled onions, a fresh vegetable salad, flakey sausage rolls, jam tarts and apple crumble with a dab of custard on top. Auntie's table wasn't just for eating; it was for feasting, exchanging gossip and spilling your guts.

I insisted on opening a bottle wine, even though Auntie kept telling me that "It ain't proper 'aving wine with tea, it ain't." I was entertaining my soul mate, a man whom I had loved in another life time. We were reunited, brought back together by serendipity or sorcery, I wasn't sure which; but I was sure this occasion demanded wine.

We ate, drank and chatted about the farm, the local folk and Jonathan's antics as a lad.

"He'd come up 'ere on weekends and do odd jobs for us," Auntie said. "We'd give him a few bob for his trouble. Most lads would 'ave spent it at the sweet shop but not little Jonny. He'd buy 'is mum flowers or get some stewing bones from the butcher's for the dog. He even went and bought a pint of milk for the cats one time. Do you remember that, Jonny?"

He nodded his head.

Her old eyes twinkled as she looked at me. "You can't go wrong with a man with a big heart, you can't."

I flashed Jonathan a warm agreeable smile. It felt so right, the three of us together, safe and relaxed, enjoying each others' company, in the hub of our cozy little cottage. It was as if nothing odd or sinister had ever happened here. Perhaps it was all just an illusion, a bad dream and I'd wake up soon and find my fairytale kingdom just the way I had always imagined it—a safe, snug fortress of impenetrable bliss. If only that were true.

"Looks like it's getting worse out there." I pulled the curtains back from the little window above the sink. Dark clouds chased each other like fierce warriors across the sky. Foliage and debris scurried around the backyard and the arms of the sturdy cherry tree tossed about like an angry serpent. One lonely forgotten dish towel swung franticly on the clothes line.

I closed the curtains and shivered as I walked away. "It's not fit for man or beast out there." I smiled at Auntie. "As you would say."

She rose from her seat, puckered her lips and gave me a nod. "Well, the beast left but the man stayed, and that's a good job and all."

Jonathan put his hand to his mouth to hide his amusement. I just rolled my eyes and shook my head. I wondered if she knew what she was saying. I decided not to ask, just in case she didn't.

Auntie slapped Jonathan over the back of his hand with a teaspoon as we proceeded to clean off the table. "Leave them alone, Jonny. Us women will do this. It ain't proper to have a man fumbling about with the dishes, it ain't."

"Oh, Auntie Em, it's not the dark ages."

"Don't you go giving me any of your lip, young lady. When in Rome, do as the Romans do."

Jonathan's hand shot to his mouth while he turned his head. He was restraining himself from bursting out into laughter. "It was a lovely tea, Mrs. Fletcher," he said through his parted fingers and muffled snickers.

"Glad ya liked it. I bet you're glad you're in 'ere and not out there, on that there motorway in this weather, ain't ya?"

"I am, and thank you so much for asking me to stay."

She looked at me and grinned widely. "Now we 'ave to decide where we're gonna put him."

He glanced at me and scanned my face with his dark expectant eyes—searching, I was sure, of some indication that I would be willing to share my bed with him.

I lowered my head just in case the burning desire I felt

deep inside showed on my face. I tried to keep my tone light and matter-of-fact. "I can make you a comfortable bed by the fire, if you like?"

There was a hesitant pause. "That would be nice, thank you." His words were sincere and polite but their undertone and his demeanor whispered, 'I'd rather share your bed.' I wanted to sleep with him, badly. But was I ready to make love with a man that I hadn't even kissed yet?

"Rubbish!" Auntie blurted out. "There's a perfectly nice bed upstairs."

My eyes widened.

"Done it up nice and proper for you, our Emily, last time you were 'ere. But you were too afraid to sleep up there, with your overactive imagination and all. Don't know why you won't sleep up there now, being as though you're all grown up."

Oh my God. I swallowed hard. She'd forgotten what happened to me up there.

Jonathan shrugged his shoulders. "Wherever you ladies want to put me will be fine."

"No. No one should go up there. The stairs are not safe, and it's cold and damp. I'm sure he'll be much more comfortable by the fire." I loaded the dirty dishes into the sink and turned on the tap.

Auntie walked away in a huff. "All right, Miss Bossy Britches, whatever you say."

She left the room.

Jonathan stood beside me and grabbed the tea towel. "I

really don't mind sleeping up there, you know."

"You are kidding! Don't you remember me telling you what happened in that room?"

"Yes, but perhaps it's gone now."

"It hasn't. Believe me."

He moved closer, leaned over and whispered in my ear. "Cuddled up to a pretty girl in a warm blanket beside the hearth sounds like a good idea."

My heart leaped in response but I wasn't going to let him know that. I gave him a poke in the arm with my elbow. "No chance." It was too defiant, I thought, but I couldn't take it back. I just didn't want him to think I was the type of girl who slept with a guy before dating him for awhile

But I also didn't want him to think that I was a prude. I had dreamt of Jonathan spending the night with me in this cottage. Many nights, back home in Canada, I had lain awake and visualized him sneaking into the parlor, taking off his clothes, slowly lifting up the blankets and crawling into the pull-out couch beside me. What happened after that was blissfully erotic. Just thinking about my vision made my nipples harden and sent rippling waves of tantalizing pleasure all over my body.

"Do you think she'll scold me for doing women's work?" he asked as he rubbed a china cup with one of Auntie's best terry tea towels.

"Women's work?"

"Well, that's what she thinks, isn't it?"

"I hope that you don't."

"Of course not. I'm all for equality, in every aspect."

I nodded my head and gave him an agreeable smile. "I'm glad to hear that."

He grinned back at me mischievously.

Auntie had tucked a warm flannel sheet around the sofa cushions and laid a feather pillow and thick hand-knitted blanket on top. She'd also stoked the fire before going to bed.

I wondered if she'd be up early again to prepare her husband's breakfast. It was something she had rarely done when he was alive. I wanted desperately to remind her that he wasn't coming home and to ask her if she remembered anything about the evening he died. But I was too afraid of how she might react. She was slowly getting back to her old self, and I didn't want to do anything that might cause her to regress.

I poured two glasses of Shiraz and handed one to Jonathan. He was sitting on top of his make shift bed. Winny was on his lap pushing her head forcefully into his hand, demanding attention. He gently ran his long fingers over her soft white back. She rewarded him with a deep resounding purr. The unbuttoned neck of his shirt revealed bits of curly black chest hair, and his rolled up sleeves exposed powerful, slightly bronzed arms.

He took a sip of his wine and stretched his long legs out in front of him. My heart sighed longingly, and as he took his hand off Winny's back, he tapped the cushion beside him, inviting me to sit. The lights were dim. Red and orange flames lapped greedily around the logs in the hearth.

I could feel the heat from his sensual body. I gazed at his exposed flesh. It was so enticing—everything about him was enticing. *Calm down,* my inside voice whispered.

"Would you like to borrow a pair of my uncle's pajamas?"

The corner of his mouth twitched as his eyes met mine. "I sleep naked."

My crotch throbbed as a vision of his naked body flashed before my eyes. Pulse racing, I raised my glass. "To us, Colrea and Golwin, reunited at last."

Our glasses clicked. There was a moment of blissful silence as we sipped.

Suddenly, a dreaded familiar sound echoed from behind the door.

*Creak, creak.*

I gasped and sat up straight, spilling the wine all over my sweater. "Did you hear that?"

"It's probably your aunt moving about."

"No it isn't. I know that sound."

# Chapter 19

"It's the attic stairs." My voice trembled.

"Do you want me to go and check?"

"Sshh…listen." The only thing I could hear now was my own short, quick, fearful breaths. "It's stopped now."

"You're trembling, Emily. Calm down."

"I'm okay." I wiped the wine from my chin and dabbed the crimson stain on my sweater with one of Auntie's hankys.

"Will it stain?"

"Oh, probably, but that's okay. I've had this old thing for years," I lied. Nothing was going to spoil this moment, this special time with the man of my dreams. Not "her," not this stupid top, not even the glaring warning signals that my inner voice was sending me. None of it mattered. All that mattered was here and now, these precious moments with Jonathan McArthur.

I gulped the remaining wine from my glass, took Jonathan's hand gently in mine and gazed lovingly into his soft brown eyes. "I've longed for this moment from the first time

I saw you. It was as if you had cast some sort of magic spell on me. I have not been able, no matter how hard I've tried, to rid myself of your presence and break the spell. It was a relentless magnetism and now I know why."

His caressed my red hair with his long masculine fingers as his eyes moved longingly, lustfully, over my face, down my slender neck to my breasts, stopping for a moment, before returning to my eyes. The scent and raunchy energy that emanated from his body was intoxicating. It was as if he had been dipped in sex.

I quivered and moved closer.

*Creak. Creak. Slam!*

I pulled away from him and shot off the sofa. "Oh my God. Auntie!" I flung open the door, flew though the passage and into Auntie's bedroom.

"Wait, Emily, what is it?" Jonathan shouted as he ran to keep up with me.

I stood at the foot of her bed, my heart racing, dread clutching at my throat. She was sound asleep and snoring contently. I gazed around the room suspiciously. All the protective herbs and sea salt were gone. Quietly, I crept to the side of her bed and slowly pulled back the covers from under her chin.

"What are you doing?" Jonathan whispered.

"Her pendent's gone."

"She must have taken it off and put it somewhere."

"No, she didn't. It was her; she took it." I had been a little skeptical about the pendent, ever since I realized what it was. "I heard her come in here. But who removed the protection that allowed her to get in?"

"What are you talking about? Who came in here?"

"Her. Merthia," I said in a loud whisper. I slipped out of the room with Jonathan at my heels and closed the door quietly behind us. My worried eyes gazed into his as I chewed on my bottom lip. "I'd sprinkled sea salt under her door, put sprigs of holly on her night stand and placed saucers of cinnamon and dill around the room. It's gone, all of it."

"She probably couldn't stand the smell and got rid of it. I can't say that I blame her."

"But she never touched it before. I think she knew it was there for her protection."

"Then it must have been Mrs. Tilly."

"I shouldn't think so. She was the one who told me to put it there." I thought for a moment. "Maybe it was your mom." My tone was full of accusation.

He took a step back and frowned at me. "Why would she do that?"

I had to think of something to say without offending him. "She must have thought that she was being helpful by cleaning it up. You did say that she was extremely house proud, didn't you?"

"Yes, I suppose she could have."

I wasn't sure that her motives would have been innocent. Ever since she had told me that the cottage was rightfully hers, I'd been leery of her and the way she treated my aunt. There was something about her, something deceitful and despicable.

I walked into the parlor and opened the bottom drawer of the buffet.

It was gone. I looked up at Jonathan, who was towering above me with a puzzled look on his face. "My bag of sea salt is gone, and no one knew it was there but me."

"Perhaps you misplaced it."

"No. It was there when I left."

He bent over and grabbed my arm and drew me up. "You don't need it." His handsome face crinkled into a warm, reassuring smile. "Nothing is going to happen to you or your aunt as long as I'm here, I promise."

There was a calm confidence in his voice that stopped my heart from racing and gave me hope. I rested my head against his warm chest and inhaled his soapy scent which was mingled with a smidgen of manly perspiration. I could feel his fine chest hairs brushing against my cheek. My spirit was soothed, my body aroused as his strong arms enveloped me and my form molded into his.

I glanced over at Winny who had followed us into the parlor; she looked agitated as she strutted back and forth in front of the door, the tip of her tail swishing back and forth. It made me nervous.

"I'm scared, Jonathan. Scared of 'her', scared of these ghosts, whoever they are, and I'm terrified of leaving my aunt alone in this place, especially without any protection. It was Merthia, I'm sure of it; she went into Auntie's room and took her pendent." I swallowed the lump in my throat. "If it's me she's after, why is she tormenting my aunt, and why did she scare my uncle to death?"

"We don't know for sure that she did."

"I do. And she's not going to give up until she has her revenge."

His slender fingers touched my lips to silence me. "Hush, don't fret. You'll be safe with me tonight."

My eyes were drawn to the library book, sitting on top of the pullout couch. It was open. I broke from Jonathan's embrace and walked over to take a look. It had been turned to the page of the dreaded legend. "Did you open this?" I asked.

"No, I left it on the chair by the window, closed, I think. Your aunt must have found it."

"I can't remember her coming in here, and I'm sure she would have had something to say if she'd seen it."

"Well, books don't open on their own." There was a hint of sarcasm in his voice. I felt like slapping him.

I looked at him and shook my head. "After all I've seen, anything is possible."

I glanced at the brown jug crammed with mistletoe stalks and wondered why they were still here, when all the other foliage had been taken. I remembered reading somewhere that mistletoe was the sacred plant of the Celts. *Does this have significance?*

I sat down, lifted the heavy book onto my knee and stared at the pictures. Merthia was strikingly beautiful, in a wretched sort of way. The more I stared at her face, the more uncomfortable I became. "Where have I seen that face before?" I mumbled.

Jonathan sat down beside me. "Probably in your recurring dream." His voice was very matter-of-fact, as though he was referring to something of no significance.

"Besides that."

My eyes grew wide as I gazed at the picture and noticed a pendant. "It's Auntie's pendant!" I pointed to the chain around Merthia's neck. "She's wearing my aunt's pendant."

Jonathan gave me an impatient shrug. "Don't you think that you're getting a little carried away with this? Do you know how old that necklace would have to be?"

Now I really wanted to slap him. "Don't patronize me. This is serious. I have to get to the bottom of this and if you won't help me, I'll do it myself!" I slammed the book closed and stood up.

Jonathan rose, stood directly in front of me and squared his shoulders. "Don't go off in a tantrum. I want to help you, but I can't get my head around it. It's all so far-fetched. I'm sorry, okay?"

I softened. "I know how you feel. It is hard to believe." I leaned into the firmness of his tantalizing body. His powerful arms wrapped around me like a security blanket; their warmth and the serene silence that shrouded the room calmed me.

All of a sudden the door burst open.

Jonathan jumped.

I screamed and dug my finger nails into his arm.

Winny hissed and flew behind the couch.

Panic rose inside me as a sense of intense fear gripped me.

It was her—the hideous creature, Merthia. Her foul smell drifted toward us as she hovered in the doorway.

"Bog ar shiul'o'e," she cried in a deep, scratchy voice.

Jonathan's arms drew me in forcefully "No, I won't. You can't have her!"

"You understood that? What did she say?" My mouth trembled in terror as I spoke.

"It's Gaelic. She said, 'Step away from her'."

Her snake-like eyes grew big, burning with a venomous rage. Slowly she moved toward us. Closer and closer she came, snarling and hissing, puss oozing from between her uneven, yellow teeth.

Winny sprang from behind the couch, back arched, fur erect, making a low growling sound like a dog. Her eyes shot to the cat.

My stomach clenched. "No, Winny," I mumbled as I closed my eyes and shook uncontrollably.

Jonathan squeezed me tight. His chin was raised, his form stiff and straight, his demeanor steadfast and defiant. But he was drenched in a cold sweat of utter fear.

Then, like a breath of magic, I heard a soft whisper and smelt the familiar scent of lavender.

The creature stopped and turned her head. In the corner of the room, surrounded by a pale pink aura, stood the angelic form of Mary Eliss. "Leave them alone, Mother," she murmured softly.

"Ta'ni' d' ma'thair, amadan!" she replied angrily.

Mary Eliss lowered her eyes and vanished in an instant.

Then I noticed the shadow of a figure slowly emerging from the darkness outside the door. I swallowed hard. It was Auntie.

I pushed back the urge to call out to her. She had a cup in one hand and her little Bible in the other. *Oh my God, what is she up to?* The knot in my throat tightened. I shook my head and mouthed a cautioning, *No.*

Auntie crept up behind the creature and raised the Bible. "I'll 'ave yer filthy guts for garters if ya come back 'ere again, hag."

The creature spun around, teeth clenched, eyes wide.

I held my breath.

Auntie pulled back her hand and threw the contents of the cup right into her face. "Be off with ya!"

The creature let out a loud-pitched squeal, like that of a wounded animal, and flew out the door and down the hall. Auntie ran after her, waving her Bible and screaming, "I've 'ad enough of ya, ya smelly hag. Stink to high heavens, ya do."

We followed close behind.

Out of the passage and into the kitchen, the ghostly figure soared, her long, tattered, blood-stained dress dragging behind her. Her pale bony fingers clutched her face as she shrieked and secreted her repulsive stench.

Then, in an instant, right in front of our eyes, she disappeared.

We looked around. There was no trace, not even a whiff

of her foul odor. She had returned to the ancient dimension from which she came.

Auntie was standing perfectly still, her arms hanging limp by her side. The cup handle was balanced between two of her fingers, and the little Bible was lying on the floor in front of her. She wore a forlorn and vacant stare.

"Auntie Em. Are you okay?"

No answer. She just turned, dropped the cup and plodded back to her room.

"She's sleep walking," Jonathan whispered.

I walked close behind her, helped her into bed and drew the covers snug around her neck. This time I left the door open.

I walked back to the kitchen and picked up the china cup and just as I had thought, it revealed traces of sea salt. But where had she got it from? I wasn't about to wake her up and ask. *She's better off sleeping until the morning.*

Jonathan was sitting on the sofa, rubbing his fingers over the tiny bristles on his chin. His eyes were downcast. It looked like he was still in a state of shock.

I sat down beside him and put my trembling hand on his. "We have to find more of that sea salt; we're all too vulnerable without it."

He said nothing, just stared at me with a baffled expression.

"Jonathan, please speak to me."

"It was her, the little girl I used to play with when I was a lad. She was trying to protect us, but why did she call that horrid thing Mother?"

"Perhaps she thought it was her mother. Mary Eliss must have seen it taking over her mother's body and assumed they were one. What did the creature reply?"

"It said, 'I'm not your mother, fool'."

"Where did you learn Gaelic?"

"From my dad, and he learned it from his dad. It's been passed on through the generations."

"When I first saw her, she kept calling me Colceathrar."

"It means cousin."

"That makes sense."

"Emily, none of this makes sense."

I took his hand in mine and gazed into his worried eyes. "Jonathan. That really was Merthia. The one in our recurring dream. The one in your painting. The legend is true and she's after us for killing her. She was my cousin and your lover."

I grabbed the book, flipped through the pages and read:

> Her spirit is said to roam the earth looking for revenge. She was given a gift from Odina, the power to posses the bodies of her female descendants. But only the ones with evil hearts could kill for her.

"When I was here before, I blacked out three times. I remember feeling like something was inside me, something dark and despicable. Jonathan, not only am I the reincarnation of her cousin, I'm also her descendant, and so was Mary Eliss and your mom and sister." I looked into his dark eyes. "And you, of course, but she can't possess you. Only her female descendants."

"Not me. I wouldn't be a descendant."

"Why not?"

"I'm adopted. It's one of those uncomfortable secrets, never talked about but always known. My parents have photographs of me when I was only a few days old, so I was probably handed over to them shortly after my birth. I think the girl that gave birth to me was the daughter of the people who lived in the cottage before us."

"What makes you think that?"

"A little research and a lot of snooping."

"Aren't you curious to meet her and find out who your real parents are?"

"My real parents are the ones who raised me," he said in a firm and defensive manner.

"Jonathan, why haven't you told me this before?"

"It just never came up. Besides, I don't really want anyone else to know—for my parents' sake, not mine."

I could see that he was a little uncomfortable talking about it, so I thought it best to leave it alone. I wasn't surprised to hear that he was adopted. He didn't look anything like his parents or his sister. In fact, Belinda didn't look anything like her parents either, but she did have her mother's eyes. Perhaps she was adopted, too—rescued by Maud McArthur from her evil birth mother, the wicked wood witch. I snickered to myself. That would be like going from one witch to another. It was a bit of a relief to hear that we were not related. I'd always felt a little uncomfortable about that.

Jonathan's long, smooth fingers wrapped around my hand. "I'm sorry for doubting you, Emily." He brought my hand slowly up to his mouth and touched it with his tender, moist lips. It was such a pleasurable sensation, but I pulled away quickly.

His brow puckered. "What's wrong?"

"Haven't you noticed that every time we get close to each other, something happens to distract us? It's her. She's watching us. Even when she's not visible, I can feel her creepy bristles pricking me."

He took a deep breath and nodded grimly.

"We have to find a way of getting rid of her," I said.

"Perhaps we can find a vicar to help us."

"Maybe, but first we have to find out whose body she uses when she kills. Someone with an evil heart. It won't be easy because once she gets inside them, a metamorphosis takes place and they become her, the hideous creature. It's like she consumes them and uses their energy. I have felt her evil essence inside me."

He cleared his throat and his chin sank into his chest. "The only female descendants we know of are you, my mum, my sister and Lizzy, but she's dead. There must be someone else that we haven't met because it couldn't be you, or my mum or sister; there's nothing evil about any of you."

I raised my eyebrows. "I beg to differ," I whispered under my breath.

"I hope you're not insinuating…" he said.

"Of course not." *But I wouldn't rule them out.* "If we do have other relatives in this area, we need to find out where they are."

I kept thinking about how Belinda treated her brother, in that provocative and possessive manner. "Does your sister know that you're adopted?"

"I'm sure that she does, but we've never talked about it."

"She doesn't treat you like a brother. More like someone she has the hots for." *That was too blatant, too crass*, I thought as soon as it came out of my mouth.

Jonathan glared at me with a shocked and hostile expression. "That's sick, Emily! Why would you say such a thing?"

"I'm so sorry. I didn't mean it to come out that way. I'm sure that it's just her way of expressing her sisterly love." *That didn't sound right either.*

"Like I said, she hasn't been the same since she found Lizzy's mutilated body. And now she's got herself involved with a bunch of hooligans." His mouth became a sour grin. "Flirting is just her way of getting attention; she doesn't mean anything by it."

There was sadness in his voice that tugged at my heart.

I decided to change the subject. "I have an idea where the sea salt might be. Come with me." I held his hand and guided him though the door and into the passage, my eyes scanning every nook and cranny fearfully, my nose sniffing the air for any unearthly smells.

The door to Auntie's bedroom was still open. I crept into

the room, Jonathan in tow, and knelt beside the wooden chest at the foot of the bed.

"What's in there?" he whispered.

"Shh…" I put my fingers to his lips and shrugged my shoulders.

I'd had a curious feeling about this chest ever since I first set eyes on it. It looked like it might have been something special to Auntie, something she kept her most private things in, and I felt guilty about snooping. But my inside voice was now signaling quietly that it was time to open it. I lifted the brass latch and started to open the heavy lid slowly, being ever so careful not to make a sound. Excitement and curiosity welled up inside me. I caught a whiff of cedar.

# Chapter 20

The lid squeaked.

I look over at Auntie but she didn't stir.

I felt a rush of excitement. It was as if I was about to open a Christmas gift that had sat in front of me for weeks, tempting me with its shinny wrapper and colorful ribbons.

When the chest was fully open, my brows shot up. Lying on top of the neatly organized contents sat Auntie's pendent. A five pointed star inside a circle made of a heavy silver metal, which I had recognized sometime ago as a pentacle and knew its association with witchcraft. I placed it gently on the floor beside me.

Quietly, my eager fingers shuffled through the other items. There was a brown paper bag full of sea salt. I handed it to Jonathan. A black velvet purse that was tied with a silky gold ribbon contained what looked like very expensive jewelry—a couple of rings set with large impressive stones, a string of pearls and necklaces and broaches studded with sparkling gems. There was a small pile of old photographs, a bundle of letters secured with an elastic band and a thick brown envelope with the words 'Private Papers' scrawled along the top.

Under the envelope, skillfully folded, was a white silk dress. I lifted it carefully out of the chest and unfolded it, one crease at a time. It was like the gown of a fairy princess. Delicately embroidered cream-colored lace hung from the neck like an intricate spider's web. The puffy arms were made of net and were gathered at the wrists with tiny studded pearls. Around the waist, a wide sash of ribbon was drawn up in an elegant bow with a long trailing tail. It was absolutely splendid and looked like it had never been worn.

"Her wedding dress?" Jonathan whispered.

I shrugged my shoulders. Surely this was too fancy, too fussy for my aunt. I started to refold the dress, trying hard to fold it in the exact same way I had found it. The silky softness of the fabric felt like baby oil in my hands. *This must be pure silk*.

I moved it aside and looked back into the chest. At the bottom I found a bundle of knitted baby clothes. I leaned into Jonathan and whispered, "Must have been for her baby; it was stillborn, poor thing." He smiled sympathetically.

I was just about to lift the tiny garments out of the chest when Auntie started to stir. She was tossing and turning and making all sorts of snorting sounds as if she were having a bad dream.

We piled everything back into the chest as neatly and quickly as we could, all except the sea salt and the pentacle. I crept to her bed side. She was still now. I lifted her head ever so gently and placed the silver chain around her neck. I had decided, in my own mind, that my great grandmother was a white witch and she'd used the pentacle to cast magic spells and to shield herself from dark forces. My gut told me that it was a good luck charm, but I couldn't help feeling a tad suspicious.

I scattered grains of salt around her bed. Jonathan stood in the doorway, his arms folded, his face wearing an expression of utter fatigue and bewilderment. "She'll be safe now," I said with a half smile as we walked out the door.

He put the back of his hand over his mouth and yawned lazily. "Sorry, I'm knackered."

"You'll be okay on the sofa?"

"Yes, but what about you? You can have the sofa and I'll sleep on the floor, if you like. I don't want you to be alone tonight, Emily." He brought my hand up to his face and caressed it with his mouth and a slip of his tongue.

I gave him a sweet, gracious smile. It was tempting, and every inch of my body craved him, but would I be able to resist the temptation? Did I trust myself? No, I couldn't run the risk of "her" coming back.

"I'll be fine, really. Don't forget to put the grate up to the fire before you fall asleep." I opened his hand, poured a generous helping of sea salt into his palm and gave him a quick peck on the cheek. "Sprinkle this around the sofa." He nodded. "Good night, Jonathan."

I tucked the brown bag under my arm and moved away

quickly, just in case I changed my mind. I knew now who this hideous creature was, and I knew that if I didn't find a way to send her back to the dark place from which she came, I'd be doomed to a savage and brutal death.

Winny had crept back into the parlor and parked her snow white form on the pull-out couch where she watched intently, curiously, as I sprinkled sea salt around the room and under the crack in the door. After I'd finished, she curled up in a tight ball on the couch, as if satisfied that we were safe now.

I poured myself a drink, pulled a jar of moisturizing cream out of the cosmetic bag that my mom had given me, and disrobed. My hands moved slowly, purposefully over my naked form. The creamy balm felt cool and luxuriously soft on my skin, its fragrance heavenly. I closed my eyes and thought of him, lying naked between the sheets. My body burnt with hunger. It was all I could do to stop myself from dashing out the door, into the sitting room, tearing back his covers and forcing myself on him. Only the thought of "her" coming back stopped me.

The familiar smell of fried bacon and the muffled sound of singing wafted through the cracks in the parlor door. I crawled out of bed. My eyes were heavy and inside my head a dull throb reminded me of the drinks I'd had before falling asleep. *You've got to stop drinking like that,* my inner voice mumbled critically. But I needed something to get the visions of what happened out of my mind. Something to calm my nerves and stop the chatterbox inside my head from going off on a tangent. Something to help me sleep.

I reached for my glass of water and painkillers. I had decided that I was going to visit Mrs. Tilly this evening, tell her what had happened, and ask her if there was anything I could do to expel this entity, now that I knew who it was.

Auntie was standing at the kitchen sink scouring a greasy chip pan. Her head, as usual, was adorned with prickly black curlers; they were poking through the mesh hair net which kept them in place. She was slurring an off key rendition of "When blue birds fly over the white cliffs of Dover." *She doesn't have her teeth in and I'm sure she doesn't remember what happened last night. If she did, she wouldn't be in such a happy mood.* The table was set for three. Uncle Reg's cup and plate were not there. *This is a good sign.* I gave her a peck on the cheek. "Hi, Auntie Em. How are you feeling this morning?"

"Right as rain, m' luv, right as rain." She looked me up and down as she reached into her pocket, brought out her false teeth, wiped them with the bottom of her apron and maneuvered them onto her gums. I shuddered. "Not looking too proper this morning, our Emily, not proper at all."

I wasn't sure whether she was referring to my appearance or to my state of health. The English use the word "proper" for so many things. "The weather's not proper." "That's not the proper way to do it." "She doesn't have proper manners." And on and on. Most of the time I can grasp what they mean, and in this instance I think that Auntie was referring to my appearance, because I hadn't washed or brushed my hair yet.

"Good morning. Something smells delicious."

I stepped back, as Jonathan's presence startled me. He was dressed and groomed, and even though he was wearing the same clothes that he wore yesterday, he looked smart, fresh and incredibly handsome. His tidy appearance embarrassed me and reminded me of Auntie's brash comment.

*I don't want him to see me like this,* I told myself as I adjusted the belt on my housecoat and fidgeted with my hair. "I'll be right back," I announced sheepishly. Scurrying out the door, I rushed into the parlor, threw on some clothes, applied a little make up, a splash of perfume and brushed my hair. The whole time, I tried to ignore the goose bumps that kept pricking my arms and the sudden tightening in my gut every time a thought of what happened here last night popped into my head. A quick glance in the mirror told me I was "proper" now.

The old farm table groaned with its abundant load of mouthwatering goodies. It was a feast for the senses. Fresh poached eggs, bacon, fried tomatoes, baked beans, mushrooms, and crumpets and scones accompanied by dishes of homemade jam and treacle. There was even a generous platter of fresh fruit—for her "picky niece," I was sure. It all squeezed together on a red gingham table cloth. Even though my stomach felt a little queasy, I couldn't resist the scrumptious aroma and tasty display of this morning spread. "You must have got up real early to make this, Auntie Em."

She wiped her hands on her apron, untied it and draped it over the back of the chair. "Wanted to give our guest a proper

English breakfast, I did." She pulled out her chair. "Well, what ya waiting for? Get stuck in, and make sure you eat plenty. You could both do with a bit of meat on yer bones."

She looked really good this morning. The color had returned to her cheeks, she was gaining back some of the weight that she had lost, and her jolly disposition seemed to be returning. *Perhaps it was the thought of having a live-in nurse that prompted her speedy recovery,* I thought. *I had mentioned it to her on a number of occasions.*

A couple of turtle doves on the window ledge outside serenaded us with their soft, throaty *coo* through the slightly open window. The kitchen door was ajar, allowing us to hear the crackling of the sitting room fire and the tick tock of the grandfather clock in the hall. We sat in idle conversation with intervals of silence, which seemed natural and comfortable now, while we savored the delicious food. It was as if nothing sinister had ever happened here, as if the horrifying incident of yesterday evening had been erased from our memories and from the soul of this charming little cottage. But it did happen, I told myself. And this place did feel so eerie at times. It was as though the walls of the cottage had soaked up the negative and positive energies of the people who had lived here and emitted them whenever it pleased.

"Isn't that right, Emily?"

"Oh, sorry, what did you say?"

Auntie shook her head. "Daydreaming again, she is. I was telling Jonny how time flies when you're my age." Her old eyes sparkled as she glared at me with a warm expression. "I remember, the first time 'er mum and dad brought 'er here as if it were only yesterday. Smashing little thing she were, with 'er carrot hair and pea green eyes."

I scowled at her.

Jonathan's mouth twitched with humor. "She's still smashing," he said as his eyes danced. "It's not just people of your age who think time flies, Mrs. Fletcher. It is elusive."

"Do you think it's some kind of cosmic joke? Or perhaps God is fed up with us, so she's trying to speed up our extinction, for a more worthy species."

Auntie rolled her eyes. "Flipping heck, our Emily, I can't make head nor tail of what you're saying half the time."

"The feeling's mutual, Auntie Em."

Jonathan snickered.

"Cheeky madam," she said in her usual playful but sarcastic tone. It was wonderful to see her jolly, hear her sing and spouting out her tactless, well-meaning English slang. Especially after what happened last night.

It was just as we had thought; she must have been sleepwalking. I suddenly remembered what she had said to Merthia: "I've ad enough of ya, I 'ave, ya hag." That would indicate that she had seen her before, and she knew enough to throw sea salt on her.

Now I was sure that it was Merthia who had scared my uncle to death. *But why won't Auntie talk about it? Is her conscious mind too scarred to remember? Has she buried that evening so far down into her subconscious that it will never emerge?*

Before Jonathan left, I told him that I was going to visit

Mrs. Tilly that evening.

"I'll come with you, if you'd like," he offered.

"I was hoping you would." I ran into the parlor and grabbed the book of legends. "Take this. I'll meet you there."

"You don't want me to pick you up?"

"No, I'll walk. I'll meet you there about seven o'clock, if that's okay."

He scanned my face compassionately. "You'll be all right, won't you?" His voice was dull and troubled. "Don't think your aunt remembers what happened last night." I shook my head. "If she comes back, call me right away."

"I will. I promise."

He leaned close and touched my cheek gently with his full lips. It was just a quick informal kiss but it felt so erotic. Everything about this man was erotic.

He walked away. The slowness of his steps told me that he didn't want to leave.

Later that day I tried to ask Auntie, in a roundabout way, if she recalled anything about last night or the incident that put her in the hospital. I thought it was best not to mention Uncle Reg. I'd wait until she started to talk about him herself, if she ever did.

She listened intently to what I had to say with a blank expression on her face and a hanky held tight in her fist. Then she sniffed, gave me a sour grin and said, "Best to let sleeping dogs lie."

"But Auntie, we have to talk about this," I insisted.

She wiped her hanky across her mouth, then narrowed

her eyes and tightened her lips. "Don't go getting your knickers in a twist. I've sussed it out and stopped it from running amok, I 'ave. So don't fret."

My interpretation of that was, she'd figured it out, she'd taken care of it and she didn't want me to worry about it anymore. Now I was really worried and confused. But I knew there was no point in challenging her or asking any more questions.

It was six o'clock. I would be meeting Jonathan at Mrs. Tilly's in an hour. Her cottage was about two kilometers from Merryweather Lodge. Auntie told me that it would take me forty minutes to walk there, but I wanted to take my time and enjoy the countryside. I hadn't had much time to be alone or find myself a private spot. I needed time to reflect on all that had happened since my return and think about what I was going to say to Mrs. Tilly. Being surrounded by Mother Nature would clear my mind and sooth my soul, just like it did when I was a child, where I would sneak away from the adult world and spend hours in the wooded area around our home. There, in my own mythical realm, I would make houses out of hollow trees for the fairies, converse with my imaginary friends, dance with the gnomes and befriend the untamed woodland creatures. I'd also gather wild flowers for my mom, who would smile and say "Thank you, honey" only to throw them away when my back was turned, because they might attract insects. She never understood me.

It bothered me to no end to leave Auntie alone, but I had somewhat discreetly placed herbs, holly and sea salt around the cottage and given her strict instructions to call the McAr-thurs if she needed help. Before I stepped out the door, I whispered in her ear, "You know what to do if she comes back."

"Right you are, luv. I believe ya; thousands wouldn't," she replied, trying to make out that she had no idea what I was talking about. But I was sure that she did.

Yesterday's heavy rain and gale force wind had given way to a crisp, calm, sunny day and a pleasant evening. I breathed in deeply. My nostrils were treated to the refreshing organic smell of damp earth and moist vegetation. The sunlight winked at me from behind a fluffy white cloud. A v-shaped squadron of birds squawked their cheerful goodbyes overhead as they exchanged positions in their follow-the-leader migra-tion. Down the old beaten path I strolled, past the chicken coop where I was greeted with loud clucking from a bossy, stubborn, ever-so-plump chicken whom I'd named Emy. Past the big red barn where I'd had my first interlude with the gorgeous Jonathan McArthur and past the zigzagged path that lead to the meadow.

I ascended the slopes of the gentle rolling hills and gazed at the landscape. It was a sea of emerald green. Its sweeping waves dotted with patches of bushes were touched with au-tumn hues and the white tufts of grazing sheep. I thought about the proud and steadfast character of this ancient land, scarred though centuries of plagues and wars, yet somehow able to retain its dignity, grandeur and charm. This place felt so much like home to me, in spite of its eerie undertones.

Flocks of sheep raised their woolly heads and gave me a bleating hello as I passed them. The brush of a gentle breeze on my cheek felt like an angel's caress. I squatted on a rocky knoll, to ponder for a moment. The setting sun was warm on my back as I sat and crossed my legs, closed my eyes, breathed deeply and went inside.

In my mind's eye, I could see myself wandering through the pasture. A little girl dressed in red walked beside me. She was swinging her arms and humming in a playful manner. Her silky black hair held traces of red that shimmered in the sunlight as she tossed her head to and fro. Her sweet face beamed with the mischievous carefree sparkle of an innocent child. "Daddy, Daddy," she called as she ran toward the tall, dark-haired man who was tending the sheep. She took his hand then turned to face me. Her forehead puckered. She squeezed her lips tight and glared at me with her sharp green eyes—eyes that cut into my soul like the blade of a butcher's knife as she whispered, "Help me, Mummy."

I shivered and turned my head, ridding myself of the horrible image. *What was that?* I stood up and tried to regain my senses. I could hear Auntie's scolding voice inside my head: "It's that funny imagination of yours playing tricks on you again, our Emily". That's all it was, I concluded; my funny imagination.

I climbed the slippery, damp bank of Beacon Hill. Uncle Reg had named it Beacon Hill. I assumed it was because he felt like a beacon of light, shining on his lowly flock when he was up there. It was the highest point in the pasture and reminded me of one of those burial mounds near Stonehenge.

The view was amazing.

On one side, Merryweather Lodge nestled amongst its enchanting garden. Just beyond that, the sprawling meadow, and looming in the distance, the dreaded woodlot. On the other side was the McArthur's home, a sturdy half brick, half stone cottage with a wraparound porch and a neatly kept lawn. I spotted a black speck running around the hedgerow. *That must be Sam.* I was glad they were allowing him to run free and not tying him up.

There were other quaint farmhouses snuggled in the lush countryside, with swirling puffs of gray smoke rising from their chimneys and neatly trimmed hedges defining their boundaries. I spotted Mrs. Tilly's cottage growing out of a tangled mass of trees and tall grasses and was reminded of the route I must take to get there.

The breeze had picked up. It swirled about my face and lifted my hair, bringing with it Mother Nature's sweet, fresh scent. I felt like a little girl on top of a storybook castle. My imagination took hold. I raised my face to the heavens and twirled around and around, swaying my head from side to side and flapping my arms gracefully, as if I were about to soar into the air. I was as light as a feather, a feather from an angel's wing, floating on the breeze in a celestial realm. Elated and fancy free, like a beautiful butterfly, freed at last from the walls of its ugly cocoon.

I threw off my shoes and squished my toes into the cool, soft grass. It felt alive and animated under my feet, like something buried beneath was trying to get out. I spun faster and faster, propelled now by a strange vortex of euphoric energy, unable to stop. A prism of multicolored lights and psychedelic patterns flashed before my eyes. Pictures of dead people and incarnations of previous lifetimes darted in and out of my mind like snippets of old movies. Faint sounds of Celtic music whispered in the ether. I hummed to the sweet bewitching echo from far, far away, as visions of my sinister dream danced in and out of my head.

I was caught up in an orgasmic, trance-like frenzy. Bright, flashing colors, corpses, incarnations, sensual music, and my recurring dream blended together, making me dizzy and out of control. I frolicked, naked now, my long red hair sweeping about my body, tickling my bare flesh and tantalizing my most private parts. The air was scented with spicy incense and fine red wine. Voluptuous, unclothed maidens danced around me, while handsome men in white robes looked on. The music rang louder and louder. Faster and faster I spun.

Suddenly—silence. I froze.

The air became bitterly cold. I ran my hands up and down my arms nervously as I tried to regain my equilibrium.

Then I heard it, the dreaded, terrifying sound of my unearthly adversary. "Colceathrar. Colceathrar."

Panic pulsated through my veins. I gazed around anxiously, too petrified to move. She was nowhere in sight. Just a creepy bodiless voice and a strong stench of cat pee burning my nostrils.

My feet thawed. I turned and ran down the hill, the soles

of my feet slipping and sliding on the muddy patches. I could feel her evil essence all around me, from behind, in front, crawling in my hair and on my skin.

"Get away from me!" I screamed and flailed my arms to keep her foul presence at bay. My legs pumped. My heart beat so fast against my ribcage that I thought it would explode. Her rancid smell made my eyes water.

Faster and faster I flew, up and down the rolling sea of never-ending green, leaping over stubble and sheep manure, skidding around untamed brambles and bushes. I could feel her disgusting breath on the back of my neck as I tried to outrun her, but my feet were raw and my legs throbbed.

Just as I was about to collapse, a burst of adrenaline gripped me and propelled me forward. A powerful invisible force that pumped me with energy, it was the same strange force I had felt five years ago when this hideous creature chased me in the woodlot. I felt no fatigue now, just desperate determination to outrun her and get to Jonathan.

I could see the little dirt road that led to Mrs. Tilly's cottage. The evil presence was fading farther and farther behind me.

My foot caught on a piece of uneven ground. I stumbled and fell.

Turning my torso around ever so slowly, I looked behind and sniffed the air. She had gone, or so it seemed. "Oh, thank you, God," I whispered under my breath.

Holding my forehead in the palm of my hand, I sat for a moment, puffing and panting, trying to catch my breath and scolding myself for not bringing any sea salt or protective herbs. The elusive power that had driven me had now left my form. I felt weak and every muscle in my body ached, but I knew I had to muster the strength and courage to carry on. She could return at any moment.

I put my hands to the ground and slowly eased myself up.

All at once I felt something heavy land on top of me, pushing me into the ground. The stench was overwhelming. I squirmed and screamed, "Get off of me, you foul bitch!" as I pushed franticly against the invisible entity.

Harder and harder she pressed her disgusting bodiless form into mine, as if she were trying to bore me into the ground. Then I felt it, that same dark, dreaded, tingly feeling I had felt in the bathtub as she penetrated my flesh.

# Chapter 21

I woke up in Mrs. Tilly's parlor, laid out on a red velvet daybed. A cold compress that smelt like eucalyptus was draped over my forehead. Jonathan sat beside me, his head slightly bowed, his eyes downcast. There was a bruise under his eye and a long red scratch across his cheek.

"What happened? How did I get here?"

He looked up and peered into my eyes with a glum expression. "We found you just down the lane, lying on the ground." He hesitated. "You were hysterical; it was like you were having a seizure or something."

It took me a moment to gather my thoughts, to piece together the frightful fragments of the evening.

My lips trembled as I raised my hand and touched the scratch on his face. "Did I do that?" He nodded his head. "I wasn't having a seizure; it was her, inside me." I shuddered as I recalled the creepy sensation of her invisible form penetrating my skin. "It felt like millions of tiny insects crawling all over my body then burrowing into my flesh."

He grimaced. I put my hand to my brow and lifted my head off the pillow, slowly. My throat was dry and a dull throb beat inside my temple. I looked down at my feet; they were scratched and my soles were raw.

"Are you in pain?" he asked, sliding his strong hand under my arm to help me up. "Sorry, we couldn't find your shoes."

The weight of my body on my sore feet caused me to flinch. "My feet hurt, and my head's fuzzy." A surge of utter hopelessness and anxiety rose up inside me. "Jonathan, I don't know how much more of this I can take." My eyes latched onto his, pleading for help, reassurance, sympathy—anything to fill the deep, dark pit of despair.

He just smiled sympathetically.

Mrs. Tilly handed me a clay beaker which contained a liquid that looked like dish water and smelt like green tea and garlic. "Drink this dear. It'll make you feel better."

I felt like I had a massive hangover, but after a few sips of the disgusting concoction the pain started to subside.

I began to tell Mrs. Tilly what had happened to me. She sat transfixed, her strange eyes gleaming as she listened intently. Her face wore an expression of sheer intrigue. It was as if she was enjoying the explanation of my dreadful experience. "Details, dear, details," she kept saying. Her eagerness and elated expression made me uncomfortable.

"You seem like you're enjoying this, Mrs. Tilly."

"Nonsense, child, but I must admit I do find it quite fascinating."

I looked over at Jonathan, who was frowning and shaking

his head. I acknowledged his annoyance with her odd, unsympathetic attitude by giving him a slight nod and a false smile.

I think she noticed our expressions, as she sniffed, then lifted herself up from the table abruptly. "I know what you need now. I'll be right back." She scurried about, gathering herbs from hand-woven baskets that hung from the rafters, things in jars and odd bits and pieces from her kitchen shelves. She flipped through some dusty, leather bound books that looked ancient, and made some notes. "You'll have to go into the woodlot and find the great oak tree. It was there that Merthia's spirit left her body and it is there that it must be banished. You will have to summon the Goddess Odina and ask her to reverse the spell. But be careful not to harm the form in which Merthia has resided."

She placed her hand firmly on my shoulder. "You, my dear, have to be the one that pours it down her throat." She sank her fingers into my shoulder blade and gave it a quick squeeze. It wasn't a gentle squeeze. "The ritual will have to be performed on All Hallows Eve, when the portal to the dead is opened, and you are to have it finished before sunrise."

She gave us strict instructions on what to wear and how to conduct the exorcism.

On the way home Jonathan sat stiff and still, his hands wrapped so tightly around the steering wheel that his protruding knuckles were white. His brow was slightly wrinkled, his lips pressed together. His eyes were distant, staring through the windshield, far beyond the road, off into the landscape of his own thoughts—searching, perhaps, for some way out of this crazy maze of uncertainty.

*Is he going to chicken out? Is he trying to think up an excuse of why he can't do this? Will I be forced to enter the dreaded woodlot alone?* I wasn't sure I could.

An awkward silence hung between us like a menacing fog. Too afraid to break the silence, I turned my head and gazed out of the side window while I fidgeted with a piece of unraveled wicker from the basket that sat on my lap. The scent of its herbal contents wafted through the chilly air.

I felt numb on the inside—my gut, my brain, my heart frozen from so many stormy emotions. *Why isn't he talking? What is he thinking? What if he backs out? I can't do this alone.*

Then, as if he'd heard my fretful thoughts, he reached over and touched the back of my hand. "We're in this to-gether, Emily. I won't let you down."

His voice was a broken whisper edged with doubt, but it was enough to reassure me. I knew that Jonathan was a man of his word. My lips trembled as I breathed a sigh of relief.

The thirty-first of October finally arrived. The day I had dreaded for the past week.

I loved this time of year as a child—the thrill of dressing up in scary costumes, carving jack-o-lanterns and going trick-or-treating door to door. Spooky decorations adorned our house, both inside and out. The trees were bare; piles of brittle, brown leaves lay on the lawns, inviting little ones to run and jump. The air was always crisp and cold, and sometimes the odd snowflake would fall, signaling the long, cold winter ahead. Skye's mom spent weeks making her the best costume, and it was always something incredibly gruesome. I always wore store-bought costumes and had to go as a princess or fairy.

I wished that Skye were here with me now. She'd know exactly what to do and wouldn't be a nervous wreck like I was. Besides Christmas, Halloween was my favorite time of year, but there were no signs of little ghosts and goblins, jack-o-lanterns, or celebrating at Merryweather Lodge—only the rustling of half naked trees and the gloom and foreboding of the cool autumn air. I reached for my journal and pen.

*Oct. 31$^{st}$*

*Dear friend,*

*This has been a fascinating journey and a dreaded nightmare all rolled into one. I am about to risk my life to banish an entity who was my cousin and my rival in another life. It is all so unbelievable, so utterly crazy, but I know, deep inside, that it's real.*

*I am terrified and worried sick. What will happen to Auntie if Merthia kills me? Will my mom be so grief-stricken that it causes her cancer to return? My dad will then have lost everyone he cares about. He'd bury himself in a deep, dark, hole and never come out. I know that for sure.*

*I've thought about going back home, since I don't think she could follow me there. But how could I leave Auntie here alone? And it would be extremely difficult to leave Jonathan now, if not impossible. I have fallen deeply in love with him. When he comes near me my heart starts to race, my stomach flutters and his touch makes every cell in my body quiver. The mere whiff of his body scent tantalizes me with a lusty sensation, making my breasts peak and the inside of my crotch throb with expectancy. Oh, the longing, so much longing. I think of him constantly. His essence stays with me wherever I go. This is a pure love, untouched by superficial things, an enduring and steadfast love. A love that was etched into my soul centuries ago.*

*If I don't come out of this alive, I leave you, my confidant, to my best friend Skye. She is the only one who will understand the content of your pages. I am scared, so utterly scared.*


I put my journal into an envelope and addressed it to Skye, just in case.

The smell of beeswax permeated the parlor, along with rosemary, fennel, wood moss, a snippet of my hair, willow bark and other ingredients that I was preparing for my potion. The only ingredient that I hadn't been able to get was three drops of virgin's blood. Mrs. Tilly had said that it wasn't essential but it would make the potion more potent.

I remembered the bashful look on Jonathan's face when she told us and when she lowered her glasses to the end of her nose, glared at us and said in a scolding manner, "You'll have to look elsewhere for that, I suppose." I had to look away when I felt the stains of scarlet touching my cheeks. I didn't know any young people here except Belinda, and the chances of her still being a virgin were highly unlikely. Jonathan wouldn't even entertain the thought of asking any of his friends; he said they'd all deny it anyway.

The other ingredients will have to do, I told myself. Mrs. Tilly said we wouldn't need to take any sea salt with us, as it wouldn't protect us now. But I decided to take it anyway, just in case.

Winny was perched on the arm of the pull-out-couch, sitting remarkably still like a stuffed animal. Her eyes followed my every move, and every now and then she'd let out a soft meow. I could have sworn that she was trying to tell me something.

I added water to the jar and stirred the concoction. It smelt like bitter incense. As I stirred, I chanted, "Three times three, three times three. Potion be, potion be, work your magic for me to see. Work your magic at the sacred tree."

A sick feeling of dread and fear churned inside my gut as I wrapped my hands around the jar and screwed the lid as tight as I could. I blew out the candles, gathered all the other paraphernalia into my backpack and left the room.

As I hurried past the attic stairs, something caught my eye. A small glass jar was sitting on the third step. I picked it up quickly and moved away from the stairs. I assumed that it was something that Auntie had left there in one of her absent-minded moments.

I took a closer look. There were a few drops of bright red liquid at the bottom and a discolored label on the side of the jar. I swallowed hard as I read the label: "Three drops of virgin's blood."

*I've seen this hand writing before.* Of course, it was Mary Eliss, but how?

It didn't matter. I had the finishing touch to my banishing potion. I tucked it into my backpack, feeling a tad more confident, and walked into the sitting room to say goodbye to Auntie.

She was sitting in her favorite chair watching TV with her stubby little legs propped up in their usual spot on the foot stool. She had taken off her corset and rolled her stockings below her knees, like doughnuts. Beside her on an old-fashioned side table sat a steaming cup of tea and a plateful of biscuits. The fire blazed and crackled. It was a picture of pure contentment.

"I'm going out with Jonathan for awhile, Auntie Em. I won't be long."

"Right you are, luv."

"Are you sure you'll be okay by yourself? I could phone Maud or Mrs. Tilly to come sit with you for a while, if you wanted."

"Don't be daft! I still 'ave all m' marbles, ya know. Just get on with ya and stop yer fussing."

I was sorry I'd asked.

She was wearing her pendant. Mrs. Tilly had told me to take it with me, but I didn't feel comfortable asking her for it. Besides, she needed its protection as much as I did, especially if she was going to be alone all evening.

I wondered as I walked away why she hadn't asked what I was doing in the parlor for such a long time, or complained about the odor that had permeated the whole cottage.

"Emily Ann," she called as I opened the door. "If ya can't be good, be careful." Auntie was still a bit of a mystery.

Here I am again, I said to myself, standing at the mouth of the dreaded woodlot. This would be the last time I'd enter this hellish portal, and if I was to come out alive, I'd never come near this place again.

I was dressed in green. Mrs. Tilly said that it would evoke the earth goddess inside me.

Like old enemies, the giant trees seemed to beckon and dare me to enter. I could almost smell the fear secreting from my body and hear the pulsating of my anxious heart.

Jonathan was standing next to me, taking deep breaths, his shoulders squared, his chin raised, and his hands pushed deep into the slits of thick sweater pockets. He was trying to put on a brave face and conceal the anxiety that must have been swirling around inside him.

He turned to face me. His dark brown eyes probed into mine, searching, it seemed, for some rationality to this ludicrous endeavor. "Scared?" he asked.

"Terrified." I sniffed and straightened my back. "But there's no time like the present."

We marched into the shadows of the formidable forest. "There's nothing to fear but fear itself. There's nothing to fear but fear itself," I chanted under my breath. It felt like I was entering the gateway to a demonic kingdom.

"Do you remember which way to go?" Jonathan asked.

"No, but I have a feeling that something, or someone,

will show me."

An unearthly stillness and gloom enveloped us as we trudged though the ominous woods. My faithful backpack hung over my shoulders, brimming with ghost-banishing paraphernalia. The air was cold, heavy and damp. A slimy mat of decaying leaves along with prickly chestnut shells clung to the soles of my shoes, as the pungent aroma of rotting foliage and wood mold invaded my nostrils with its bittersweet farewell.

"This way," I called instinctively, as my inner guide pointed the way.

A red squirrel scurried up the tree in front of me, causing me to wince. I had an uncanny sense of being watched, as if the trees themselves had eyes, peering at me from their ancient moss-covered trunks. They were like burly old giants dressed in droopy damp leaves, watching, crooking their cold spindly fingers, beckoning me. "Come closer, Emily, deep within our clutches, if you dare."

I tried hard to thaw the icy cold wad of anxiety that had formed in my gut by thinking pleasant thoughts, but they were clouded by dark eerie visions of dead, blood-covered bodies, ghoulish phantoms and "her".

I shivered as I started going over the ritualistic procedure in my head. It was to be performed after we'd summoned Merthia. Would I be brave enough and strong enough to stop her from overpowering me? Jonathan had promised me that if she possessed my body before I had time to cast the spell, he would do it himself. But would he be too afraid of harming me?

I reminded him of what Mrs. Tilly had said: 'Don't allow Merthia to frighten or manipulate you, no matter what she says or whose body she has possessed. But be careful not to harm her host physically.' "She kept emphasizing that."

There was so much noisy static inside my head that I couldn't hear my inside voice. I looked around in despair, at the gloomy shadows and decaying thicket. I didn't recognize anything. "I'm not sure if we're going the right way." My trembling voice mirrored the feelings of hopelessness and anxiety that I felt inside.

"Shh…"

"What is it?"

"Did you hear that?"

I stood still and listened, but all that I could hear was my own rapid, heavy breathing and a cold ominous silence all around us. "I don't hear anything."

"I was sure I heard a noise. Maybe it was the old wood witch following us."

"Would you stop it! This is not the place or time for jokes. I'm scared stiff as it is."

He paused and took my hand; with the other he brushed a spot of dirt from my cheek. "I'm sorry. Look, maybe we should turn back. It'll be dark soon and we could get lost in here."

I pulled my hand away from his. "No! We've come too far to turn back. We have to keep on going. If we don't put a stop to her now she'll keep coming after me until she gets her revenge."

I was on fire with utter determination but smoldering painfully on the inside with fear. Was I really trudging through a haunted forest, searching for an evil druid priestess with my reincarnated lover by my side? It was all so surreal, so utterly unbelievable. But I could feel it, smell it, hear it and see it so clearly. If this was a dream, I had to experience it fully, live through it and wake up alive.

We ploughed our way through the dark kingdom, dodging low-hanging branches, nettles and woodland debris, our eyes and ears alert, our hearts pounding in fearful anticipation.

"Emily, I really think we should turn back."

I caught a glimpse of an opening between two groves of trees. "Wait! It's over there."

"Are you sure?"

"Yes, this is it." I reached for his hand and gripped it tightly.

We moved slowly, cautiously, hand in hand into the formidable den. The great oak tree stood before us like a majestic icon, flamboyant and drenched in secrets, its roots pushing up from the ground like thick, long tentacles, wallowing in the nourishment of Mother Earth. Its ancient trunk was covered in wrinkles and its outstretched arms held drying leaves of green, yellow, saffron and brown.

We walked over to the gray slab of stone that lay close by. It resembled the one that held the mutilated body in my dream and there were no other large rocks in sight, so we assumed that this was it, the sacrificial altar.

I placed my backpack against the cold stone slab, pulled out the bag of sea salt and sprinkled it in a large circle around us. It was called a protective circle, and I got the idea from a book I found in the bottom drawer of Auntie's buffet. It was titled *Basic Witchcraft*. I wondered what Auntie was doing with a book on witchcraft. I also wondered why Mrs. Tilly had told. us not to bother with sea salt.

My cold hands trembled as I lit the thirteen candles and poured the potion into the old clay beaker that Mrs. Tilly had provided. I added the drops of virgin's blood and stirred slowly. The concoction was to be poured down Merthia's throat. Jonathan would hold her down while I forced her to consume the potion. We knew that it would be an extremely dangerous task and one that would take an immense amount of strength and courage.

I scattered willow twigs around the rock then glanced at Jonathan who was shuffling his feet back and forth in a nerv-ous manner. He caught my glance, grinned awkwardly and nodded his head, signaling me to proceed.

I raised my eyes, lifted my arms to the sky and chanted loudly, with as much confidence as I could muster: "Three times three, three times three. Great Goddess Odina, I call on thee. Take back Merthia's immortality and set her spirit free."

I lowered my arms and turned to the great oak tree. "Oh sacred tree, oh sacred tree, I summon Merthia here to me." A sudden rush of mastery and exhilaration surged inside me, as if I were a powerful witch casting an ancient spell.

Then I shivered as the air around me got colder and colder. The hush and stillness of the forest was eerie and threatening, like the calm before the storm. Jonathan's eyes scanned the woods fearfully as his long fingers rubbed the tiny bristles on his cleft chin. I wanted desperately to move close to him, to feel his strong arms around my trembling form, to mold into his embrace for a little comfort. But I was worried that it might provoke her and make her more dangerous.

"It's not working," he mumbled.

"Pray, Jonathan. Pray that it works."

"I didn't think you believed in God."

"I do, just not the conventional one."

He gave me a puzzled look.

"Just pray, for God's sake!"

Then we heard the dreaded sound of breaking branches and rustling leaves. I took some long, deep breaths as I felt icy cold fingers of panic and fear clutching at my heart.

Jonathan stood motionless, his eyes wide.

From out of the shadows the figure of a woman emerged.

I gasped. Jonathan grabbed my hand.

She strutted toward us, shoulders back, head held high. My eyes were wide, every muscle in my body clenched. Her form was wrapped in a long velvet cape. It was the color of ripe plums and had a wide hood that draped over her shoulders. Her hair was crowned with a tight circle of braids.

"What on earth are you doing here?" Jonathan asked, with a sigh of relief.

She came closer, looked down at the salt with a frown,

then at me. Her eyes were wild and glassy and more green than hazel now. They bore into me like a drill, trying, I was sure, to penetrate my soul. She looked stunningly attractive and much more mature.

A delightful fragrance of vanilla and roses drifted toward me, but I knew that beneath that fragrant, alluring exterior lay a dark and ugly soul. "Hi, Belinda. I should have known it was you."

She screwed up her face and snarled like a vicious dog as her evil eyes raked over my body. "My mother told me you'd be here."

"How did Mum know we were here?" Jonathan asked.

"Not her!" She lowered her voice. "My real mother."

"Belinda, you're not making any sense. Are you on drugs? And why are you dressed like that?" He stepped out of the circle. "You have to leave; it's not safe for you here."

"For God's sake, Jonathan, are you blind?" I screamed. "It's her! Get back into the circle!"

He ignored me and walked toward her. My hand shot to my mouth as my inner voice rose up inside me. *No. No!* "Get back here!"

"Calm down, Emily, it's all right. It's obvious that she's not coming. You can come out of there now."

"Are you really that dumb? Can't you see it's Merthia? Look at the way she's dressed, and look at her eyes!"

"Don't be ridiculous, Emily." His gaze wandered up and down his sister's form. "Are you going to a fancy dress party or meeting one of your freaky friends here?"

She scoffed.

"Why are you here, Belinda?"

"Do you love her?"

"What?"

She pulled her hand out from under the lush velvet cape and pointed her finger in my direction. "I said, do you love her?"

He glanced at me warmly. Then he replied, in a defensive tone. "Yes, but what's it to you?"

"He does? He does!" I mumbled to myself.

Before I had a chance to give his words anymore consideration, I noticed Belinda's hand coming down fast and hard on the side of his face. The sheer force of her slap sent him stumbling to the ground. He held his hand to his red cheek, his dark eyes glaring at her in tortured disbelief.

"Why did you do that? Where did you get all that strength from? I knew it, you're on drugs." He hesitated, then drew in a quick breath. "Or, has she possessed you?"

"I'm sorry, Golwin; I don't want to hurt you." She pointed at me and screwed up her face. "It's her I want." Her voice was deep now and raspy with a bitter edge. My soul recognized it as the voice of its adversary. She walked toward me with an air of arrogance and stood directly in front of me, just outside the salt circle.

"Hello, Merthia. I see you've found a worthy host."

She snickered. "How long do you think you can stay in there?"

"As long as it takes to banish you from the face of this

earth, back to the dark world from which you came."

Her face grew red with rage. Her fists clenched as she took a step back and hocked. A wad of thick yellow phlegm shot out of her mouth and into my face. I heaved as I wiped the spit off my face with the back of my hand. "I will kill you, Merthia!"

She grinned. "That will not be easy, cousin."

Impulsively, as if suddenly instructed, I threw my arms up into the air and called out, "Odina, Goddess of Immortality, I call on you. Take your gift from this evil soul. Banish her from the face of the earth."

She tossed her head back and cackled like an old witch. "She's not listening, Colrea."

Suddenly a soft breeze picked up and a cold current of air swept around me, blowing a path through the protective circle.

# Chapter 22

I gasped, spun around and made a dash for the sea salt. She flew past me with tremendous speed, knocked me to the ground, grabbed the bag and tossed it into the woods.

I lifted myself up from the damp earth, gritted my teeth and clenched my fists as my heart sank in utter despair. She strolled toward me, wearing a twisted smirk on her face and with wild eyes that gleamed with satisfaction like an evil sorceress that had just reclaimed her dark kingdom.

Her long, slim finger pointed to the ground. "On your knees, Colrea. Beg for mercy."

I didn't move.

"Now!"

My chin rose as I straightened my back and stood my ground. "You are the one who will be begging for mercy." I tried to sound confident and assertive, but my voice was hoarse with terror and every cell in my body trembled.

Her green eyes grew wide and her gaze latched onto mine, blazing with a fiery anger. I flinched as I felt it burning into me like a red hot poker.

Then I noticed, out of the corner of my eye, Jonathan's powerful silhouette creeping up ever-so-slowly behind her. He looked like an agile panther sneaking up on its prey.

I had to keep her attention and stop her from noticing him.

Taking a quick deep breath, I pulled back my shoulders, twisted my mouth and drew my eyes into slits. "You don't scare me, Merthia. I pity you. Having to roam this earth not dead or alive, slaying innocent people and looking to revenge the soul that took your man." I glared into her raging face; my lips were tight and firm, but inside my guts were churning over and over like a cement mixer, and my heart was pounding so hard, I was sure she could hear it. "He's mine now, Merthia."

She snarled, and her face was red with fury as she stretched out her slender hands and reached for my throat.

Swiftly Jonathan's muscular form pounced on her from behind. Wrapping his strong arms around her torso, he pulled her back. She roared like a caged lioness, tossing her head from side to side, kicking her feet and thrashing her arms. He tightened his grip.

I scurried over to the rock, grabbed the potion and waited for the opportunity to pour it down her throat. He had to subdue her, get her flailing arms under control. I couldn't run the risk of spilling the precious concoction.

"Let go of me, Golwin! It's not you I want!" Her pleading cry echoed through the ghostly silence of the woods. She threw back her head and bared her teeth like a ravenous vampire. Then she thrust them fast and forceful into Jonathan's arm, sinking them though his thick sweater and into his flesh.

He let out a bloodcurdling scream and loosened his grip. She spun around, lifted her knee and drove it hard up into his groin. He let out an agonizing screech that made me cower. My heart ached as I watched him grab his crotch and fall to the ground. On his knees, with his back hunched over and his face wracked with pain, he moaned pitifully.

I could feel his suffering. "I'll kill this bitch! I'll kill her! I'll kill her!" I chanted to myself.

She stood in front of him like a wild animal protecting its wounded young, then she glanced at the beaker. An odd, eager look flashed from her eyes.

I held it close to my chest. Then I carefully, cautiously, with trembling hands, set it on the ground and proceeded toward her. A fiery wrath of revenge and loathing blazed inside me as she tuned and moved in the direction of the beaker.

I couldn't let her get it. I had to do something. "You will not go down without a fight, Emily Fletcher," I mumbled as I strutted toward her, held out my quivering fingers and reached for her hair. Latching my hands onto her head, I dug my nails into the circle of braids and tugged hard, with all the strength I could muster.

She flinched and whipped her head around, loosening my grip. Her face was lit with rage. Her long fingers extended then grabbed my wrists and clasped tight, like a pair of steely pliers. Her pointed nails dug into my flesh as she whipped back my wrists, sharply, painfully. I screamed in agony as a stabbing sensation shot up my arm. She threw back her head and chuckled triumphantly like an old witch.

"Leave her alone," Jonathan cried feebly.

Her mouth drew tight and her eyes grew wider and wider like balls of fire as she marched toward him, her deep purple cape flapping behind her like the wings of a huge vampire bat. Grabbing him by his sweater, she lifted him up with ease and tossed him into the air, as if he were a rag doll. He landed hard against the trunk of the giant tree, his body limp, his head tilted to one side.

"Oh my God. She's killed him," I mumbled as my heart plummeted. "Are you okay, Jonathan?" I called hopefully, desperately.

He moaned and lifted his head, just enough to give me hope.

Merthia ran over to him, dug into the pocket of her cloak, pulled out a bundle of rope and tied him to the tree. He struggled feebly, pathetically, to try and free himself, but she seemed to have the strength of ten men and I knew now that any effort to contain her would be futile. The only hope we had was the magic potion, but we had no way of getting her to drink it.

Only a miracle could save us now, I concluded, only a miracle.

With haste, I gathered grains of salt from around the remaining circle and sprinkled it into the gap. My wrists throbbed as my fingers moved. At least I was safe for now.

The gloomy shadows of dusk were looming and the cold damp air was seeping into my bones. I shivered, took a long, deep breath, closed my eyes tightly and went inside, deep inside, to my safe place, my private inner world, a world where there are no ghosts, goblins or evil Druid Priestesses; just blissful peace and beautiful pictures of anything I could imagine.

Nothing came. I tried harder to quiet my mind and feel my spirit. "Breathe deeply, Emily. Concentrate," I whispered to myself. I wanted so much to escape from this nightmare, if only in my mind, if only for a moment. Perhaps something would come to me, a sign, a clue, some sort of direction from my inner voice. Or perhaps, when I opened my eyes I'd be back home, snug in my own bed, waking up from this hellish dream. "Oh please, God, let it be so." All I could see was darkness, a black hole of infinite darkness, and I had a feeling of utter despair.

Slowly, despairingly I opened my eyes to the horror of my hopeless situation.

Merthia was kneeling down beside Jonathan, staring into his eyes and running her fingers over his cheeks, gently, lustfully, in a circular motion. He flinched and turned his head away. She snarled, shook her head from side to side, then brought her mouth close to his ear and said, in a soft innocent voice, "Jonny, it's me, Lindy, your little sister. I need to drink the potion. It's the only way to expel this evil entity inside me. Help me, big brother, please." It was Belinda's voice we were hearing, but I knew it was Merthia speaking.

Jonathan frowned, "How did you know about the potion?"

"No more questions! Just tell her to give it to me."

"Emily, give her the potion," he called meekly.

It didn't make sense. The concoction Mrs. Tilly had prescribed was supposed to banish Merthia, unless this really was Belinda coming through. *No, she wants me to give it to her so that she can dispose of it.*

I grabbed the clay beaker, held it tight in my hands and called teasingly, "Come and get it."

Her eyes lit up and she grinned like a spoiled child that had just gotten its way. "Put it outside the circle," she demanded.

"No, I have to be the one to pour it down your throat. Come close to the circle and open your mouth."

She crept toward me. I swallowed hard.

Again, in a soft innocent voice, "I can't drink it over the sea salt. Give it to me, Emily. Set me free, for Jonathan's sake. Please."

"Just give it to her!" he shouted.

"How do we know that she won't pour it out?"

"We have to trust her. What choice do we have?"

Trust her, was he kidding? But we had no other choice, he was right about that. It was a risk, but it was a risk I had to take; what else could I do?

I placed the beaker tentatively just outside of the circle and prayed. "Please God, make her drink it. Don't let her throw it away."

My inner voice started to vibrate inside me, a deep resounding, *Take it back. Take it back!* I leaned over the circle to retrieve it but her swift hands were there before mine.

She held the beaker gently between her hands and gazed at it lovingly, as if it were made of pure gold. Slowly, tenderly, she brought it to her lips. Her eyes closed. Her mouth watered like a famished goddess about to bite into a rare and exotic fruit.

Something was terribly wrong. This was too easy. My heart started to sink. The warning voice in my gut rang.

I tried desperately to remember the ritualistic words I had to recite to banish her soul, but nothing came. She sipped and savored until every drop was gone. Then she ran the back of her hand across her mouth and tossed the cup into the woods.

Her eyes caught mine, gleaming cold, glassy and sharp. A smirk of utter satisfaction lit her face.

I shivered. Why wasn't she screaming in agony and defeat? Why wasn't she releasing the form of her human host? Disappointment and alarm chewed at my stomach muscles. It felt like hundreds of insects were gnawing on my intestines.

She tossed her head back, gazed up at the heavens and spread her arms wide as if she were about to take flight. "Odina, Great Goddess of Immortal Youth, I have been your loyal and faithful servant. I call upon you now to bestow upon me your final gift."

A dark, eerie hush enveloped us. The candles danced erratically, as if caught by a sudden gust of wind. The dusky woods all around us emanated alarm and despair. The air reeked of trepidation. I wanted to cry out to my mother, just as I had done as a frightened little child stirred in the night by a bad dream. But my mom was thousands of miles away and this was no dream.

Gradually, she started to mutate—first into the hideous creature, snarling and clenching her teeth, discharging her foul stench. Then, like Cinderella, her stained and tattered dress became a pristine white gown, fresh and flowing. Her ugly, distorted face grew into that of an exquisitely striking and bewitching young woman. Her almond-shaped face held high cheek bones, a perfect straight nose and full, ruby lips. Matted strands of yellow hair melted and grew back into soft, silky, locks that trickled over her shoulders and down her back like a fountain of red and gold, crowned with a wreath of ripe red berries. Her features were similar to those of Belinda but bolder and much more stunning.

She walked toward me in a slow, meticulous motion and across the salt circle, her long gown trailing behind her. I stared, dumfounded and numb with fear. She stood directly in front of me. Her chin rose in a regal and pompous manner. Her outer appearance was that of a powerful, exotic and en-chanting temptress, but her frigid eyes revealed the evil within.

"Hello, Colrea."

It was my rival as she was in my dream, as she was in the picture, as she was hundreds of years ago—my cold-hearted cousin, Merthia.

A strange feeling came over me, as if there was something inside me struggling to come out. A mysterious voice from deep within me, that I did not recognize as my own, spoke. "Why did you do it, Merthia? All of those poor animals and innocent young girls slaughtered, and for what? Vanity? You made a pact with the goddess of darkness, and you lost it all in the end: your man, your babies, your life, your soul. You carry the seed of your wicked mother, the one who deserted you at birth, as you deserted your own infants."

"My mother did not desert me. She has always been with me and is still with me here!"

I stared into her face, confident and fearless now. "I pity you, Merthia. I have always pitied you."

Her green eyes poured over me, like hot acid burning a hole in my soul. Her lips twitched as she spoke. "Pity yourself, Colrea. For tonight I will have my revenge and claim what is rightfully mine."

"He could never love you. He couldn't love anything so ugly. Go back to the dark, demented world from which you came. Your soul does not belong here."

She threw back her head and laughed scornfully. "Don't you see what you have done? You imbecile. You have given me back my soul. Thanks to the elixir of immortal life, I am whole again." She turned and glanced at Jonathan. "He's mine now, Colrea."

A smug grin that was not my own tugged at the corners of my mouth. "You are mistaken, Merthia, he is mine. Tell me, cousin, why have you waited so long? I have lived numerous lifetimes since our encounter. Why this incarnation?"

She snarled. "Do you know nothing? Is it not obvious to you? You should have learned the magic of the goddesses when I tried to teach them to you as a child. You could have had it all, but you were too afraid. You are still a coward and an imbecile."

"What would I have gained by using your kind of sorcery? Beauty, charisma, it is all so fleeting and look where it got you. I choose the way of the true goddesses, the goddesses of light."

She laughed. "They have no magic; they are powerless. I had to wait until you returned to this place, until you were reunited with my betrothed. Everything had to be in perfect order. Tonight is the night I have waited for, for so long. Tonight, Colrea, I will finally have my revenge."

I tried to shake off the strange feeling that I was someone else, someone from another lifetime. My insides quivered as I cleared my throat, shook my head and regained my composure. "No! That was hundreds of years ago. I am not Colrea. I am Emily Fletcher and that is not Golwin, his name is Jonathan McArthur. We might share the same souls but we are not those people anymore. And you, Merthia, you are dead. Slaughtered unmercifully by the one you loved."

She raised her arm and slapped me hard across the side of my face with the palm of her hand, causing me to stumble. My hand flew to my cheek as the sting of the blow pricked my skin. Then she grabbed hold of my arm and pulled forcefully, dragging me across the greasy sea of damp moss and leaves. It felt like my arm was being wrenched right out of its socket. I clenched my teeth and pushed back the cries of pain.

She shoved me against the wrinkled bark of the ancient tree, next to Jonathan, and bound my sore wrists with rope.

"Leave us alone, you monster. What have you done with my sister?" Jonathan's voice was feeble and tainted with extreme fatigue.

Merthia bent over and brushed his messy hair away from his swollen face with her finger tips and whispered, "She was never your sister."

Then she rose with authority, straightened her back and lifted her eyes and arms to the heavens. "Oh mighty Odina, I call upon you to accept this offering from your loyal and faithful servant."

Instantly, a primitive axe appeared in her hand. Its steely, rough blade was tarnished with blood. She marched toward me, eyes wide, mouth tight, seething with an ancient rage.

*Surely this is not real. This cannot be happening. It must be one of my visions out of control, or perhaps I am trapped in some sort a hellish dream world, unable to wake up.* I blinked my eyes rapidly, frantically, while I prayed for a miracle. Nothing changed.

A gasp of breath caught in my throat as she lifted the axe. Her face beamed with glee. The pupils of her eager eyes grew and grew until the small black dots became big blots of ink. "Now, Golwin, you can watch as the life blood drains out of her, just as you did with me."

Every inch of my body trembled uncontrollably. My insides shook with the bleak, fearful, gut-wrenching sob of imminent death.

Jonathan struggled desperately to free himself. "No! No!" he cried.

Something moved in the woods. The angel of death, perhaps? A shadow appeared. I cringed and covered my eyes.

*Smack!*

I gasped. Someone had crept up behind her and was whacking her over the head with a shovel.

"Sod off. Be gone with ya, ya hag!"

It was Auntie. She was dressed in the same comical clothes that she wore when we came here to solve the mystery five years ago.

Dazed, Merthia stumbled and dropped the axe.

Auntie grunted and tossed her head like a crazy woman, as she whacked Merthia again and again on the side of her head and across her back with an incredible blunt force. Her strength was like that of a burly man, not that of a fragile old woman "This one's for m' man. Scared the life right out of 'im, ya did, and put me in a nut house. Take that! Ya hag." She gritted her teeth and swung the shovel. "This one's for m' mum. This one's for m'—"

Merthia turned swiftly and yanked the shovel out of her hand, growling and gnashing her teeth like a mad dog.

Auntie fumbled inside her pocket as she fell back on the hard ground. "I'll hex ya," she said feebly, holding out her silver pentacle and a handful of sea salt.

Merthia raised her chin and snickered. "Those things can't hurt me now." She ripped the chain out of Auntie's hand. "But I'll take back my Father's amulet." She held it out in front of her eyes and grimaced. "It's the old symbol of the goddesses of light, much misunderstood by the ignorance of your past generations, especially the males who feared the power of wise women. My Father made me wear it all the time. It was his feeble attempt to protect me from sorcery and rid me of my mother's seed. They should never have dug it up and built their pathetic little cottage on sacred ground." She twirled it around then tossed it into the woods. "All that it did was burn a hole in my chest."

Her eyes widened as they bore into Auntie. "My mother warned me about you, you stupid old fool."

"Who's yer mother, and what 'ave ya done with little Lindy?"

"The one you call Mrs. Tilly is my real mother, Hag-manis. My loyal host, the one you call Belinda, is your child."

"Rubbish, she ain't yer mother, and Lindy's Maud's girl."

"You thought your baby was stillborn, you fool, but she was not. My mother stole her from you and told you she was dead. When she delivered Maud's baby three days later, she exchanged it for yours. Her offspring is buried at the bottom of my mother's garden." She snickered.

Auntie's jaw dropped. "Yer lying!"

"Why would I lie? You imbecile. I needed a descendent with an evil heart to perform my sacrifices, after my faithful host Elisabeth Eliss died. I waited for many long, infuriating years for someone to replace her. When your baby was conceived, my mother sensed the evil seed within her. Even as a child, she fooled you all with her false innocence as she practiced her butchery on small animals. She has been a loyal and devoted servant."

Surely Auntie could not have given birth to such a monster. "No! You made her do it, and why would your mother give Auntie's baby to Maud?" I yelled.

"We could not have her raised in a place built on sacred ground or by the daughter of a white witch and the aunt of my adversary." She glared at Auntie. "I would have killed you a long time ago, but I needed you to lure my cousin back here." She picked up the axe. "Now I have no use for you."

The knots that were tied in my stomach tightened and moved up into my throat, causing me to heave. I swallowed hard, pushing the sour taste back down my gullet, and screamed. "Stop! Stop! Don't hurt her. It's me you want."

The breeze shifted. Something stirred in the ether. My eyes searched the ominous darkness as my heart quickened. From the eerie stillness of the foreboding woods came the dreaded sound of breaking branches and rustling leaves.

Merthia stopped and cocked her head.

Out of the gloomy shadows of the tall giants emerged the radiant form of Mary Eliss. In her arms she cradled two snow white kittens. Behind her trudged an army of gruesome specters. Pale, blood-soaked young girls with amputated limbs and gaping wounds, moaning and wailing. In their arms they carried the mutilated, hissing, spitting bodies of cats, cats of all manner.

I squirmed and gagged, every muscle in my body tightening as the stench of the gory procession came closer.

Merthia raised her axe. "Don't come any closer." Her voice cracked and trembled slightly, revealing for the first time a hint of weakness.

Mary Eliss stood back. The gruesome army picked up speed and flew toward Merthia in a floating motion, their blood-soaked feet hardly touching the ground.

"Get back! Get back!" she pleaded, her tone more desperate than before.

One by one, her unearthly victims descended upon her, clawing, scratching, and gnawing at her flesh. Shrieking and harrowing cries, like that of a thousand wounded animals, echoed all around.

I could never have imagined, not even in my worst nightmare, such an intensely horrifying and sickening scene.

Jonathan squirmed and twisted his bound wrists in hopeless desperation. "Belinda," he cried feebly as he watched what had once been the body of his younger sister being ravished and ripped apart.

I could hear Auntie praying meekly from her spot prone on the ground, "God 'elp us. God 'elp us."

I glanced over at Mary Eliss. She stood by the gray rock, motionless like a cold inanimate statue.

Merthia's tortured, bloodcurdling screams were searing. My body was saturated with a cold, clammy sweat of repulsion and horror. I turned my head as a shred of pity tugged at my heart. She flung her body about in a fierce and agitated manner, trying desperately to free herself from her gruesome avengers. Lifting her eyes to the sky, she pleaded weakly, in a raspy tone, "Odina, help your loyal and faithful servant, I beg of you."

The low-lying clouds started to move, round and round, swirling like coal-clad ghosts above our heads. A sudden clap of thunder rumbled in the distance.

Slowly, Merthia began to mutate. From the scared, blood-stained appearance of an evil Druid priestess into the body of an innocent young girl. Belinda let out a chilling scream and shook violently. The vengeful spirits backed off.

Like an ugly moth from its cocoon, the hideous creature emerged from its human host. With a high-pitched shriek, it dashed into the shadows of the gloomy woods, its ghoulish avengers close behind.

Belinda lay on the blood-soaked ground, curled up in a fetal position, rocking back and forth like a baby. Auntie rushed over and knelt down beside her. Cradling Belinda's damp head on her lap, she brushed it gently with her motherly, old hands.

"Is she all right?" Jonathan cried.

"She'll be as right as rain in a few days, she will." Then in a whisper, "I 'ope." She lowered Belinda's head to the ground and came over to untie us.

"I think you'll need the axe," I said.

She looked at the blood-stained instrument of death and cringed. "I wouldn't touch that thing with a ten foot pole."

"Pull hard on the knot," Jonathan told her as her stubby fingers fidgeted awkwardly with the rope.

"Auntie, you'll have to get the axe. You'll never get it

untied like this. It's too hard for you."

"Who said I won't?" She jerked it and pulled hard. It slipped off my sore wrists with ease, as though it had been dipped in butter.

I looked into her dear old eyes. "Auntie Em, you never cease to amaze me." As soon as we had untied Jonathan, he ran over to aid his sister.

I glanced over at the slab of rock. Mary Eliss was still standing there, unmoving, like a large porcelain doll, with two snow-white kittens at her feet. I walked toward her. As I stood in front of her and gazed into her pale, angelic face, her eyes lit up like sparkling little gems. It was as if I had turned a key and switched her on. Then she put her dainty hand into her dress pocket and pulled out a small bundle of lavender. "For you, Emily," she whispered sweetly.

I sniffed the tiny bouquet. "Thank you, Mary Eliss. You saved my life." She turned her head ever so slightly toward the opening in the thicket. "It wasn't just me, Emily."

My eyes grew wide in utter amazement. There, standing in the dark shadows, was the luminous form of my dead grandmother. She looked exactly like she did in the framed portrait that hung above our living room fireplace. She beamed with a radiant smile.

"Grandma," I called as I moved to go toward her.

Mary Eliss put her hand on my arm gently. "She just wants to let you know that she loves you and will always be with you."

I watched in wonder as the unearthly ghost of my dead grandmother slowly disappeared into the shadows of the dreaded woodlot. I turned, looked at Mary Eliss and sighed. "There was so much I wanted to ask her. And you, why do you haunt this place?"

"It is my home, Emily." She touched my face with her alabaster fingers. They were cold and felt like ceramic. "And there's more of the mystery to be solved." She bent down and gathered the kittens in her arms "Goodbye, Emily, and remember, things are not always the way they seem. Watch out for the malevolent spirit. She is a master of disguise and deceit." Then she turned and walked away.

"There are more spirits? Mary Eliss, wait! I have more questions. Do you know where your mom is buried?"

She turned her head. "In the hill, of course, with all the others." In an instant she was gone.

Belinda was dazed but coherent. Auntie had her snuggled inside her big yellow raincoat. Jonathan was kneeling beside them. "How is she?" I asked him.

"I think she'll be okay, but she's in no condition to make it back on foot.

I put my hand on his shoulder and gazed into his worried eyes. "She'll be fine."

He chewed on his dry lips and nodded hopefully. "I'll have to go and get help."

"No!" Auntie hollered. "I'll go, you two 'ave been through enough, and little Lindy's sleepin' now, she is."

"Auntie, we can't let you go in those woods alone, and it's getting dark."

She walked over to Belinda, fumbled with her raincoat and pulled a large silver flashlight out of the pocket. "I've got this 'ere torch and I left a trail of salt though the woods, so I could find m' way back."

"I'll go with you. You're not going alone."

Jonathan cleared his throat. "It would make more sense if I went and you two stay here with Belinda."

"Shut your bloody cake holes, both of ya. If the hag comes back, I want the two of ya..." she pointed to Belinda, "'ere with 'er."

I knew there was no use in arguing with her once she had her mind made up. She tightened her head scarf, shoved the flashlight into her apron pocket, picked up the axe and shovel, and headed for home. I knew, somehow, that she would return in a few hours with help.

I could see my breath now and feel the cold damp air of nightfall soaking into my skin. Exhaustion and hunger gnawed inside me, but the dense cloud of foreboding and fear had left me, for now. I wrapped my arms around my weary form and shuffled my feet back and forth. Jonathan stood up, drew me close and ran his firm hands up and down my back briskly, to warm me up. "How are your wrists" he asked.

"Sore. How's your arm?"

"Sore." He pulled back, just a little, and stared into my face. His sensual gaze wandered lovingly over my soiled features, while a gentle smile rested on his lips. "She won't be bothering us anymore. It's over, Emily."

I sighed deeply as I remembered Mary Eliss' words. "I

hope so." Drawing my face close to his, I touched the dent in his chin, softly, with my parched lips. "I love you, Golwin."

"I love you too, Colrea."

The steely gray clouds that had shrouded us in gloom parted as if by magic, exposing a full, plump, luminous moon. Its radiance lit Jonathan's bruised but handsome features and made his dark velvety eyes glow. Slowly, he drew his face to mine. Lightly, seductively, he skimmed my neck with his silky, succulent tongue, making the inside of my thighs tingle. His mouth drew to my ear. "How old are you, Emily?"

I closed my eyes. "Old enough." My body quivered with anticipation. Then I felt the long awaited, heady sensation of his lips on mine. Passionately, hungrily, I took his tongue into my mouth as my body molded into his firm embrace. I had been though hell, but now I was in heaven with the gorgeous Jonathan McArthur.

\* \* \* \*

I set my pen down on the antique writing desk in front of me and reread the last few words I'd written.

Is it over, I wondered. And what will it be like here in the winter?

# ABOUT THE AUTHOR

I grew up in southeast England, in a mining village lovingly nicknamed "the place that time forgot." I came to Canada when I was 21 years old, in search of adventure and a new life. I live in Spruce Grove, Alberta, with my hockey-crazy husband, lazy ginger cat, and adorable Shetland Sheep dog. We have two wonderful children.

As far back as I can remember, the pen and paper have been my faithful companions and story telling my forte. As a child I would sneak away from the mundane adult world, find a private retreat (usually behind the garden shed) and imagine. There in my own little sanctuary, I'd conjure up all kinds of intriguing tales and colorful characters. In my teen years my journal became my confidante, revealing all my hidden secrets, private fantasies, and wild notions within its pages. Later I started to write poems, articles, and short stories, and pondered the thought of becoming a writer.

When I immigrated to Canada I buried my dreams under layers of real life clutter. I chose a safe and practical career in child care, married, and raised a family. But my creative spirit kept trying to dig its way out. I was asked to write articles and editorials for our local church. I taught a story time class at the school, which lead me to writing a children's book. I wrote an article about my husband's prestigious grandfather and sent it to our local newspaper. They printed it. I kept sending them articles; they kept printing them. I was surprised at the compliments I received from the editor and readers. It was evident to me then that I had excavated my creative spirit.

I decided to take a comprehensive writing course to improve my technique. With help from a proficient and supportive tutor who told me I had a gift, I began to cultivate my skill. My articles started to sell and I received an assignment from a major Canadian magazine. I have spent the past few years working on my novel (a trilogy) and two children's books. I have a diploma in creative writing, along with a certificate complementing my creative skills.

*For your reading pleasure, we invite you to visit our web bookstore*

**WHISKEY CREEK PRESS**

**www.whiskeycreekpress.com**